The Mysterious Partner

A Chief Inspector Pointer Mystery

By A. E. Fielding

Originally published in 1929

The Mysterious Partner

Published by Resurrected Press

This classic book was handcrafted by Resurrected Press. Resurrected Press is dedicated to bringing high quality classic books back to the readers who enjoy them. These are not scanned versions of the originals, but, rather, quality checked and edited books meant to be enjoyed!

Please visit ResurrectedPress.com to view our entire catalogue!

For news and updates, visit us on Facebook! Facebook.com/ResurrectedPress

ISBN 13: 978-1-937022-96-9

Printed in the United States of America

Other Resurrected Press Books in *The Chief Inspector Pointer Mystery* Series

The Uttermost Farthing: A Savant's Vendetta

Arthur Griffiths
The Passenger From Calais
The Rome Express

Fergus Hume
The Mystery of a Hansom Cab
The Green Mummy
The Silent House
The Secret Passage

Edgar Jepson
The Loudwater Mystery

A. E. W. Mason
At the Villa Rose

A. A. Milne
The Red House Mystery

Baroness Emma Orczy
The Old Man in the Corner

Edgar Allan Poe
The Detective Stories of Edgar Allan Poe

Arthur J. Rees
The Hampstead Mystery
The Shrieking Pit
The Hand In The Dark
The Moon Rock
The Mystery of the Downs

Mary Roberts Rinehart
Sight Unseen and The Confession

Dorothy L. Sayers

Anybody but Anne
The Bride of a Moment
Faulkner's Folly
The Diamond Pin
The Gold Bag
The Mystery of the Sycamore
The Come Back

Raoul Whitfield
Death in a Bowl

And much more!
Visit ResurrectedPress.com
for our complete catalogue

FOREWORD

The period between the First and Second World Wars has rightly been called the "Golden Age of British Mysteries." It was during this period that Agatha Christie, Dorothy L. Sayers, and Margery Allingham first turned their pens to crime. On the male side, the era saw such writers as Anthony Berkeley, John Dickson Carr, and Freeman Wills Crofts join the ranks of writers of detective fiction. The genre was immensely popular at the time on both sides of the Atlantic, and by the end of the 1930's one out of every four novels published in Britain was a mystery.

While Agatha Christie and a few of her peers have remained popular and in print to this day, the same cannot be said of all the authors of this period. With so many mysteries published in the period, it was inevitable that many of them would become obscure or worse, forgotten, often with no justification other than changing public tastes. The case of Archibald Fielding is one such, an author, who though popular enough to have had a career spanning two decades and more than two dozen mysteries, has become such a cipher that his, or as seems more likely, her real identity has become as much a mystery as the books themselves.

While the identity of the author may forever remain an unsolved puzzle, there are some facts that may be inferred from the texts. It is likely that the author had an upbringing and education typical of the British upper middle class in the period before the Great War with all that implies; a familiarity with the classics, the arts, and music, a working knowledge of French and Italian, an appreciation of the finer things in life. The author has also traveled abroad, primarily in the south of France, but probably to Belgium, Spain, and Italy as well, as portions of several of the books are set in those locales. The books attributed to Archibald Fielding, A. E. Fielding, or Archibald E. Fielding, are quintessential Golden Age British mysteries. They include all the attributes, the country houses, the tangled webs of relationships, the somewhat feckless cast of characters who seem to have nothing better to do with themselves than to murder or be murdered. Their focus is on a middle class and upper class struggling to find themselves in the new realities of the post war era while still trying to maintain the lavish lifestyle of the Edwardian era. Things are never as they seem, red herrings are distributed liberally throughout the pages as are the clues that will ultimately lead to the solution of "the puzzle," for the British mysteries of this period are centered on the puzzle element which both the reader and the detective must solve before the last page.

A majority of the Fielding mysteries involve the character of Chief Inspector Pointer. Unlike the eccentric Belgian Hercule Poirot, the flamboyant Lord Peter Wimsey, or the somewhat mysterious Albert Campion, Pointer is merely a competent, sometimes clever, occasionally intuitive policeman. And unlike, as was the case with Inspector French in the stories of Freeman Wills Croft, the emphasis is on the mystery itself, not the process of detection.

Pointer is nearly as much of a mystery as the author. Very little of his personal life is revealed in the books. He is described as being vaguely of Scottish ancestry whose father was a Coast guardsman on the Devon coast.. He is well read and educated, though his duties at Scotland Yard prevent him from enjoying those pursuits. In an early book in the series it is revealed that he spends a week or two each year climbing mountains, his only apparent recreation, though in *The Mysterious Partner* it is revealed that he had once played forward for the All-

England International football team. His success as a detective depends on his willingness to "suspect everyone" and to not being tied to any one theory. He is fluent in French and familiar with that country. He is, at least in the first two books, unmarried, sharing lodgings with a bookbinder named O'Connor, in much the manner of Holmes and Watson, though this character is totally absent in the later works. Amongst his skills, we discover, is the ability to pilot a small plane, while his most endearing quirk is a tendency to look down at his feet when thinking.

One intriguing feature of the Pointer mysteries is that they all involve an unexpected twist at the end, wherein the mystery finally solved is not the mystery invoked at the beginning of the book. *The Mysterious Partner* is no exception to this rule. Not only does Fielding introduce the usual red-herrings and subplots to confuse the reader, the real mystery of the book is not so much who committed the murder, but rather who the victim's mysterious partner is and what role, if any, did he play in the crime. *The Mysterious Partner,* published in 1929, is the eighth book in the series featuring Chief Inspector Pointer. The author's style was maturing from the earlier books in the series, and devices such as disguises, secret Scotland Yard gestures and codes, and tactics that are somewhat dubious from a legal standpoint play less of a role in the story than previously, replaced by the more mundane aspects of police work. There is, perhaps an over reliance *in The Mysterious* Partner on some unlikely coincidences, to the extent that the author might not be playing completely fair with the reader. Still, the Pointer mysteries have a certain flair that separates them from the "humdrum" school of mysteries that were starting to appear at the same time. Stylistically, they fall somewhere between the works of Agatha Christie and those of Ngaio Marsh or E. C. R. Lorac.

The Mysterious Partner deals with the death of Edgar Danford, a wealthy businessman and the owner of an ancient estate called Farthing. He is found strangled in his bedroom in an out-building called the Chantry which he used as a retreat. The call to the police reporting the death was made by the victim's partner, Digby Cox, but when the police arrive at the scene a few minutes later, Cox has vanished without a trace. While a number of the characters are supplied with motives enough for wishing Danford dead to become suspects, it is the missing partner that becomes the real mystery, and not the murder.

As much as the various characters, the house Farthing has a palpable presence in the story, and Fielding adopts atypically atmospheric language in describing the house and the surrounding estate. Though some of the characters are drawn to Farthing, others feel it as an oppressive force to be shunned. Though architecture plays a role in a number of the Pointer mysteries, in no other book does a single building assume such importance.

Beyond the mystery itself, *The Mysterious Partner* is interesting for the clues it gives us about the identity of the author. During the course of the investigation Pointer travels to the cities of Venice and Riva in Italy, and the description of those places could only have come from someone who had spent some time in those locales. Another Italian connection, is the fondness that Digby has for Montepulciano, an Italian wine that would presumably have been unusual in the London of the 1920s, but would have been more familiar to one who had traveled in Italy.

Despite their obscurity, the mysteries of Archibald Fielding, whoever he or she might have been, are well written, well crafted examples of the form, worthy of the interest of the fans of the genre. It is with pleasure, then, that Resurrected Press presents this new edition of *The Mysterious Partner* and others in the series to its readers.

About the Author

The identity of the author is as much a mystery as the plots of the novels. Two dozen novels were published from 1924 to 1944 as by Archibald Fielding, A. E. Fielding, or Archibald E. Fielding, yet the only clue as to the real author is a comment by the American publishers, H.C. Kinsey Co. that A. E. Fielding was in reality a "middle-aged English woman by the name of Dorothy Feilding whose peacetime address is Sheffield Terrace, Kensington, London, and who enjoys gardening." Research on the part of John Herrington has uncovered a person by that name living at 2 Sheffield Terrace from 1932-1936. She appears to have moved to Islington in 1937 after which she disappears. To complicate things, some have attributed the authorship to Lady Dorothy Mary Evelyn Moore nee Feilding (1889-1935), however, a grandson of Lady Dorothy denied any family knowledge of such authorship. The archivist at Collins, the British publisher, reports that any records of A. Fielding were presumably lost during WWII. Birthdates have been given variously as 1884, 1889, and 1900. Unless new information comes to light, it would appear that the real authorship must remain a mystery.

Greg Fowlkes
Editor-In-Chief
Resurrected Press
www.ResurrectedPress.com
www.Facebook.com/ResurrectedPress

CHAPTER ONE

A PORTER placed the lady's luggage on the rack, then he said to one of the boys with her:

"You see those two gents passing? They're from Scotland Yard. Going down about that there mail-robbery at Hanton, I'll be bound."

"Scotland Yard!" echoed the boy, thrilled.

The porter nodded.

"Ah, only one's going down, I see," he amended, "t'other's just come for a few last words by the look of it. The one getting in is Chief Inspector Pointer. Young for such a post, ain't he? But there, as he was an International before he joined the police, why, it stands to reason that they'll send him along fast, don't it! Not likely they'd let one of the best forwards who ever played for England stick in the ranks, is it! Many's the time I've cheered him in the field. Thank you, mum." And the porter, a football enthusiast, moved off without waiting for the obvious agreement.

A young woman in another corner of the compartment got up and spoke to him.

"I wish you would point out to me the man whom you said was from Scotland Yard."

The porter extended a vast hand.

"There he is, miss. Buying a paper. Yes, that's him, and no mistake I allers think if he was still—"

But Mrs. Danford lost the remainder of the porter's constant reflection, for she had re-entered the train, and passed swiftly down the corridors. She paused at a third-class compartment where sat a tall, lean, brown-faced man, reading a paper. He was alone.

He glanced up for a second as Mrs. Danford stepped in, and closed the door behind her. It was the merest sweep of dark gray eyes, but it cataloged every detail of the woman. Guessed her age, correctly, as around thirty, boggled a little over her position, but put her down as very likely some country magnate's wife or daughter, who was not interested in clothes. Fond of gardening he would expect, landscape gardening for choice.

"I'm told that you're a chief inspector from Scotland Yard," Mrs. Danford said at once, as she took the seat opposite the newspaper.

As it was instantly lowered, she saw a good-looking face set in very firm lines. The eyes were pleasant in expression, but absolutely non-committal.

"You wished to speak to me?" Pointer made a gesture to knock out his pipe, but Mrs. Danford stayed him. She lit a cigarette herself.

Pointer had an idea that she was nervous, and that she was under the impression that she concealed that fact perfectly.

"It's such a silly seeming thing," Mrs. Danford said after a pause, "but it's worrying me. Badly. May I tell you about it?"

"Do," Pointer said with genuine interest. He did not think that the woman facing him was one to be worried by silly things. She looked to him quite unusually intelligent, with a kind of intelligence not common among Englishwomen. He put her down as quick-witted, vivacious, and stimulating. She could be malicious, he thought, and quite possibly she could be sly. At any rate, he would expect her to be determined to get out of life all that it could give her of happiness, and in its pursuit, she might possibly, he thought, not be much concerned with the happiness of those around her. Though of that he was not sure. At any rate there were possibilities in the face— of many kinds. There was love of beauty in it and of some large kind. Which was why he had guessed landscape gardening since, to his eye, she belonged to the country.

Among other possibilities she could be charming— when, and if, she chose. Pointer had an idea that she did not often choose.

"A member of my family," Mrs. Danford went on, "owns a place with which a local sort of banshee—only it isn't a cry, it's a laugh—is associated. Heard three times running, the laugh means a violent death for the owner. It's been heard twice—just lately. Now what ought to be done?"

She looked at him eagerly. Chief Inspector Pointer was silent for a moment. He had not expected this kind of a tale.

"Why don't you believe that it's a spirit's warning?" he asked.

"Because I don't believe in occult things. I'm supposed to, for my people were all firm spiritualists, but as it happens, secretly, I've always been a sceptic. A firm sceptic, if such a thing is possible."

"But you're more than sceptical here, you're *certain* the laugh is not the family ghosts." He spoke casually.

She nodded.

"What makes you so certain that it's a—well—a fake?" he asked.

She hesitated.

"I don't think that would be quite easy to say," she said slowly, "but I have an idea that something grave is being planned against my husband. My husband is the owner of the property, and I have an idea that some person who intends harm to him, is staging this ridiculous piece of family superstition." She stopped. She had spoken with great care, like one stepping from stone to stone in crossing deep water.

"With the object?" the chief inspector asked. He never showed himself as quick of apprehension in talks of this kind.

"Of having whatever happens to him appear as something foretold—occult."

"You have an idea who this person is?" he said quietly.

She shook her head.

"Not the slightest."

He asked her a few more questions, chiefly as to why she felt so certain that this was not merely a practical joke, but had some evil intent behind it. She gave evasive answers, pointing out that she had only her woman's intuition to go on.

"But a woman's intuition, you know, chief inspector—" she wound up smiling. A surface smile. Her eyes were fixed and intent.

"Is very often based on acute observation of many small things," he finished. "At least in my experience."

She flashed him a glance at that in which he would have sworn that for a second, there was a gleam of mockery.

"I should very much like some one from Scotland Yard to look into the matter," was all she said.

"I'm afraid it's not a case for us. We have all too few men as it is for very pressing needs. But how about a chat with your local police?"

"Over a ghost's laugh? I really haven't the courage. But can't you give me any advice? Make any suggestions?" she pressed.

"If I were you," Pointer said after a moment's thought, "I should go to a first-class private investigator, one whom I could introduce to my friends, and to any house-party that you may have at the moment."

"That's what someone down at my husband's place advised. Someone who, I know, has nothing whatever to do with what's afoot. He suggested a Mr. Marjoribanks. Is he any good?"

"Mr. Stephen Marjoribanks? None better. You can put yourself unreservedly in his hands. He's a gentleman by birth as well as by character. He would fit in very well as a guest."

"And he's clever, you think?" she asked, frowning a little.

"Clever, I know," Pointer assured her.

She thanked him, took down Marjoribanks's address, and left with a cool nod, saying that she would try and see the man at once, since Scotland Yard could not come to her assistance.

Not an effusive woman evidently. She did not look it. And apparently not over-pleased with the result of the interview. Or was that only the impression which she intended should be left?

She had struck the chief inspector as both sincere, and oddly, deeply insincere, throughout the short interview. It was an idea based not on anything psychic, but on observation of tone, half smile, and fleeting gleams of an eager, yet ironic, kind in the cool bright eyes.

And that feeling, too, of both sincerity and insincerity, was what struck Mr. Marjoribanks most, when within the hour she sat talking to him in his large room. A room so large that his clients could feel at ease about eavesdroppers. Though, had they known it, there was a recordaphone connected with the telephone extension standing beside a typewriter.

To Mr. Marjoribanks, Ivory Danford gave her name and the name of her husband's place. The one told the other, to him. Farthing was one of the oldest houses in England.

Marjoribanks knew vaguely too of the tradition that a spectral laugh, three times repeated, heralded a violent death to the owner of the place.

"You don't think it's some silly idea of a joke?" he asked when she had repeated what she had told Chief Inspector Pointer.

She looked at him with a glance in which he too, like the Scotland Yard man, caught something mocking.

"Who would be so cruel as to play on a wife's fears, or on my husband's fears—though he pretends to scoff at such things? I'm sure no one at Farthing would. Besides, all of us were in the hall at the time."

She explained that the house was empty of guests. The persistent bad weather had ruined any idea of cricket, and there was only her husband, her husband's stepdaughter, the land agent, and herself in the house at the moment. The first time when the laugh had been heard, other people had been there, it was true, men hoping for cricket, but not yesterday. Yes, the laugh had been heard the second time yesterday at lunch, and had sounded as though in the room with them.

Marjoribanks questioned her a little further, and again something evasive flitted through the sentences. It annoyed him.

He told her that he did not think he could be of any use to her, and that he was working very hard just now on a case which threatened to last another week or more. Probably the twice-heard laugh was a joke, he said suavely, to frighten her husband. A joke on her own part, Marjoribanks was half inclined to think. The idea of getting a detective down was, or might be, he fancied, merely a cloak, a sort of alibi for herself.

Should he unexpectedly find himself free . . . he ended, with the insincerity of which he suspected her; and should she still care to have the laugh investigated, they might discuss the matter once more.

Mrs. Danford got up reluctantly. He thought she looked more baffled than anxious.

"By the way," he asked, as he held the door open, "who sent you to me? I never advertise."

"Our land agent, a Mr. Rivers. He spoke of you as particularly good at seeing through frauds," she murmured.

The door closed, and Marjoribanks returned to the case on which he was working. But Mrs. Danford haunted him. He experienced a quite unusual difficulty in driving thoughts of her from the field of his mind. She made him think of a sentence of Conrad's in a book which he had been re-reading on his way up to town only that morning. "You may take it from a man who has lived a rough, a very rough life, that it is the subtleties of personalities, and contacts, and events, that count for interest and memory—and pretty well nothing else." "Subtleties of personalities, and contacts, and events . . ." Yes, he felt them here. He was almost sorry that he had another piece of work on hand. Then with an impatient frown at himself, he managed this time to concentrate on the task before him.

Meanwhile his would-be client's husband, Edgar Danford, owner of Farthing, whose life the ghostly laugh was supposed to menace, was just stepping into his handsome private room in the suite of offices in Fenchurch Street, where Cox and Plumptre, Metal Merchants and Agents, had settled over a century ago.

The firm, of which he was the only active partner, had been one of the most successful, and still was one of the most respected, in London. He himself was around forty, with a fresh-colored, clever kindly face.

Something about him still spoke of the artist, the out-of door painter which he had once been, which he would still like to be. Something about him, too, suggested anything rather than a business man, and there again it suggested the truth. He was one. And a remarkably astute one, a ruthless one, his enemies whispered, but he did not care for business in itself, and whether for that reason or not Cox and Plumptre had only just been able to pay the dividend on their preference shares this year. All other shares were held by members of the firm equally.

"Well, Pippa, come and welcome Mark as the new partner. The papers have been duly signed, and the event duly celebrated." Edgar Danford had a pleasant deep voice. He laid his hand on the arm of a tall, smiling young man who entered with him.

His stepdaughter, Philippa Hood, came forward. Since leaving Bedford College she had insisted on acting as a sort of unpaid private secretary to Danford.

"Did you have champagne?" she asked Mark Ormsby in mock anxiety.

"Chateau Lafite Rothschild." And Ormsby added a notable year. He was a young man who looked clever, and as though he were quite aware of that valuable asset.

Without being handsome, he was quite passable looking, though his eyes might have been larger and wider apart with advantage. For the rest, one would put him down as a young man with whom the good things of life, and some not so good, were usual, and to whom they would appeal very strongly.

"You must think he's worth his weight in gold," Pippa—her full name was only used on formal occasions, even the servants never employed it—said laughingly to her stepfather.

"Don't you?" he asked in return, with a twinkle in his eyes.

Pippa and Mark Ormsby had become engaged only this morning, and Mark was coming on down with them to Farthing presently, to spend the week-end. Pippa pursed her lips as though considering the matter objectively. Ormsby laughed and would have caught her hands in his, but she put them behind her. He took a short leave and hurried off.

Pippa stood looking after him with a little pucker on her smooth young forehead. She was slight, small and very pretty, with a hint of what might be called the post-war look, the same look that Ormsby had, that Mrs. Danford, her stepfather's second wife, had; the look of a person determined to have a good time and to let little pass them by, whether worth while or not worth while. In her case, even more than in his, it was too early to tell what else the look covered, for she was barely two-and-twenty; but something about her chin suggested a tendency to a vacillation which might be only a surface blemish, or might be part of the core of her.

"Come, Pippa, don't be shy. Don't you think Mark worth his weight in gold?" repeated her stepfather teasingly.

"I'm not sure," she said doubtfully and rather unhappily. "Awful, isn't it? After this morning."

"Come, come, Miss Weathercock, or weather hen!" he reproved in mock indignation, yet watching her keenly.

"I'm only terrified of making a mistake," she said slowly. "With whom did you lunch?" he asked suddenly.

"Kate and her brother, and—Beaufoy." The last name came hastily and yet unwillingly.

"Ah, with Rivers!" There was a short silence.

Then Danford said:

"My dear girl, you're not regretting not having taken Beaufoy Rivers instead of Mark Ormsby are you?" He spoke bluntly but very gravely.

"That, Chief, is entirely my own business." Her head went up.

"Not exactly." Edgar Danford spoke very kindly. "Your mother was far too dear to me for that to be possible. I stand to you in the place of your dead father. And I know that he would say, as I do, that Beaufoy Rivers is no husband for you."

"Oh I'm aware that it's supposed to be the best way, if you want a girl to marry a man, to warn her against him. But that's only in books. You're far too sensible for that twaddle to be true of you. And I do warn you against Rivers. He's unstable—shifting—"

"Oh!" A glow came into her cheeks, "He's a dreamer with wonderful dreams."

"He's no husband for you," Danford repeated gravely. "He's a good land agent, but just because I like him, and he's my own kinsman, I see his faults. More of them than I care to talk about to you. Now Ormsby has a fine character. He too comes of a good family, and he happens to have ample means —unlike Rivers."

"And unlike Beaufoy too, he's more than conscious of those points you mention."

Danford said nothing for a moment. He stood with his quiet, kind glance on the girl, apparently thinking how best to put what he intended to say.

"Ormsby tells me that you won't sign the notice of the engagement to be sent to the papers," he said after a little while.

"Not till the week-end is over." She spoke a trifle shame. facedly. "I do want to be quite, oh, quite sure," she added in excuse.

"I think I had better tell you something, Pippa, that I had meant to keep silent about." Edgar Danford spoke slowly, weighing his words. "And I want your word of honor—of honor mind, that what I now tell you will not be told by you to any one. To any one. Ever."

He waited, very impressively. Pippa's eyes widened. "I promise," she said wondering.

"A solemn promise," her stepfather insisted.

"A solemn promise," she assured him, firmly.

"Then this is what I have decided to tell you and what you have pledged me your word not to divulge to anyone. On your marriage to a man with whom I think you can be happy, a man worthy of you, I intend to hand Farthing over to you both as a home, and on my death it is to pass to you, and whomever you marry, absolutely. Farthing, and everything that belongs to it and is contained in it."

"Farthing! You mean, it's always to be my home? I'm to live on there after my marriage, and it's to come to me when you've done with it?" Pippa had risen in involuntary start. "Beautiful Farthing! The only place in the world I really love. Oh father!" She rarely indeed called him by that name, fond though she was of him.

"I bought it originally from Colonel Rivers because your dear mother fell in love with it when I showed her our old family place. We were very happy in it." He sighed. "But as things are, I should like to see you, and your husband, and your children, happy there instead. I bought it partly with your mother's money, you know. You'll have the nice little sum your father left in charge for you on your marriage, and that will help to keep the place up, besides Ormsby's means."

"But it's too much! Much too much! And surely Uncle Harold—"

"Harold agrees with me that Farthing needs youth. We've talked it over many times, he and I. Besides, he feels about the place rather as Ivory does. And she hates it. Says it crushes the life out of her. As for me, I should be equally at home in something smaller, and frankly, more fitted to my purse just now."

"But—but Beaufoy Rivers," she protested, half-heartedly.

"Well? What of him? His father had to sell the place through extravagance and weakness. Just as the son would if it ever came his way. Which it won't. He's no earthly claim on Farthing, Pippa."

"No, of course not!" she agreed.

"He's no relation. A distant, most distant, kinsman."

"He's your next-of-kin, barring Uncle Harold," she said a little feebly.

"Next-of-kin!" he repeated testily. "Farthing isn't entailed. No, no, Pippa! I should not be doing my duty if I let you, with such an inheritance coming to you, marry the wrong man. And Rivers would be the wrong man. He's no husband for you, and no master for Farthing. Now, Ormsby has character. A woman could trust her happiness to him. A place would be well looked after under his care?"

She nodded a little wistfully.

"Come, come! You know that you love him, or you wouldn't have accepted him. It's something Rivers said to you at lunch that's put your eye out—for the moment." He looked accusingly at her.

"Only talking of his dreams. Mark never dreams."

"And a good thing too," he said promptly, but with a humorous half-smile at her.

"You have dreams!" she countered, "or you wouldn't have painted pictures once."

"I was young then. I don't paint now."

"But you look out of a window when you're kept here in town on a fine day, as if you'd like to. You listen to the barking of the wild geese passing over Farthing in the Spring and Autumn as though you'd love to be off with them."

He laughed, but he did not deny what she said.

"I've earned the right to dream," he said finally.

"Mark will never dream." She was twisting her gloves around her fingers "He would be too afraid of their losing him the best of a deal." Danford laughed again, a laugh of intense amusement.

"That may be rather a fault of his," he conceded, "but there's sterling stuff in Ormsby. And there isn't in Rivers." Pippa was silent.

"You mean?" She turned a little pale, "you mean, that if I married Beaufoy, you wouldn't let Farthing come to us either to live on or in, or—or—when you had done with it? But you would, if I married Mark? Is that what you mean?"

"It comes to that—yes," Edgar Danford agreed. "I know that in your heart you really love the better man, Pippa. The rest is only glamour—"

"Dreams," she half whispered, half sighed.

"Ormsby is the right man," he persevered. "He loves you and he's just the man to make you happy, That's what I want to secure. What Harold and I both want to secure."

"It isn't fair!" Pippa said suddenly facing him almost , angrily. "Oh, it's not fair to've told me! How can I let Farthing slip away? To own Farthing! I never dreamt of such a thing. Never to have to leave it. Oh, it's not fair to offer me such a gift. Of course I'll marry Mark as I've promised—"

There was something fierce, defiant, in her voice.

"And among all the young men whom I know, Pippa," Danford said again very earnestly, "there isn't one whose character I respect as I do his. That's why I want you to marry him. You say it's not fair to tell you about my intentions. But remember, my dear girl, that it's only your happiness I want. And, quite apart from Farthing, if you were penniless, I should think any girl who got Mark Ormsby, got a prize."

"So would he!" She said it half in fun. Then her face sobered. "Or—I wonder! If I were a penniless girl? Mark doesn't know of your wonderful plan of giving us Farthing to live in as our wedding present?" she asked quickly, suspiciously.

So it was to stay "us" and "our." Danford was glad. "Ormsby? Not an idea! A fine surprise for a disinterested lover, eh, Pippa?"

"But—poor Beaufoy!" she said ruefully. "I shall feel a sweep. After all, it was to have been his inheritance— once. Before his father had to sell it. Before the crash."

"My dear, if you're going to be sentimental I shall be sorry I ever offered to take him on as agent. Only he hadn't a bean. And he is a distant kinsman. And he knows the place thoroughly, and really is well up in all the by-laws, and regulations, and all that sort of stuff, that agents have to know nowadays." Danford spoke tartly.

"Besides the work he's doing on that wireless crash preventor you're interested in," she put in. "He's really awfully clever. Because his father couldn't keep his head above water, in the changing times of the war, doesn't mean that Beaufoy couldn't. There's nothing he couldn't do, and do well, if he gave his mind to it."

"Perhaps—if he gave his mind to it. Pippa," Danford caught the twisting fingers and held them gently, "you know that I've only your good at heart?" He waited for the answer. It came at once.

She felt quite sure of that.

"And so I say, take Mark Ormsby and ultimately take Farthing with my blessing, and lead a full, happy, honored life, useful to every one around you, or take Beaufoy Rivers, break your word to Mark, and slide with Rivers, gently at first, then steeply down, and down—and out!" There was the ring of sternness in Danford's voice. "Mind you, don't think I'm coercing you. I'm speaking to you as man to man. I know putty, and I know solid metal. Rivers is putty. What has upset you so? Why this sudden swing over to him?"

"Oh, nothing," she said evasively.

"No, no let's talk the thing out fairly. We've always done that, you and I. What has cast such a spell over you?"

"Oh, Chief, he explained some of his work after lunch to me. He's getting on splendidly."

"I know. I'm financing his researches. I and Ormsby together from now on. But you're not interested in wave mechanics. Don't try to make me believe that you are tempted to break off an engagement only a few hours old because Rivers is doing good wireless work." Danford was grimly humorous.

"He told me he loved me," she said very gravely. In the tone of a woman turning away after a last look into the coffin at a loved face. "You see, he doesn't know I have just got engaged. And because his work was promising to be a success financially—or because it's such a wonderful July day—he—he talked—of his dreams." She choked. Then she straightened up.

"Well, that's over—or rather it never was. And there's Mark coming up the stairs. Mark always walks as though he owned the earth."

She was quite charming to Mark Ormsby though, when he opened the door and told them that the car was below. It would have taken a close observer to detect any coolness in the smiles that she gave him, the laughter that seemed to spring so readily to her lips. It was quite a seemingly cheerful trio that drove down to Norbury. It so chanced that Ormsby had never been to Farthing. Something had always prevented his accepting an invitation there. He knew of it, of course. Every one knew of Farthing.

His first sight of it was as a stately silhouette, and the nearer they got, the more imposing it grew, rising with a certain stark power in its thick old walls from the inner side of a filled-in moat. Its mellowed brick and stone work, its massive buttresses, its gabled roofs and its mullioned windows made a splendid picture. It seemed to tower above short-lived mortals conscious of a vitality which they did not possess, a strength greater than their's. Farthing had been big and brawny even in the early, unregenerate days of King Canute, when some *huscarl* of "the Mighty and Old," after murdering the then owner, had taken his land, and as much of his neighbors' land as he could. "Fourthing" he called his spoils, and in truth it represented a most goodly fourth of all the regions. He kept them moreover, though they lay outside the Dane law, and his descendants, Danfords or Rivers; all of them, had owned it ever since, though many another unlovely tale of greed and treachery accompanied the transfer of its mighty bulk from one generation to another, or from kith to kin.

The car drew up before a portico.

"Welcome to Farthing," Edgar Danford said warmly. There was the usual agreeable stir that an arrival in a friendly house makes. Ormsby's man had already arrived with his suit cases, and a little later he came down from the comfortable rooms assigned him into the great inner hall to find his host reading a letter. He waved it at his guest. The two were alone.

"It's from Digby Cox. He writes that he isn't coming to us for the week-end after all. In common civility he should have come. I told him expressly you'd be here. But he writes that he can't manage it."

The Cox of whom they were speaking was a great-nephew of the original founder of the firm, who, by the uncle's will, under favor of a clause in the original articles, had been appointed a partner in the dead Cox's place, but without a voice in the company's management.

Digby Cox must have written more than an excuse.
Ormsby thought, to account for the vexed look on
Danford's usually cheerful face.

Danford went on to explain his expression.

"Cox called in to see me about a perfectly mad claim of
his only yesterday; he still writes in the same strain."

"Claim?" Ormsby looked his interest.

"Oh, too preposterous to discuss," Danford said
contemptuously, "but I'll just speak to him over the
telephone. He's staying for the moment at Brighton, it
seems. But before 1 try to catch him, just a word. Pippa
asked me if you knew that Farthing is coming to her on
her marriage and will be left her on my death. I said that
you hadn't an idea of it. It wouldn't do to have her think
anything else. She might imagine heaven knows what
absurd and quite. Untrue stuff. She's shockingly
romantic really—"

"Quite so," Ormsby agreed heartily

"Besides," Danford went on, it was only by the merest
chance that you saw that paper—"

Ormsby again agreed, and Danford hurried away into
a room opening out of the hall.

While his host was busy with the telephone, Ormsby
looked about him with a sort of grudging appreciation.

The big hall was very fine, he acknowledged, but it
was also very gloomy with its walls, and musicians'
gallery, and raftered ceiling, all of oak, darkened by the
slow passing of the centuries, and perhaps the good
brown ale with which it had been tended. The windows,
with their tiny panes and bright heraldic insects, flung
soft patches of color here and there on to the polished
boards, but they were powerless to cope with the
shadows.

Under the gallery two glimpses of the lawns, and
trees, and flowers outside showed like twin oblongs of
glittering enamel where the slatted doors stood open. The
light they let in fell on some wonderful things, Ormsby
had to acknowledge He was used to good houses, came

from one himself, where generations of taste and means had had their way, but there was not another commoner's house in England to touch this one. Some of the carved chests and "joyned" stools around him were by rights museum pieces.

In a corner, facing him, gleamed a suit of plate-armor as perfect and complete as on the day when an owner of Farthing had tilted in it at the Field of the Cloth of Gold. A fake he told himself, but he knew that it was genuine. He had come down there determined to at least pretend to himself that the fact that Phillippa Hood was some day to inherit Farthing had played, and played now, no part in her attraction for him. But the fact remained that it was only after he had seen a copy of Danford's will that he had asked her to marry him.

The document in question had been handed him among some which the incoming partner had to look through. Ormsby had given it back with an "I say! This is some mistake!"

Danford had taken it from him and looked it over. It was a signed copy of his will marked to be kept in the safe of the estate room at Farthing.

"How on earth did it get in there? Shows how this constant bother with Digby Cox has rattled me." Danford had said apologetically. "Here's the paper that should have gone in its place."

Ormsby had read the other paper through, but so he had the first one. And its contents, the contents of the will, not of the new metallurgical process in which "Cox and Plumptre" were interested, had staggered him.

After a moment, Danford had said a little awkwardly, but very much as though he meant it, "by the way, that will is to be an absolute   secret, of course. My brother Harold knows of it, but no one else has a notion. I don't want a land-grabber to get on the track of the future owner of the place," he had continued.

"The very future owner!" Ormsby had thrown in lightly. On that, Danford, who hoped very much that he and Pippa would make a match of it, had told him briefly, but as a definite promise, that on her wedding day, Farthing, and all it stood for, passed onto her, and her husband's occupation and use, until such time as his death should make it theirs absolutely.

"Pippa is a very charming girl," Edgar Danford had wound up. "I think her more than that, but we're talking, what's in a way, business now—the business of her happiness. She's charming, she'll make any man a wife in a thousand, but until she's married, she's rather difficult to count on. Her mother was like that. She led me a pretty dance until the very altar steps, but after them she was constancy and loyalty itself. Pippa is, and will be, just the same."

Ormsby had murmured something to the effect that he was sure of it. He did not add that he was also sure that Farthing was a noble dowry.

Ormsby loved land. It was in his blood, that strange call of the earth, the actual earth and all that grows on it and is rooted in it. His mother came of a great land-owning family, and all his early days Mark Ormsby had been looked on as, her brother's successor, but the uncle had married, and three boys stood definitely between the one-time heir and Great Scaw.

He had now gone into business, after a couple of years in a minor government post, but, though he knew it was no good to a man who wished to make, not to spend money, the landowner's life was to him the ideal life. Also, he wanted to try later on for some of the big parliamentary plums, and an estate was a fine stepping-stone. Well, he would have it now. The will had been duly executed. Nor was Edgar Danford a man to change his mind. Quite the other way. "I hold," their family motto, applied to plans as well as possessions.

Of course he was very fond of Pippa. But a pretty girl becomes no less attractive because such a gift accompanies her. It would be a good match, for both of them. He, though he was but a younger son's son, came of

as good a family as did Pippa herself, and, like her, he
had a sufficient fortune of his own. Between them they
would keep Farthing up as it deserved. It had never been
neglected, though Edgar Danford frankly, admitted that
it might have come to that in these last years of intense
depression in the metal trades but for his brother Harold
who now lived with him, and contributed more than his
share to the upkeep of the place. Harold was unmarried.

Still, Ormsby had reflected as they drove past the
home farm on the way here, a man keen on the place, a
man like himself, would change several things for the
better when he was master.

The sunlight outside seemed to beckon him with a
promise of glitter and gold. Judging by the tone of
Danford's voice near by, his conversation over the wire
was not nearly ended, so Ormsby stepped out into the
gardens.

Along this side of the house ran a terrace with little
bays in it here and there dipping into the thick walls.
Going down to a lower grass-walk, less open to the hot
July sun, he saw a young woman standing with her back
to him, pressed in flat against the wall, close to a jutting-
out window, a window of the room where his host had
gone to telephone, or Ormsby was much mistaken. She
seemed to be listening intently. She was not in any
uniform, but wore a crumpled frock of some pale material
that almost matched the stonework. Ormsby frowned. He
had half a mind to walk along the upper terrace and
make her beat a most inglorious retreat, but she might be
a guest in the house, though she did not look it, and in
that case—well, awkwardness could hardly go further.
For a second he watched her.

There was something positively painful in the
straining intensity of the small, dark head, of the hands
pressing the light skirt closer mound her, lest a stray fold
should show itself to anyone in the rom.

Ormsby returned as he had come, walking over the grass to the hall again. He had hardly stepped in when Danford hurried back, looking very much put out.

"Can't get him. The hotel was sure they could find him, but it was no use."

He stopped as Pippa came in, with the sunlight turning her pretty brown hair into a sort of halo as she stood a moment in the door.

"Beaufoy wants you, Chief. Something about some elms that need topping, but which no one can be got to top, apparently. I told him to have tea with us and talk it over with you afterwards." There was just a hint of defiance in her voice, but her stepfather smiled approval.

"Good. Beaufoy Rivers is my land agent," he explained to his guest. "He's also a distant kinsman, and the son of the late owner of the place."

"—and he's awfully like that portrait there," Pippa finished inconsequently, looking up at a painting inset over one of the big hearths. Electric candles, perfect copies of the real thing, showed a man in the dress of the late Tudors. In his long, pale, narrow face the eyes were boldly painted. There was power in them. They were dominating eyes that followed you wherever you moved in the hall. They seemed not so much to observe you as to command you.

"Oh, come now!" laughed a rather gentle voice—for a man—behind them, "I hope that's only your vivid imagination, Pippa, and that I'm not really like that devil incarnate!"

It was the land agent himself. A slender young fellow whose sensitive brown face and deep set, rather veiled, eyes bore a certain structural resemblance to the painting, in spite of their owner's denial, and in spite of his youth.

A silence fell on the little group. It struck Ormsby, who was a quick observer, that it was a silence full of constraint. Pippa continued to stare at the portrait with something in her glance that suggested that she would have liked to look away, but was held, either by her thoughts or by something in the skill of the painting.

"May one inquire the story, or is it too bad for words?" Ormsby asked Pippa. She hesitated. Then turning resolutely from the portrait she said with a tone of almost forced gaiety.

"He's the demon of the family. Yet he was a perfect little gentleman until middle age and Queen Mary came along, when he turned Roman Catholic. But he was suspected of heresy all the same, and was to lose his property—in other words—Farthing. So he promptly told on his wife, and had her burned, in order to gain merit in heaven and on earth. And incidentally in order to keep Farthing. It was there, in front of that very fireplace that he stood, when they dragged his wife, Dame Anne, off—" Pippa went on.

"And very glad she may have been to go and be rid of Farthing, even though by way of the faggots," remarked a cool, brisk voice from the stairs.

Ormsby saw that it was the listening woman whom he had seen on the terrace. A moment later he was introduced to Mrs. Danford. Quite apart from his first glimpse of her; she was a surprise to Ormsby. He would have expected beauty in the mistress of such a place. He only saw a carelessly dressed young woman with wispy hair badly in need of tongs or water-waves, or whatever it was women do that makes their hair look like rippling silk. Her complexion—Ormsby was shaking hands by this time—was shiny. Distinctly shiny. And rather sallow. Her hand-clasp he considered too firm for a woman.

"Do you mind giving me that executioner's block beside you, Edgar," Ivory Danford turned to her husband. "It is a shade higher than this one." And with that she sat down at the tea-table, refusing a cocktail. These remarks were Mrs. Danford's only contribution to the conversation.

She sat most of the time looking through one of the open doors, like a captive out of a prison slit. Her face wore an expression of extreme boredom, yet Ormsby noticed that she seemed always to be listening, that when she sat with her eyes on her hands hardly seeming to be conscious of the presence, of others, there would come an unexpected, swift, upward flash. of bright eyes for a second that showed a most alert watchfulness.

Though she was so quiet, far too quiet for a hostess, discord had entered with her. There was a vague but quite perceptible feeling of something, or someone holding aloof from the others, inimical to closer intercourse.

For one thing Ormsby thought that between herself and Pippa there only reigned a sort of cold civility. That would not have surprised him had not Pippa when he had first met her this last winter at St. Moritz, spoken in enthusiastic terms of her stepfather's wife.

Fortunately Pippa did the honors and did them charmingly, except for the fact that she let young Rivers monopolize her, thought Ormsby.

Before the tea was more than begun Harold Danford came in. In looks he was very like his elder brother, but thinner and quieter, yet with the same pleasant smile and manner. He seemed around forty, though he was a couple of years younger, but his thinning hair was gray on the temples, and he wore glasses. He was making a name for himself as a composer, and was living for the time being at Farthing in order to finish an opera that needed seclusion.

After shaking hands with Ormsby, whom he knew already he held out a bunch of wild flowers to his sister-in-law.

"I picked them as I walked back through the spinney. They'll go well in that piece of pottery against that Meriel sampler."

"Any tomb will do," she said negligently. "Ring the bell and Dawson will see to the death ceremonies."

"You don't like flowers?" Ormsby asked civilly.

"Why should you think that? Because I don't like to see them dying all around me? Flowers die when they're cut, and suffer cruelly. I like to see them growing."

"I forgot!" Harold said penitently, "I only thought of their color. Let's hope Pippa won't disdain my little gift for her quite so thoroughly." He began to get something out of a box in his hand.

"Oh, Uncle Harry!" Pippa dashed over to him. "What is it? Oh!" Pippa fairly hugged the little piece of porcelain that was finally unwrapped.

"It's the mate to the Drinking Boy we have in the China Room—Oh, how splendid! Look everybody!"

"Splendid!" Edgar echoed with appreciation.

"Splendid!" Ivory repeated with a note of sarcasm in her voice. She reached out a hand, a very well-shaped hand, and picked up the china in her turn. She gazed at it with a sardonic smile. It represented a stout and blowsy young woman sitting on a stool, her head sunk back in drunken stupor against the wall behind her, while from a full cask beside her, the beer was running away. "Rockingham ware, ,I see. A truly lovely thing!" She handed it back as though it were a treasure indeed.

"Ivory, you're jealous!" Pippa said good-humoredly, "jealous of anything given to Farthing. But Farthing's awfully pleased, Uncle Harry, that at last it's going to have a mate to the piece that's waited so long—over fifty years since the Drinking Boy was picked up by—let me see, not Colonel Rivers, but his cousin, the then owner."

"I think you know the history of every pin in the place," Mrs. Danford said with a little laugh, that for the once sounded like genuine amusement, as she watched her run off with her new acquisition. Then she turned to her husband.

"Mrs. York tells me that Mr. Cox is not going to be here to-night after all."

Mrs. York was the housekeeper.

"So it turns out," Danford said irritably, "he's written no sort of an excuse, merely said he can't manage to-night, not even for dinner. It's too bad. I wanted him and Ormsby to meet."

Mrs. Danford dropped her eyes to her lap, then she lifted them and gave Ormsby one of her quick, brief, intent glances that he had already noticed.

"The old and the new partner?" she said finally.

"Exactly. And I wanted Digby Cox to meet you too—" Danford went on.

"How do you know that we haven't met already else where?" she asked, smiling a little. A bright, but very intriguing smile.

"He's not spoken as though he had ever met you." Danford looked puzzled. "Have you met?" he asked, wheeling rather sharply on her.

"Ah!" She smiled gaily, but it was not a friendly gaiety, "wait until you introduce us, and then you'll find out!"

Pippa rejoined them.

"The Drinking Boy nearly dropped his flagon for sheer joy," she said in the pleased tone of the collector.

"But I meant it for you, my dear girl," Harold Danford said, smiling at her look of pleasure, "not for the Drinking Boy."

"*Tout pour Farthing* should be Pippa's motto." Ivory Danford rose with a little gesture as though suddenly weary. "Pippa, do come out into the sunshine, and look about you, and realize that there's a whole wide world which is not Farthing. Which is much bigger than Farthing, and much more beautiful. Farthing is an ogre, or rather a witch-doctor, and casts black spells, I think."

Harold Danford only shook his head indulgently.

"There have always been plenty of us Danfords and Rivers, Ivory, who kept Farthing where it belongs— outside, not inside, their souls."

Pippa had not condescended to reply to Ivory Danford's outbreak. She was talking to her stepfather over in one of the long windows now.

"Happy, Pippa?" he asked her fondly.

She nodded, rather over-forcibly.

"You'll never regret the step you're taking," he said gently.

"May one ask what earthly thing it is that one never regrets?" Mrs. Danford had evidently very sharp ears.

He told her of the engagement. Mrs. Danford did not glance at Pippa. She turned to Ormsby with so cold and probing a look that it amounted almost to a challenge.

"I congratulate you," she said icily, "and you too, Phillippa. A most excellent arrangement, I fancy. Congratulations to you too, Edgar." Her gaze swept her husband. Pippa rose hurriedly, unheeding Harold Danford's little mild staccato notes of surprise and pleasure. It was almost as though she fled from the hall, and she did not so much as glance at where Beaufoy Rivers sat with a sort of incredulous, horrified stare in his eyes, like that of a man suddenly shot through the heart by someone whom bethought his friend.

CHAPTER TWO

THERE was a large dinner party at Farthing that night. Ormsby met all the neighboring people. Cricket was the one topic of conversation—cricket which was being done out its rights by the shocking weather—except where Mrs. Danford sat. She did not care for games of any sort or sport in any form. Ormsby decided, as he glanced at her, that she was not so easily "placed" as he had thought. She was evidently a most entertaining talker, the corners near her seemed to sparkle with her light, rapier-like wit. Even her looks had changed. Her green frock, bright as a beetle's wing, suited her. Her little gold turban tight around her head with its large mock pearls dangling over her ears, framed a face that could, he saw, be bewitching. And yet, he thought, there was something about Mrs. Danford—it was difficult to see what—that always kept that barrier up between herself and others.

Ormsby told himself that it was not his knowledge of her eavesdropping, but some quality in her smile that suggested, to him at least, that she was laughing at, as much as with, those around her. She conveyed, intentionally or unintentionally, a sense of an inner meaning to many of her remarks, he thought, inner hostility to those around her.

And, though her end of the table sparkled and rippled, Ormsby did not think that she was popular as Danford, for instance, was popular, as he himself intended to be popular in his time. For Mark Ormsby was a very good cricketer indeed, in itself and by itself an *open sesame* down here. And it would not be by itself nor of itself, it would be backed by Farthing.

The dinner was not very good. Good cooking has gone out of fashion. It is so dangerous to the slim outline, but the wines were superb. Ormsby decided that it was no wonder that the late Colonel Rivers had died a bankrupt if he had laid down this cellar. It was just before the break-up that Danford suddenly leaned forward in his seat.

"Forgive the old-fashioned touch, but please fill your glasses, ladies and gentlemen, and drink to the engagement of my stepdaughter, Pippa, with Mark Ormsby here. He is going to be her partner as well as mine."

Pippa turned scarlet, something in her eyes looked as though with as much vexation and surprise. Ormsby too was not prepared for this but he made a very amusing reply to all the good wishes that rose around them. As for Rivers, he did not lift his eyes from his plate, but sat composing diagrams with green almonds around a peach-stone center.

Afterwards Danford got a chance for a word aside with Ormsby.

"Surprised you, eh? Well, frankly, I thought it just as well to put up the county banns as far as Pippa is concerned. She's very popular, you know."

Ormsby murmured some civil word of agreement. But he thought that he knew why Danford had made his little announcement. Not so much for the sake of the county as for Beaufoy Rivers. Ormsby had caught that young man's eyes resting on Pippa's face—just after the little toast, and he decided there and then, that he would have another land agent.

In the drawing room he noticed that Pippa was not there. Was she in the gardens? He had seen Rivers step out. Ormsby strolled promptly onto one of the terraces. It led to a path which in its turn led onto a rustic bridge that crossed a trout stream. Two figures were on the bridge leaning on the railing looking back at the house. But though one was Rivers, the other was Harold

Danford. Ormsby joined them and he too looked back. He was startled at the beauty of Farthing seen from this spot. Silently the three men looked up at it. Ormsby heard Rivers beside him draw a deep, almost a quivering breath. It was like a man making a vow, he told himself. Glancing at him, he saw the younger man's eyes alight with an eager, covetous look. The look of a miser who seeks a sack of gold. A moment more and Rivers seemed to notice who stood beside him. He drifted away. Had he felt at least one pair of eyes on him, Ormsby wondered? He saw Pippa standing in one of the drawing room bays, but the next moment he was lost in contemplation of the house and its setting. Farthing rising from its gardens was a vision this evening. A great possession. After all, such a place would cover many faults . . . after all, would the girl herself greatly matter who brought this noble pile to a man? It was a chance in a thousand to acquire even a prince consort's right to such a spot, and Edgar Danford's will had been very generous. Farthing would be as much the husband's as the wife's, and he loved Pippa, very much indeed; it was as if out of the gloaming the sirens were singing to Mark Ormsby from the roofs of the old house.

He felt eyes on him. Turning, he met Harold Danford's quiet scrutiny. He flushed uncomfortably. "Fine place," he said brusquely, carefully choosing words cooler than he felt. As cool as he could muster. "I was never able to come down before."

Harold Danford nodded a little disparagingly.

"My sister-in-law and I agree in our opinion of Farthing," he said with a smile, "the place is too old. And too powerful. And too jealous," he went on, "Edgar tells me that by some inadvertence you are aware of his intention to hand it over to Pippa and whomsoever she marries. No one must know, of course, of his plan, but one likes to think of youth and freshness in these old halls, of children's feet running across this very bridge. But whether the place will bring her happiness? Do possessions ever do that? *Acres* spells *cares* if you transpose but the first two letters."

His voice held a doubtful note.

"Possessions certainly don't prevent happiness," Ormsby said with sound common sense. He hardly knew what he replied. Nor what his companion had said. He felt as though the walls before him were magnets drawing him—drawing him—

"That's very tr—" by a last-second swerve, Harold Danford changed "trite" into "true," and led the way indoors.

Card tables were spread, for Mrs. Danford refused to go into the card room itself. She wanted music. As so often she wanted Harold to play to her—and to her guests. She did just barely include the others in her gesture.

"Play something from your Symphony of the Heavens," she begged. "The duet between Mira Ceti and its companion star for choice. I heard the village orchestra practising it last evening."

He refused, though pleased at her eagerness. "It would sound horrible on the piano," he assured her. "The fact that the oboe is above the clarionet in those consecutive fifths makes all the difference—a line of silver on vermilion. Your color vision is too good not to be stunned by it in one flat sweep."

Mrs. Danford replied. They talked a language quite unknown to those around them. But it was an intelligible language. They understood each other, with their talk of color thinking, of perspective and focus, of vertical and horizontal lines, tone depths and tone washes. They might have been two painters.

"But play something!" she urged, "violin or pianoforte. Play the devil asleep again in me, Harold." She spoke under her breath. "The others don't matter. They'll only hear the bids, anyway."

He sat down. The touch of his fingers on the keys, big-boned and vigorous, spoke of the master. All his notes meant what they said, and said what they meant, and said it clearly, because the player-composer thought clearly. There was a strength, a grave sweetness, yet an austerity in the soft harmonies that seemed to float out from the piano, to have nothing to do with strings or hammers, that kept Ivory Danford spellbound. What was he playing? Now it sounded like bells, far-off bells, not like some resigned leave-taking—now a lament—

She jumped up. There were tears on her cheeks.

"No, no, Harold! Don't preach patience to me," she begged, still under her breath, "and that everything passes. I want something bright—gay. I want life. Real life. My own life." She spoke in a tense whisper. "Play something else. Anything else!" she persisted almost angrily.

The musician nodded. He glanced at the others. Pippa, too, was listening.

For a few minutes his fingers strayed softly among the keys. He was evidently thinking aloud. Then coherence came.

Built up on a rough and rugged tune something rose steadily, expanding without let or hindrance, clear cut and towering. Its massive proportions seemed to darken the very sky, whose buoyant clouds and sunshine he sketched with a few light and glittering notes. Then, bit by bit, the darkness spread and enveloped the whole structure which he was rearing chord by chord, and span by span. It grew cold. Cold as steel and as cruel. Dark and dangerous it seemed to fill the big room, to weigh on the listeners' hearts. The largeness of the design, the clarity and the force of it, and in the end the menace of it, was extraordinary. And it was a menace that had existed from the beginning, that had been woven into the initial theme, working itself out to an inevitable conclusion.

"Oh, what is it?" gasped Pippa, coming near to the player. "What *is* it?"

"Farthing." Harold Danford looked at her with a flicker in his eyes not unlike the light that often played in Mrs. Danford's. "Farthing—as *I* see it, Pippa dear."

"You're a great genius," his sister-in-law said, not rapturously, but quietly with all sincerity. "That is the real Farthing."

"It's not!" Pippa protested, "though you make it grand and wonderful. But put some love into it, Uncle Harry. That's all it needs. Just love."

"Love and dreams, eh?" he asked. And she flinched as though from a blow. He did not notice it, as with eyes on his fingers he smiled to himself, a quizzical, sceptical smile. And, in a few minutes, he had dissolved that which he had wrought into smooth chords, smooth as enamel. Vaguely the outlines of the building showed through at first, but he played them down into the merest shadows. After a *finale* of almost oily finish, he got up and closed the Pleyel. There was an outburst of grateful thanks from all around. There were compliments on "that last charming bit" from every one. Only Edgar Danford, who was one of the dummies, shook himself as though he had been far away. He gave a little shiver.

"By Jove, Harold, you can express yourself in music! But no one would call that thing cheerful."

Ormsby cut one rubber with Rivers as a partner. He never met a worse player. Half the time his partner forgot what were trumps. Later on, Ormsby saw that he fell to Edgar Danford's lot. Finally, when it was time to make an early move to a dance, a charity dance, to which every one was going, the host turned to his wife with a laugh.

"Thanks to River's remarkable talents we're both of us broke." The land agent was out of hearing for the moment, and he went on. "Evidently I am quite remarkably lucky in love." He gave his wife an affectionate glance.

"You are!" she said with a smile like a purr.

She was about to add something, when a woman's laugh rang through the room. High in pitch, unnatural in some way, it sounded both mocking and menacing. There was an instant silence. Ormsby, who had no clue, was as much surprised at the quality of the silence that followed, as at the laugh itself, for there was in the immobility of the guests a suggestion of horror.

Edgar Danford stared around the room as though unable to believe his ears. Harold, who had been talking to a retired diplomat on Janacek's music, stood still with an expression of amazement that was almost ludicrous had it not been for the terror in it.

Only Mrs. Danford showed no emotion except a sudden, alert, and therefore to Ormsby very strange, watchfulness, as her glance swept the room, and darted among her guests. Her eyes rested on him for the fraction of a second with a very probing look as though, he thought, wondering just how the sound that they all had heard had affected him.

"What is it?" he asked her. His words seemed to break a spell. The guests began to whisper in startled groups. The women to rise from the card tables.

Now Mrs. Danford sprang to her feet. She grasped the back of her chair wildly.

"The laugh again! Dame Anne's laugh! Oh, Edgar! Edgar—" He soothed her gently.

Harold Danford turned to Ormsby who was near him

"You must think us all mad, but—well, perhaps you don't know our family superstition," he broke off, biting his lip.

"Edgar, we must have this investigated," Mrs. Danford was saying, with something hysterical in her voice. "Some body's trying to frighten me. It's not possible, oh, it's not possible that any harm is coming to you!" The words, the tone, were those of a loving, half distraught wife

Edgar Danford looked at her affectionately.

"It's just some maid servant or her friend laughing in a room upstairs or downstairs and the laugh is carried in here by a defective flue," he explained to the room in general.

"Of course" came in an outburst from all the guests The men spoke in a confident, would-be completely satisfied way, the women crowded around Mrs. Danford, but she waved them to silence.

"It's not!" she said imperatively. "Oh, no! It's no servant!" Danford crossed the room to her and took her hand

"My dear, you're a believer in the occult. But I'm not. If not some joke, then it's a builder we want."

"If it's not a warning, then we need a detective down," Mrs. Danford persisted vehemently.

Ormsby turned to Pippa.

"What does it all mean?" he asked in a low voice. She was looking behind chairs and stooping under couches. As she stood up he saw how pale she was.

"That was Dame Anne's laugh! Oh, I forgot, you don't know. Every one else here does. Dame Anne, the wife of the man whose portrait we showed you out in the hall, laughed as they dragged her out of Farthing. And again when they sentenced her to be burnt, since she would not turn Roman. And again, a last time, when she saw the faggots and the stake. Oh, yes, they burnt her. And since then, she's supposed to laugh three times before a violent death overtakes the owner of Farthing. And—Mark, that's the third time we've heard the laugh just lately. Of course it must be a hoax—"

"Of course it is," Harold Danford chimed in, patting her hand. "Or as Edgar suggests, it's some timber out of place deflecting a stray sound in some novel way."

"Evidently Beaufoy doesn't think so," Pippa said looking at the land agent.

His cards lay around his feet, and he was gazing about him with an effect of trying to recover some semblance of self-control. Ormsby thought the pose extravagant, and a piece of acting.

But as regards Mrs. Danford, what Pippa had just told him did explain, he thought, that strange watchfulness on her part. It even cast a more seemly light on her eavesdropping of the telephone conversation. If she were a believer in spirit warnings, and thought that her husband had been given, or was being given, one, she might well be on her guard, and, distrustful of everything that could come near him. Since he so obviously was not a believer himself.

Ormsby glanced at his hostess. She was looking at her husband who had turned away. It was a long look, and if there was not dislike in it, Ormsby told himself that he was a Dutchman. Yet he had just been thinking—He frowned. He disliked mystery. And the so-called spirit-laugh, and Mrs. Danford's solicitous, almost hysterical fears lest it should mean some danger to her husband, and now this most perplexing, because it seemed most illuminating, look at that same husband when his back was turned. . .

The laugh itself, Dame Anne's laugh. . . . Ormsby was a thorough-going materialist, and therefore disbelieved in anything occult. It had seemed to come from this very room, but what about some mechanical means?

A portable, hidden gramophone. There are some small enough to go into the palm of a hand. Or what about a concealed loud speaker and a wireless laugh? This last idea kept recurring to him. Rivers was a wizard where wireless was concerned. He, Ormsby, knew this. "Cox and Plumptre" were backing him in some very intricate experiments which wiser people even than they believed might revolutionize flying, by eliminating crashes. Could Rivers be possibly connected with this laugh? But he had seemed so strangely disturbed at the sound. More so than any one else in the room, not even excepting Mrs. Danford. Ormsby thought again that there had been something positively theatrical about his way of marking that what he had heard was a ghost. And on that came, quite unbidden, the reflection that in Mrs. Danford's wail of terror, in her entreaty to her husband to have someone down to investigate, in the very way she clutched her husband's arm, there had been something just a trifle overdone. Ormsby tried to shut out the thought, but it grimaced at him from the recesses of his mind. It whispered that Mrs. Danford's outburst had not carried that note of conviction that genuine emotion bears. Could this be some joke to be explained and laughed at later? But there's no point in a joke, even a practical one, unless it's amusing. No one had seemed in the least amused just now.

Edgar Danford was saying something affectionate under his breath to her at the moment. Some one near Ormsby murmured something about "poor Mrs. Danford being naturally wrought up, as she was a daughter of Grant Beardsly, the well-known spiritualist painter."

Ormsby had forgotten who she was. He remembered the many tales of Beardsly's credulity. His groups of "Those Beyond" were famous. Incidently Grant Beardsly, Ormsby reflected, was one of the few artists who leave large fortunes behind them. And on that came the reflection that Danford's first wife, Pippa's mother, had been very wealthy too, far wealthier than Miss Beardsly had probably been. Well, why not? Why should one not marry a girl, who, besides charm and affection, had lasting gifts to bring to the common household? Why not the system of *dots*? It made for the happiness of the wife he had heard Frenchwomen maintain.

He saw that people were beginning to pass on out of the room. They were off to a big dance near by. He was not going. An effort to play on wet asphalt courts yesterday morning had given him the kind of sprained ankle that only needs a little negligence to become tiresome.

"You'll be late, my dear," Edgar Danford was saying to his wife. She flashed a reproachful look at him.

"Do you think I'm going to dance now—after that!"

"Nor I either!" came from Pippa.

"I should quite expect to hear that something terrible had happened to you on my return home," Mrs. Danford went on apprehensively.

"We should be frightfully nervous, Chief, and uneasy," Pippa chimed in.

He pinched her chin.

"Nonsense! Of what should you be frightened? That Ormsby and I should hear some girl laugh once more? We will try not to scream with fright should that happen? Or are you worried of Ormsby harming me?" He chuckled at the question.

Pippa replied with some half-protesting reply, and Ormsby assured them all that he really was a most terrible fellow if he were crossed, ever so slightly. And again Mrs. Danford surprised him by the steady stare she fastened on him.

Finally, with every appearance of genuine unease and reluctance, Mrs. Danford let them ring for her cloak, and she and Pippa followed in the wake of their guests. Rivers, Ormsby noticed with approval, did not accompany them. Harold Danford went off to his own upstairs suite of rooms.

The two men left behind, played billiards for a while. Then Danford suggested a move to the Chantry for a talk.

"Chantry?" asked Ormsby.

"My own particular dug-out. A chapel built originally by her loving husband for masses to be said for the soul of Dame Anne. Grim old jester, eh?"

Danford led the way through another, room to a deeply recessed Norman arch. A stout door was inset between the curves which he unlocked and opened. They stepped out. Ormsby saw that they were at the extreme end of the wings. Across a wide gravel path a little squat building of Tudor brick faced them.

A door, similar to the one by which they had just left, was unlocked in its turn, and Ormsby followed his host first into a tiny lobby, and then into a large, handsome room with windows running around three sides.

"This is my study." Danford motioned the other to a chair beside a table provided with everything that a smoker could want. He looked about him as a man looks around a place that he likes.

"There wasn't such a thing at Farthing when I bought the place. Colonel Rivers used the business room, and my great-grandfather, who owned it before him, never needed such a thing. So I installed myself here. It had been unconsecrated for centuries, though Mrs. Danford maintains that even so it's use will bring bad luck. I've had it thoroughly put in order. There's this room and a couple of bedrooms above it. It's my retreat when I want to be quite by myself, or bring some business man down whom I don't care to introduce to my wife or Pippa. I often work here, and as often sleep here. But the great charm is that no servant ever enters until, or unless, I ring, and, no one has a key to it."

Ormsby agreed that not being interrupted was one of the most difficult things to secure in this world of interruptions.

They chattered for a while of politics, in which Ormsby was keenly interested.

He mentioned a few of his more modest hopes. Danford promised help. Finally, for it was very close even in this airy, spacious chamber, they sauntered out into the gardens again, walking down paths fragrant with flowers that the shadows hid from sight. The talk veered around to business, and finally to Digby Cox's absence which seemed to annoy Edgar Danford more than a little.

"It's ridiculous your never having met him," he said almost testily. "He and I both waited for you last Tuesday at the office—"

"I know. I was I unexpectedly detained," Ormsby explained.

"And now *he* doesn't turn up. I particularly wanted your opinion of him."

"Why?" Ormsby asked.

"Because my own is none too favorable, for one reason. I'll tell you, another and greater reason later on—"

He stopped abruptly. Walking over the lawns they had turned a corner of the drive. By one of the powerful arc lights, Pippa and Beaufoy Rivers could be seen talking earnestly together. It certainly looked as though he were holding both her hands.

Rivers seemed to melt away as the two men appeared on the scene. Pippa hurried up to them.

"Ivory and I only just looked in at the dance for the appearance of the thing," she explained. "But what on earth are you talking about so solemnly?"

Her voice sounded as though she strove to make it light. She passed an affectionate arm through her stepfather's and looked up at him with great affection.

"Digby Cox," he said promptly. "I would like to bear Ormsby's opinion of him."

"I'll give you mine," Pippa volunteered. "He dopes."

Her stepfather burst out laughing.

"Nothing like a woman for giving you a well-founded opinion," he said, still convulsed. "Pippa has never met Cox!"

"But I've read most of his letters." Pippa was undismayed at the hilarity her kindly opinion of the absent Cox had caused. "And they're quite extraordinary. Psychically, I mean."

"Psychically!" Her stepfather cast up his eyes "This comes straight from Bedford College. Psychically!" He went off into another burst of laughter.

"Why not? They are, as I say, extraordinary." She shook him gently. "Either they're the work of two people, or they show a most unbalanced mentality. I have quite a clear idea of Cox's inner man after reading as many of them as I have at the office."

"What is that idea?" her stepfather asked indulgently, but with quite evident curiosity.

"He could be a most dangerous enemy," she said gravely. "I say that because I feel sure that he is absolutely without any standards. Absolutely mercenary, and yet cloaks himself, even to himself, in a sort of garment of respectability."

Danford laughed again under his breath.

"My dear girl! I should be impressed if I hadn't read the letters—the very same letters myself—naturally— seeing that they were sent to me. To me they were merely rather incoherent for the most part—"

"With an intentional incoherence. Like ambassadors' letters," she put in firmly.

"Nonsense, child," he retorted.

"Neither nonsense nor child." She drew herself up with mock indignation. "I'm frightfully disappointed that he didn't come to-night."

"So that you could find out how true your idea of him is!" scoffed Danford.

"Oh, I shan't find that out," she said quietly. "Any one who has any business dealings with him will. But *I* shouldn't. I should only meet a very ordinary, and probably very pleasant person, as I told you. I do assure you, Chief, that you mustn't trust Mr. Cox an inch further than you can see him." She gave his arm a squeeze and wished the two good-night. Ormsby tried to maneuver a trip around the nearest rose bush or at least up to the house with her, but Pippa would have none of him.

They watched her out of sight, her frock of silver gauze making her look rather like a dragon-fly flitting between the bushes. For a moment Ormsby was silent, then:

"Your land agent seems to have rather lost his head over Pippa," he said bluntly.

"Looks like it," Danford agreed ruefully. "But her's is screwed on the right way. Of course, in the ordinary way, I could get another land agent, though I should be sorry to have to do that, but Rivers couldn't carry out his experiments anywhere else so well. What we call the

Roman tower near his cottage is ideal for his work. And of course he has stored all the materials down here now— no, Rivers must just get over it as best he can. I'm sorry for the boy. But he is doing really fine work as we both know."

Ormsby nodded grumpily. Yes, he knew. The two men had had a great expert, Sir Halliday Barnstaple, down only a month before and his report had been enthusiastic.

"I believe his oscillator-controls are all but perfected now. If so, the Universal Aviation group will offer us— well, you know that the figure is—"

Again Ormsby did. He nodded. A little less grumpily.

"We can't quarrel with our ether-mechanics partner. And in the experimental field, of course, he is our partner," Danford said more lightly. "Not that I mean, or think, you or he would quarrel. Beaufoy has a remarkable even temper. The Rivers's temper." And he led the way into the house.

There he left Ormsby, who sat on smoking in the big empty inner, hall. He fingered a board of Saxon chessmen on a table near his great, leather-thonged chair. Quaint and ungainly the big bone pieces were, with rudimentary animals' heads and with faint Anglo-Saxon characters carved on their fluted bases. It was believed that King Canute had played with these. Or King Edgar. Wonderful place, Farthing. A never-ending source of interest, whether you thought of what its thick walls held, or of its spreading acres. And he would one day own it—together with Pippa of course. His first act would be to get rid of Rivers, however, Ormsby knew the importance of the land agent's wireless experiments. But other places could be found for that. And then came the reflection that it was only on the death of Danford that the place would really pass to him jointly with his wife. Only on the death of Danford could any changes such as that of Rivers be made except by Edgar Danford himself, who, after all, remained the owner till he died. And as men live nowadays he was good for another forty odd years, probably. A feeling of resentment rose in Ormsby. Why had Danford not made up his mind to give the place outright to Pippa as her dowry, instead of leaving it to her in his will. Danford did not intend to live there himself, or to have the use of what little money the estate brought in after all the outgoing expenses were paid. Then why did he only purpose to let it pass from his hands on his death? That distant death. Probably distant. Though of course one never knew. . . . And a man might change his mind about a will. Even such a man as Edgar Danford. Pippa could have told him that Edgar Danford never altered any intention that he had deliberately taken, that he invariably carried out any, plan of his to the end, once he had thought it over, and weighed it well. Mark Ormsby moved uneasily in his chair. Supposing, after all, that Danford were to alter his will some day. . . . Or Mrs. Danford might die and he might marry yet again. Of course his own and Pippa's marriage settlements would take up the question, but he doubted if Danford would let them so tie up Farthing that he could not leave it to someone else eventually should he so decide. He must have another talk with Danford. Not at once of course, but before he left Farthing. Though talking . . . promises . . . especially promises for the distant future— the very distant future. . . . .

How that portrait over the chimney seemed to be staring at him. Ormsby returned the look. Rather a pleasant expression in the eyes from this distance, something quite friendly and pleased about the mouth. He had disliked the face when he saw it first, but somehow, sitting here, it was almost the face of a friend. Approving . . . encouraging. . . .

A cold draught suddenly seemed to chill him, and, without knowing why, he got up hurriedly and went on into the library.

CHAPTER THREE

PIPPA was up early next morning. The day was even hotter than last night, though rain had fallen heavily. Thunder was in the air. First she made her way with a little basket of chopped apples and carrots to the paddock. The hunters, unshod, grass-distended, rough of coat, pushed and jostled about her, a very different sight from the lean, satin-smooth shapes that they had been when turned out to grass a couple of months ago, with a rib or two showing, and more than one strained tendon.

She patted and fed them and finally slipped under the rails and walked back. As a rule she thoroughly enjoyed that part of the daily round. But her face showed no pleasure to-day. She was looking very plain this morning, Ormsby thought, as from a window he saw her pause and stand up at the building in front of her. She was very pale, and her eyes looked red and puffy. But it was more than that. It was as though some hard, cold, element in the girl had obtruded itself, and made her seem tired and almost old. For a long minute she stood staring up. A finch that had finished moulting hopped towards her along a bough and asked her opinion of his beautiful new waistcoat. She never even glanced at the little chap, who retreated thoroughly snubbed. Her thoughts were on Farthing, concrete stone and brick Farthing. Her home, her house if she married Ormsby, and not her home, not her house ever, if she married Beaufoy Rivers. Edgar Danford was not a man to say what he did not mean. Nor a man to change his mind. She knew both facts by knowledge as well as intuition.

Suddenly she caught sight of Ormsby. She turned away quickly. She felt that she loathed him. But that would never do. She had liked him very much up till now. And she had flirted with him rather more than she usually did, though Pippa was a flirt. She ought to be very much in love with him, she told herself. She had promised to marry him. And she intended to marry him. If only there were some third way out. The sunshine seemed to run loving fingers over the old bricks that it had known for so many centuries, but they were red hot fingers to-day.

She turned into another path. Rivers appeared suddenly, wearing the rubber-soled shoes which he always wore at his electrical work, she had not heard him. She stiffened. Her face grew unresponsive to his agitated one.

"Pippa, why wouldn't you give me the chance to finish what I was saying last night? You seemed at first half inclined to listen—"

"Fortunately I remembered that I'm engaged to Mark Ormsby," she retorted.

"But you don't love him. You love me as I love you. I know you do. And you know it too."

"How—how dare you!" It was old-fashioned, but she could think of nothing else to say, and she felt as though she would choke if she said nothing.

He came quite close to her. So close that she thought he was going to kiss her and edged away.

"Pippa." He spoke with a strange eagerness. "What if I could give you what you most love in the world?" He whispered the words.

"What do you mean?" Her voice, too, had dropped in tone.

"Never mind what I mean. But think what you love most." He spoke in a still lower whisper. "And tell me. Would you marry me if I could give it you?"

She stared at him. His eyes were on Farthing's towers too. It was ridiculous. But what did he mean?

"I love Farthing more than anything else," she said in a tone of finality. "Can you give me Farthing?" He gave her a queer, hesitating look.

"You say your stepfather objects to our marrying," he said briefly, instead of replying to her question or rather to her impatient expostulation. "He has no right to object. Nor you to listen to him, when it's a case of following your heart."

"It isn't my heart," she said on that, "it's—it's just—glamour. You're all wrong in thinking that I care for you."

"At this moment perhaps. But you did yesterday noon. You know you did. Pippa, why won't you follow your heart. Your heart wouldn't change and hop about from day to day, almost from hour to hour. But if Cousin Edgar stands for anything in your hesitation, I intend to talk the whole matter, out with him, and as soon as possible, and as plainly as possible." There was an edge to Rivers's usually gentle voice. "In any case, I think I can promise you that his objections won't stand in our way much longer."

"They don't stand in the way," she said weakly.

"Listen," he said peremptorily. "Give me a month before you bind yourself to anybody. At the end of four weeks, I'll ask you to marry me, and—I don't think you'll refuse me then!" His voice came close to her ear. Even so, he looked around him to make sure that they were alone.

What did he mean? Pippa knew how close he stood to great discoveries, but she also knew, that by his agreement with her stepfather made a couple of years back, Rivers could reap but very little money reward from those same discoveries for some time. Danford had backed him well, but not from philanthropy.

"What are you talking about?" she began, when he laid lightly a slender, but very unexpectedly strong hand over her mouth.

"Hush! I shouldn't have said what I did. But don't forget it, Pippa!" And with that he was gone, as though he could not trust himself to say more.

Pippa was bewildered, but his earnestness had impressed her. Also, there was curiosity. Yet on the other hand it came too late, so she told herself virtuously. A promise is a promise. Unspoken was the knowledge that Farthing was Farthing. And with that she walked towards the house and the breakfast-room. She had some grape fruit, toast, and a little tea. Pippa was fetish-ridden when it came to her figure. A peck or two, and she was off again, this time for a stroll with the terriers. She did not acknowledge it to herself but she quickened her step none the less when she heard Ormsby's descending the central staircase.

As for that young man, finding the breakfast-room empty, he promptly buried himself in the papers.

A little later Danford came in. Cheerful of face as always.

"Just read that!" Ormsby showed him a page with a photograph inset. Danford read it.   The gist was contained in a notice at the top which read: "It is feared that Mr. Charles Fairbairn, of Fairbairn and Paget, the well-known. brokers, met with an accident while out walking on the cliff near Brighton yesterday. A coat and hat identified as his have been found on a patch of grass near to a sheer fall of several hundred feet. The grass was slippery from the recent rains, and it is feared that Mr. Fairbairn may have lost his balance and not been able to avoid a fatal tumble," etc., etc.

"Good heavens, what a fatality!" Danford seemed very startled. But Ormsby himself was in no condition to notice this. His own hands were not quite steady as he went on.

"And now read this letter that I've just received, it's from my solicitor who happened to be down at Brighton. Read it!" Edgar Danford did so with a dropped jaw.

The writer told of a very acute doubt as to whether there had been any accident at all to Mr. Charles Fairbairn. The writer's own investigations made on the spot caused him to doubt it. The police—he told this in confidence—doubted it too. He recommended Ormsby to doubt it also. The writer thought that the man in question was not killed or injured, but merely missing. In which case the City would soon want to know why. The writer hoped that Ormsby had not placed a deal of which they had talked only last week with this very Fairbairn, and went on to suggest some quite harrowing reasons for this hope. Harrowing and obvious.

Ormsby took back the letter and put it away. His clear color had faded a little.

"Arnold—that's the name of the writer—wouldn't send this if he weren't quite sure. Well, Danford, I wish I had had this earlier. Say, before yesterday morning. I should have put off coming in as your partner just yet. Had to. For Fairbairn is running some heavy shares for me. I've a fine sum coming to me next settlement day, as I explained to you. But now—" He broke off and set his teeth. "I must find out how things are. I must go up to town at once. Do you mind if I ring and have my man pack at once?"

He went off himself to hurry up this operation. There was a train which, if he could catch it, would rush him to town faster than any motor.

Ivory Danford came in at that moment.

"I'm off to town," she said in her disengaged way.

"Saturday matinée?" her husband asked.

She flashed one of her level inquiring looks at him before she turned away. As though something in his voice had caught her attention.

"Something of that sort. Ah, here's Pippa! Pippa—a word with you." She was out after the girl.

"I'm off to town," she added quickly, "but there's something I must say first. No, don't think I'm going to repeat what I said to you the other day. That's done with. I'm not fond of repetitions. This is something else. It is, that if you don't marry Rivers, you'll be sorry for it all your life. And now good-bye." She kissed Pippa and was gone.

Pippa flushed with what looked like keen vexation, then with a little twitch of her lips that was the equivalent of a shrug she walked on.

For a car was drawn up before the portico, and Ormsby's man was putting in some cases. Ormsby himself appeared a second later.

"Walk with me to that tree at the corner," he said, tucking her hand in his arm. "There's plenty of time for me to get in there."

When they were clear of the servants he began.

"I've had a blow, Pippa. A financial one. Can't tell how bad a one until I make some inquiries in the City this morning. That's why I'm rushing away. Perhaps I shall be down again to-night." He told her briefly what he had learned from paper and letter.

"Are you deeply involved?" she asked.

"To over my head if the firm can't pay."

He kissed her, in spite of the windows, and in spite of her lack of enthusiasm, and hurried to the car. She walked back into the house and into the breakfast-room. It was empty by now. She tried the business-room, where her stepfather was generally to be found at this hour of a Saturday morning. He was there. His face startled Pippa. It was that of a man who sees all his future tottering.

She took a swift step to his side. There was nothing hard about her looks now.

"Oh, father! Are you involved too?"

He stared at her with eyes that seemed to see her entrance only now. Then he glanced behind her at the door. It was shut. He struggled hard, she saw, to get back his usual imperturbable, pleasant look. But in vain. He only showed the effort.

"Hush, Pippa!" he said in a voice that was not quite steady. "I didn't hear you enter. Was the door standing open?"

She told him that she had opened it. He seemed relieved, she thought.

"I'm going up to town as soon as I've seen Beaufoy, and got through the usual weekly business with him. But I shan't go near the office, and I expect to be back here in time for dinner."

With that he left her.

Meanwhile Marjoribanks, the private investigator to whom Mrs. Danford had gone, found his mind constantly recurring to her and her story, if story one could call it. The task on which he was engaged suddenly fell away. A clever piece of work on his part knocked the ground so completely from under one of the parties that they instantly made terms. By Saturday he was free, and more and more regretting his dismissal of Mrs. Danford's suggestion that he should investigate the laugh heard at Farthing. He looked up the warning in a book on Family Portents. It was fully described. Dame Anne's threefold laugh, first heard a month before her one-time husband was burnt to death when paralyzed.

The laughter, always heard three times running, had been recorded six times in all at the date of the book's publication, and it was only a couple of years old. All the times were apparently duly vouched for, all could really be considered authenticated. All invariably preceded a tragedy to the owner of the place.

That much of Mrs. Danford's story was true therefore. Not that he had doubted that much. He did not think her a liar. He had a feeling that facts would be as she said, but as for other things—?

The book called to his mind a talk which he had had some months ago about warnings of that kind. It had been with a young man who had seemed very keen and well-informed on the topic, at the rooms of the "Other World" Society. What was the young man's name? Ah, yes, Rivers. That was it. Oddly enough, the article on Dame Anne mentioned Rivers, or, de Redvers, as the name of her husband. And as the name of one of the two families who, as constant owners of Farthing, were directly concerned at the present time with the portent. And it occurred to Marjoribanks on that, that Mrs. Danford had murmured something about a "Mr. Rivers" from whom she had first heard of him. Perhaps it was this last little straw that finally decided him to go down to Farthing after all and look into that curious warning, if warning it were—or hoax, if hoax it were.

He tried to get Mrs. Danford on the telephone, but she was away from home. Probably for the day, he was told on inquiring further.

"May I ask who is speaking?" Marjoribanks said, half inclined to ask for the husband, half uncertain whether Mrs. Danford would like that done or not, and certain that he had heard the voice before.

"My name is Rivers," came the reply. "I'm Mr. Danford's land agent. And you?"

It was one of these coincidences that are always happening in connection with thoughts about people or things.

"Aren't you the Rivers who talked to me at the 'Other World's' rooms some months ago about family warnings? It's Marjoribanks speaking."

The voice replied that he was that same Rivers and went on in what sounded an eager and pleased voice, "So Mrs. Danford did go to you yesterday! I didn't like to ask her. And you're looking into the matter? Good!"

"Well—unfortunately, Mrs. Danford is away for the time being, and I did not take on the job yesterday. I was at work on another case that has unexpectedly fizzled out."

"She is coming back later on in the afternoon," Rivers reminded him. "Come down meanwhile and have a preliminary look round."

"What do you yourself think about the affair?" Marjoribanks asked. The reply came rather slowly.

"I don't know what to think. But—I'm awfully glad you're going to clear it up. Mrs. Danford is nearly off her head with fright."

The description of the lady's state of mind intrigued Marjoribanks. Neither worry nor any likelihood of her going off her mental balance had been a feature of his opinion of her. Two hours later he was shaking hands with Rivers at Norbury station. Past the lodge gate, the inner, gate— there were two on the drive, one at the entrance to the park, one of the gardens proper, Marjoribanks got out of the car and walked slowly up to the house. Rivers would join him as soon as he had run his car into his garage, but a few minutes' drive further on. Marjoribanks looked up at the vast building, vast more in height and thickness than in actual spread of circumference. There were many larger houses in the country, but even Marjoribanks had never seen a building that impressed him more. A place like this, he thought, staring hard at it, might get a strangle-hold of you, supposing you lived here, belonged here. For there is power in old houses Marjoribanks always maintained. A power of their own. As though they acquired life from all the lives lived within them. As if they had sucked at the vitality of the living, until they had stored up a vitality of their own, and then began to take the upper hand, owning their owners, steadily draining their life-power, growing bloated as the. years passed, and victim after victim faded into the family vault, generally placed conveniently close.

Yes, he thought, here in this old, old house might be invisible, but most potent forces at work, that could be very terrible. And the recorded history of the place which he had read in the train coming down was steeped in treachery and greed. Not through and through. There were golden threads woven in as well.

The land agent interrupted his musings. He led the way in, and explained that Miss Hood was looking forward to seeing the visitor.

"She'll be thankful to have someone like you to talk to. It's no use my telling her the laugh we heard is as much Dame Anne's as that suit of ring-mail at which you're

looking—it belonged to King Stephen, by the way. Like
that nose-guard helmet over there."

Rivers left Marjoribanks to make an enthralled tour
of the great hall. He was not given much time to see its
treasures, for very shortly the door opened and Pippa
came in. In her bright summer frock she made a pleasant
picture amid the surrounding gloom. And then too, she
was no kith or kin of these dark walls, which were by this
time literally bone of the bone and flesh of the flesh of the
Rivers and Danfords, for every breath breathed within
them had left its residue behind it, Danford breaths and
Rivers breaths, touch of Rivers hands or Danford hands.

Rivers introduced him, spoke of his interest in things
psychic, and of his skill in unraveling mysteries, then he
left them together. Pippa welcomed the investigator most
cordially. She only regretted Mrs. Danford's absence, she
said, as she knew how thankful her stepfather's wife
would be to have some qualified person try to explain
those puzzling, and, Pippa confessed, terrifying laughs.

Marjoribanks made some suitable reply. Then he
learned to his dismay that the laugh had been heard
again, since Mrs. Danford had talked to him, had been
heard for the third time last night. That meant that they
would not be repeated, unless there was some perfectly
innocent explanation of them. And since they would not
be heard again, he could not unmask them on the spot as
he had hoped. He would not have come down had he
known. Still, since he was here, he would have a look
round.

He inquired about the origin of the legend, or fact,
whichever it was. Pippa told him.

"What a horrible story! And how pleasant to
remember the justice of the man's own end."

He crossed over to the painting which she pointed out.
He had noticed it already for a certain curious strength, a
sort of dramatic intensity that made it one of those
disturbing pictures which refuse to stay on the wall,
which will intrude into the center of any room.

The day was dark. Pippa turned on the candle lights. Alive and solid the figure looked, with that curiously truthful effect which tells the spectator that the portrait is a good likeness though the subject be never seen. The greatness of a picture is not in the subject but in the treatment, and in some deep way this picture was truly great, with its distant view of Farthing behind the standing figure. It was far and above any other that Guillim Stretes, the boy-king's court painter, had ever done. He had drawn the two sides of the face unlike each other, so that the expression seemed to shift with the changing angle of view.

Even had he not known the tale of the man's life, Marjoribanks would have considered this a sinister face, cold, penetrating, and obdurate, with traces of cruelty and avarice in the lips and chin.

"So rather than lose Farthing, he doomed his wife to such an appalling end! Another instance of the possessor possessed. Well, the world has improved since those bad days." He turned away with a shudder, as though from the living man.

And as he turned, by that trick that the portrait had, a faint but sinister smile seemed to flit across the face in the dimly lit hall.

Marjoribanks eyed it from the center of the room with growing distaste. It might, he thought, have belonged to one of Goya's most terrible frescoes, with a hint of some living and awful reality that belongs not to the thing seen, but comes from far beyond it, from a spiritual world of horror.

And then he saw the likeness to Rivers. He started. But though he acknowledged that it was only a case of a certain similarity of brow, eye-socket and head shape, and that there was nothing unpleasant to be read in Beaufoy Rivers's face, the thought remained, and went to join the fact that the land agent had been extremely interested in warnings and portents not long before the laugh was heard at Farthing this last time.

"Is the Mr. Rivers I know any connection of the original of that portrait?" he asked.

"A very, very distant one. He's descended from a collateral. But my stepfather's mother was in direct descent from that horror. She was a Rivers too. Danfords and Rivers intermarried dozens of times, in order to keep the property in the family."

"It would be a tempting dowry."

He noticed the sudden cloud that crossed Pippa's fresh and pretty face, and speculated on its cause.

"Is he in the running for the property at all?" he asked vaguely.

"Mr. Rivers? Oh, no!"

And again Marjoribanks felt that he had trodden in some way on her toes.

"To whom would the place go if anything were to happen to the present owner?" he persisted.

"That would depend on Mr. Danford's will," Pippa said stiffly. "The place is not entailed. Has not been for generations."

He next asked her where everybody had sat on each of the times that the mocking laugh had been heard. The only person who seemed to have been present all three times was Mrs. Danford. Danford himself and Pippa had heard it twice. Harold Danford, Rivers and Mark Ormsby only this last time. Pippa described also the curiously inhuman character of the sound. That was one of the attributes spoken of in the book on Family Portents, Marjoribanks remembered. It was also the attribute of a phonograph laugh—or of a laugh reproduced by wireless.

"What do you think of the laugh yourself?" he asked.

Pippa hesitated.

"Well, by daytime it seems so silly, doesn't it. But it has been heard. And it did come three times, exactly the same laugh. I heard it twice, and Mrs. Danford, who heard it all three times, says that it was exactly, the same each time, in length and in pitch and in expression. Always weird, eldritch, unhuman. And last night, when it came for the third time, I was—well, I certainly did get the wind up! Like my stepfather's wife. My stepfather laughed at us, and at it, and by day—" She puckered her forehead. "I wonder if, after all, it could be a servant laughing, when she thought herself unheard? They do speak, and laugh, with quite different voices from any they ever let us hear them use, you know."

Marjoribanks thought that Pippa was speaking frankly, was telling him all that she knew about that laugh. Why had Mrs. Danford given him such a different impression?

"How did Mrs. Danford take it?"

Again he was told of that lady's state of terror.

"And Mr. Harold Danford? Mr. Danford's brother?"

"I don't think he liked it at all. Though he pretended to agree with my stepfather that it was some woman laughing somewhere."

"And probably is the explanation," Marjoribanks said at once. "And Mr. Ormsby, did he agree?"

"I think he was too puzzled to know what to think."

"And Mr. Rivers?"

"He—it quite upset him," she said thoughtfully. "But then, you see, he too is a Rivers. It shocked him tremendously."

Now that was not the impression that Rivers's account of the affair had made on Marjoribanks when they had talked of it driving up in the car. Sceptical, not shocked, was the word that he would have used.

"Is Mr. Rivers a believer in things commonly called occult?" he asked next. Pippa said curtly that she did not know. "There's no one else staying in the house?"

Pippa explained that the bad weather had driven away the houseful of guests that they had had last week, and had prevented any others being asked in their place. Norbury offered nothing to a visitor in summer except first-class cricket.

There was a little silence. Though all the lights were on, it was very dark in the great hall.

"Mr. Marjoribanks," Pippa said suddenly and rather timidly, "what did you mean by that phrase you used just now. The possessor possessed? You were speaking of the Sir Amyas Rivers of that picture."

"Great possessions have a way of exacting their own payment," he said, looking at her; her voice had sounded stirred. "You can't have anything in this world—nor in the next—without paying for it. And sometimes the price paid outweighs, to an onlooker, the value of the article bought."

"That man of course paid his soul away for Farthing," Pippa said dreamily, going once more to the canvas and peering up at it. "He's still supposed to have a sort of wicked power. The country people wouldn't pass by the family vault at night for anything. Just because he lies there. And Mrs. Danford's father—but then he believed in such things—came down here once. He was writing an article on the painters of Edward the Sixth's period, and wanted to see it. Do you know he begged Mr. Danford to destroy it!" She gave a faint and derisive laugh. "Fancy destroying the gem of all the pictures here! He said it radiated evil."

Marjoribanks said nothing.

"You don't believe that sort of thing, do you?" she asked.

"I don't disbelieve it," he said quietly. "Granted, and anyone of an open mind must grant, that relics have strange powers, Miss Hood, powers of healing and help that in many well authenticated, historic cases have nothing to do with the faith of those healed, or helped, then I think we must agree that the reverse is possible. Not likely, nor probable, but possible."

"But surely that's rather hard to believe," she said doubtingly. He noticed that she was easily swayed to and fro.

"Not more difficult to, believe than some of the powers of wireless. Not more so than the beam, for instance. The relic, we might say, has been for centuries regarded and thought of with veneration and piety. Blessed in all men's minds, it has stored up powers of blessing in itself. It gives out, as it were, all the good put into it by the minds of those who have believed in it. Just as coal gives out the sunshine stored in the trees ages ago.

"Well, in the same way"—he too now looked at the portrait—"in the same way, as I don't suppose that anyone ever looks at that picture without thinking of, or speaking of, or being told of, the terrible crime committed by the man painted there, feelings of horror, thoughts of the fate of Dame Anne, might well have been accumulated on that square of painted wood, and might—might—be given out again to very sensitive minds. Or minds in tune with it. But now, may I roam the house a little and have a look at some of the rooms down here?"

He had brought a pocket phonograph with him and experimented with sounds above and around the drawing-room. Harold Danford had by now heard of his presence and came down to speak to him. He felt sure on thinking it over, he said, that it was either a hoax of some stupid and cruel kind, perhaps the work of one of the discharged housemaids of a month back, two girls who lived near by and could slip in and out with care. Or it was some chance reflection of sound? Here, too, Marjoribanks received the impression of a man concealing nothing. Then what was Mrs. Danford concealing? What was back of her reticence? As for the land agent, he might well have adopted in all honesty this simple solution, since both the Danford men held it so firmly, which would account both for his agitated manner when he heard the laugh—he, a Rivers —and when to-day he had doubtless thought it over and scoffed at the whole thing, himself probably included, for his momentary perturbation. From Harold Danford Marjoribanks learned the history of the land agent.

His father, Colonel Rivers, had committed suicide, either because he was up to his neck in debt, or because he had to sell Farthing. Rumor said the latter.

Another instance of the possessor possessed, thought Marjoribanks. Both men started. A distant roar sounded around them, a tremendous thud made the windows rattle. The first might be thunder, but the second—? Rivers put a red face in at the door to say that he hoped no one was alarmed. Something had fused. He was very technical, and therefore quite incomprehensible to his listeners.

"He's a wireless genius," Harold Danford explained to Marjoribanks after the face and explanations had disappeared. "His experiments are all made on the top of an old tower near his cottage, but just now he's setting up something quite new on the roof in the way of wireless. I don't understand the passion for it myself. For men in some lonely spot, yes. For invalids, and so on. For rapid communications I can see its use, but otherwise! And when it comes to transmitting music! Well, heaven preserve me from ever being transmitted."

Marjoribanks, as soon as he was free to move about the house again, and he received carte blanche from Harold Danford, strolled up on to the roof for a chat with Rivers, whom he found like a spider in a most complicated web of wires.

"My knowledge of wireless is limited to swearing at atmospherics," Marjoribanks said, coming closer. "If you could tell me how to cut them out, I should not have wasted my time, as I have otherwise, in coming down here."

"Atmospherics?" Rivers turned a dreamy eye on him. "Of course, in thundery weather like this, they're pretty awful."

Marjoribanks, while he listened, was looking about him carefully. His knowledge of wireless was not so slight as he had represented it. He too wondered whether a loud speaker, well concealed and muffled, might not have—

"Personally I love them," Rivers said suddenly. "They're literally the pulses of the world. We really do hear in them the actual beating of the tropic heart of nature. They're pure energy. But about your question—" and Rivers went into a disquisition the upshot of which was, that, so far, you could not hope to keep the atmospheric out and only let in the signal, tune as you might.

"Atmospherics are nature, you think. . . ." mused Marjoribanks. "Well, of course, nature will always creep in." And with that he made his way downstairs to find that Mrs. Danford had just telephoned saying that the coming storm would keep her in town for the night. It looked like being a very unusually bad one.

Even here at Norbury the outlook was so threatening that Marjoribanks decided on returning at once to London. The warning laugh always came at least a week before the misfortune of which it warned. He could not waste a week of his time in waiting for what might never eventuate, for it stood to reason that a real criminal would not herald his intention beforehand. And if some spiteful parody of a jest were about to be played, in which the wife had a part, or of which she was cognizant, well—that did not appeal to Marjoribanks.

He had an idea that Danford was to be stampeded into something, a life insurance perhaps—change of his will—a dozen things . . . but, at any rate, nothing that he would care to touch. Or else, since Rivers and Mrs. Danford seemed linked by their definite scepticism of the laugh it might be a divorce court in the offing. Also nothing he ever touched. Rivers saw him off, and they just made the station before the storm broke.

Pippa, alone in the great hall, watched the rain lashing at the trees, and the trees beating back at the rain. Saw the wind trying to tear off the leaves in passing, saw it break all the flowers that withstood it, and howl around the house as though maddened by the calm defiance of that massive bulk. The sky was all but pitch black, great rivers of lightning showed at close and closer intervals till the countryside seemed bathed in alternating light and darkness. The thunder crashed

almost in time to the flashes. As always, the storm was
traveling in a circle, and Farthing seemed to be on one of
the worst sweeps. It was very close indoors, and outside
was impossible. The rain was coming down in moving
walls of water with intervals of furious wind, and then
another swirl around of lightning, and thunder and
lightning.

The smell of electrical discharges pervaded the air.
She began to go over the thoughts which, this last day or
two, had been milling in her head. But to-day they
seemed to have taken on a stormy tinge. Farthing . . .
Ormsby . . . Rivers.

Farthing. . . . She shifted her seat restlessly.

She told herself in sultry discontent that very likely
Farthing would not come to her in the end. But her
stepfather had spoken very definitely. So much so, that
he must have already made his will. So that if he died
unexpectedly, as men did sometimes, she need not fear its
loss too, as well as the loss of him himself. Not that
anything would happen to him, of course. Still—men did
die unexpectedly—and if anything should happen, why
then in that case—it would not matter whom she
married, or if she married. And supposing—in that most
hypothetical case—that case that was of course not going
to happen until she would be long past the marrying age,
why then, she could marry Rivers and give him back the
home of his father, the house where he had been born.

A flash jerked through the great room. From its place
over the chimney the portrait showed up oddly brilliant.
She had never disliked the face before, never been able,
as had others, to read into it any hint of what came later,
but now it seemed to glow, with a horrid, anticipatory
look. Its lips parted in almost vampire greed, its gleaming
eyeballs straining into the room as though quivering with
eagerness. They seemed to fasten on Pippa with a sort of
gloating triumph. And surely that thought that had
swished through her mind, with great black wings

outspread, was none of her's. That thought that on the whole it would be tremendously to her advantage if—

Pippa jumped up with a shudder of revulsion. It was high time for her to dress for dinner.

When she came down again, she glanced involuntarily at the portrait. The light on the canvas had gone. The picture was barely discernible in the intense gloom. It gave her an odd relief. At that moment she heard a sound in the outer hall and pressed a switch. Great bronze electric torches burst into flame. The lanterns down the body of the hall shone through their horn slides.

Her stepfather was standing in the doorway with a stranger behind him.

"This is Mr. Cox, Pippa. You've read so many of his letters, and talked to him so often over the telephone, that it seems quite ridiculous to introduce you solemnly to each other. But this is my stepdaughter, Miss Hood."

Pippa looked curiously at the "well-known stranger," to use an expression which she had heard in Dublin. She saw a tall, slender, red-bearded, red-haired man. He limped as he walked.

"He got flung out when his own car skidded and overturned," Danford went on. "I had to fit him out. But where's Ivory?"

When he learned that his wife would not be back that night, Danford looked definitely annoyed. As for Cox, he burst into a chuckle that sounded to Pippa much too amused to be sensible.

He grinned again in the same over-amused way, when Danford said, "Well, at least you and Miss Hood have met. Ah, here's my brother Harold."

The usual conversation on the weather began. Harold Danford thought it wonderful. "Even the clouds seem to sweep past in a harmony of their own, wild and primitive. Ever heard any of the Hebridean songs? I understand that you've traveled far and wide"—this to the visitor— "'The Song of the Seal-woman' for instance? You should when you get the chance. They're the wind, and the sea

and the calls of the birds and the seals put into music."
He broke off to turn out a light near him. "I don't like any
more electricity than I can't help having around me in
such a storm. I only hope Beaufoy isn't on the roof, still
playing with aerials."

"In which case, I think we should have heard a call of
something more than a bird or a seal before now," Edgar
said grimly.

"He's in his cottage. Shall I order the wooden knives
and forks that we have, to be laid for us to-night?" Pippa
asked gaily. "I mean the set that Snorro brought Earl
Tostig over from Denmark?"

"Wireless?" Cox had a muffled and yet a high-pitched
voice. "Have you a wireless here?"

"Not yet," Edgar Danford said quickly, and changed
the conversation. Rivers's experiments were private, and
very important financial issues hung on their success.

Dinner was very silent. Pippa had an idea that her
stepfather and his guest must have fallen out coming
down from town. As for Cox, he ate sparingly, and drank
only water. When he was absolutely forced to speak, he
replied in the shortest of sentences, but his eyes were
active.

Pippa noticed them always at work, roaming the walls
and the raftered ceiling above them. The great
banqueting hall, in the corner of which their round table
was set, was worth looking at, with its carved panels, its
great fireplaces on which stood out in faded colors the
arms of the Danfords and the de Redvers, its frieze of
carved shields each charged with the arms of a family
with whom the owner of the place had intermarried, but
Cox did not seem to pay much attention to the carvings.
His gaze was oddly sweeping and general, and yet very
searching. Also, she fancied that he tried to make his
observation unobtrusively.

Harold Danford rose when she did, pleading his
symphony and a new combination that had just occurred
to him as the wind whistled past the windows.

"But I forgot—you wanted me to act as witness to some signing or other, didn't you?" He halted, halfway to the door.

Danford frowned at him, the frown that enjoins silence, and has no connection with ill-temper.

"Thanks no. You won't be needed. Cox and I aren't going to do any business, or even talk of it to-night. Though we shall chat on for a while in the Chantry, where we shall both sleep."

Pippa drifted into the library. She knew that a box from one of the booksellers patronized by Mrs. Danford had arrived, and she helped herself to a couple of new novels.

To her surprise her, stepfather looked in before she had done. He seemed rather excited, she thought, as he carefully, closed the door behind him and came up to her.

"Pippa, just a word. If the Chantry should ring you up in a few minutes, and Cox should ask you, after saying that he's speaking for me, whether Ormsby took a paper, of which he and I are speaking, up to town with him, I want you to say that you 'think so, but aren't certain.' Keep to that, will you. Don't pretend to know anything about the paper, except that Ormsby took one which I had handed him and put it in a safe in town. Cox won't press for further details. The fact is, I want to be able to produce a certain document if I think it well; or not show it to him, if I think that better still. You mustn't mind if Cox sounds annoyed. I rather fancy he'll be more than that!" Edgar Danford laughed a laugh of intense amusement at some project which was going well, Pippa thought. She knew that laugh. She promptly told him that he could count on her to do exactly as he had asked.

"Good girl. And do you think you'll feel up to starting off with me at five tomorrow morning? Wet or fine? I'm going up to town, and we could just run over your translation of the letter to Messieurs Jacques at Stutz."

"Are you proposing to attend early service at Westminster Abbey?" she asked curiously.

Danford laughed.

"I want to deposit something in the office safe and get back here before the world, our world, is astir. I want you, partly because of that translation, and partly because I think it's just as well you should know what I intend putting in the safe. But I can tell you about that too on the way up. Will you come? But no keeping me waiting, young lady!"

"I shouldn't think of keeping my boss waiting," she said in shocked tones. "Why, I might lose my job!" And with that he left her.

A few inquiries of the housekeeper told her that a breakfast of some sort would be provided by a kitchenmaid, and Pippa decided to turn in early. In spite of the storm she was soon fast asleep.

As for Mr. Marjoribanks, he had set out all right from Norbury station on his way back to town, but a fallen tree had blocked the line after some half-hour's traveling, and the train had to put back. But before reaching the station another tree fell on to the rails and it was late at night when he was told at the inn that quicker travelers who knew how to find their way to the hostelry in the darkness and through the howling wind had taken all the available beds, yea, even to the time-honored one on the billiard table. There seemed nothing for it but a couple of arm-chairs. But Marjoribanks had just spent a night in them while at work on his case, the case that had petered out. He decided to think of something better than that. And he thought of Rivers and the land agent's cottage. An inquiry over the telephone told him that Mr. Rivers was out at the Tower. He was put through in another minute. Yes, Rivers replied he had a spare bedroom. Two of them. Marjoribanks would be heartily welcome to whichever he preferred, and would he excuse him, Rivers, from being there? He was at some work that could not be put off, and would take some hours yet. The maid at the cottage knew all about the ingredients for hot toddy, or rum and milk, or anything else in the line of cocktails. He would tell her to stand by with whatever his small cellar offered. Marjoribanks thanked him, and explained that he wanted to catch the first train up in the morning. Rivers regretted that he himself never put in an appearance before ten on Sunday, as Saturday night was always a night of extra work with him. However, if Marjoribanks would understand his absence at both ends of his short stay at the cottage, the land agent would be delighted to have him.

Marjoribanks assured him that his hospitality would be accepted in the same spirit as it was offered, and then was able to get a lift on a car to Farthing's gates, where one of the lodge keeper's children directed him to a cottage, which in the daylight could almost be seen from Farthing's windows. Here Marjoribanks found everything ready for him, and fell asleep to the sound of driving rain on the windows.

CHAPTER FOUR

MARJORIBANKS looked at his watch. It was only a little after three. He had slept well and felt thoroughly ready for the day which was not due for another two hours yet. He was disinclined to turn over again. The light in the room was not convenient for reading in bed. He opened his window and looked out. The storm had quite died down. The air smelled and tasted washed and clean, and softly perfumed with the flowers that the storm had strewn over the gardens. All yesterday afternoon and evening the windows had had to be almost battened down, the force of the rain had been so great. He suddenly decided to walk part of the way back to London. He looked at his map and timetable.

Yes, by starting now, he could walk to Undershaft, and catch the same train there that would leave here later on.

He knew of a good inn in Undershaft, an inn where breakfast for a hungry man could be ordered blindly. A three hours' tramp, and an hour's rest at the little village, would send him back to town refreshed and invigorated.

He dressed quickly and noiselessly. He had turned on his cold tub last night, as the train which he had expected to catch from Norbury, would take him out of the house before any one else might be astir.

A little later he made his way softly down the stairs. As he did so, he heard voices talking. Very low voices. He hesitated. If Rivers were up he might thank him for his hospitality in person better than by the letter which he was about to leave on the hall table. But the sound came from Rivers's bedroom. A voice was speaking which Marjoribanks had not heard before, a man's voice. He heard the words, "Suppose we call ourselves partners—"

Marjoribanks made up his mind not to disturb the talkers. He did not want to spoil the fit of his timetable which allowed of no lee-way this end. Nor did he want to intrude. And, since he was not investigating the mysterious laugh of Farthing, conversations had no interest for him. He left his note of thanks, let himself out, and started down one arm of the drive that would lead past the big house and out through the two gates. The rain of yesterday had made the gravel soft and noiseless as velvet.

The stars were wonderful. Against them, Farthing showed up as dark and vast as a prison. It did not fit in with this summer night that suggested tents and loggias. The sight of its walls brought back to Marjoribanks the reason for his coming here. He was not pleased with himself for leaving like this, and yet the case—whatever it was—was not in his line at all—even supposing that Mrs. Danford had really wanted him to investigate that laugh. The private investigator is supposed to be a sort of passer-on of anything that he finds out. Was that the reason that made Mrs. Danford seek one? That would look as though something serious . . . but no criminal ever warned people beforehand. . .

Marjoribanks threw off that recurring doubt, that the matter might be graver than he thought it, and reiterated to himself that some petty scheme was afoot, that Mrs. Danford hoped to clear herself of any suspicion of being implicated in it, by being able to state that she had asked for a detective. . . Or did she guess that he would not take the case? And merely want the credit of having tried for him? Marjoribanks walked on slowly deep in thought. Suddenly a light was flashed into his face, and after traveling very swiftly down and then up him again, remained on his face.

Marjoribanks promptly side-stepped and peered at the man holding it.

"Are you staying at the house, sir?" a voice asked, a voice that Marjoribanks would have recognized the world around as belonging to an English police officer, civil, business-like, and imperturbable.

"I'm at the land agent's cottage. Why?"

Again the light traveled over Marjoribanks very swiftly.

"Up early, aren't you, sir!" the voice went on. "I'm Superintendent Lang. We've just had a telephone message from Farthing, from a Mr. Cox—"

He paused. "Know the name, sir?" he asked, as Marjoribanks said nothing.

"I know it as the name of one of Mr. Danford's business partners, that's all. Well?"

"Well, the message said that we were to come at once. That Mr. Danford had met with an accident in his bedroom at the Chantry—meaning what we call the chapel, I suppose."

The superintendent had wheeled. "Do you mind coming with me as fast as we can leg it, sir? You must know your way about pretty well to be able to take a walk before daylight." The superintendent kept very close to Marjoribanks, and just a thought behind him. Marjoribanks knew that position well.

"My name is Marjoribanks," he said now. "I'm a private investigator working for Mrs. Danford."

He had instantly decided to take on the case, which no longer seemed as trivial as he had thought.

"Mr. Marjoribanks? I know the name." The superintendent spoke civilly, as he almost hustled his companion over a lawn. "And working for Mrs. Danford? But on what? What's brought you here, sir?"

"She was disturbed about a laugh, that has been heard lately at Farthing."

"Ah! Dame Anne's laugh. We heard about that to—funny. . . . But here's the chapel. Mr. Danford sleeps here often heard his head gamekeeper say. No one seems to be about. The big house itself looks all dark too. Wonder where Mr. Cox is? Do you happen to know which is Mr.

Danford's room?" whispered the police officer. "That message may turn out to be some one's idea of a joke."

The superintendent rang at the Chantry door. All remained silent and dark. Flashing his light up, both men saw that most of the windows on the floor above, the only floor of the little building, were open. Marjoribanks recollected a ladder that he had seen yesterday lying not far off. He led the police officer to the spot.

"Dropped when that first deluge came down probably," the police officer suggested, stooping over it. Straightening up, he mentioned that he had a stiff arm. Could Mr. Marjoribanks manage to carry the ladder for him? He would be exceedingly obliged.

Marjoribanks, amused at the still rampant suspicion, carried the ladder around to the front of the Chantry. There he placed it against the first of the open windows.

"Shall I go up?" he asked. The superintendent again thanked him, and came after. Marjoribanks's head rose over the sill, and there it stopped.

By chance he had put the ladder against Danford's bedroom. Looking in, he saw a big, pleasant room, a bed not far from the window, and on the bed, lying with its face turned towards him, its terrible face turned towards him.

"Good God!" he gasped, and would have leaped over the ledge into the room, but the Superintendent, staring over his shoulder, had him by the arm in a second.

"Stay where you are, sir!" came the quick order. "He's dead." A whistle sounded. A constable appeared in the darkness below them swinging a stable lantern.

"Guard the ladder, Tompkins. Now then, sir, be kind enough to go down. And wait down at the foot till I join you."

There was no time to argue. The police officers passed him from one to the other before he could have said a word, had he been so minded. The superintendent then crooked a leg over the sill and stepped into the room, taking off his cap as he did so.

Some minutes later a low murmur reached Marjoribanks's ears. Someone was using a telephone and speaking through a mouthpiece that would let him use the lowest of tones and yet be heard over the wire.

Another minute and the superintendent's lamp showed as he stood on the window.

"I'm telephoning to the chief constable. Anything you can tell us that I ought to add? Anything bearing directly on what's happened behind me?" He jerked his thumb over his shoulder.

"What has happened behind you?" Marjoribanks asked quietly.

"Murder," was the reply.

"Of whom?" persisted Marjoribanks. "Who's the dead man, officer?"

"Mr. Danford himself, sir. Now then please, anything you can tell us we ought to know at once?"

Marjoribanks shook his head. He would have found it difficult to speak had he wanted to. It was a dreadful position for him. The wife had come to him, had appealed to him to save her husband, and he had turned her down. He could have immediately hung up the case on which he was working; he would have hung it up, had Mrs. Danford's story seemed urgent —or real—to him. And he had not done so! He had come to Farthing it was true, but with a dilettante, a scoffer's interest almost, never believing for a moment that he trod near an open grave. Yet that was what he had done. He must have stepped over it in his careless stride. Marjoribanks bit his lip hard while the Superintendent continued his low-voiced conversation with the chief constable of the county.

It was horrible. He might have saved Edgar Danford—the man whom he had seen for the first time just now with features choked out of all semblance to what they should look like —had he trusted the wife's story. Never before had such a thing happened to him. He had always hitherto in accepting, or rejecting cases, been able to rely absolutely on his instinct—he always gave his unconscious observation that convenient name. But never again. Not after this. It seemed to him, that next after. the murderer, he was guilty of Edgar Danford's death. And it had been his great chance. The chance that every man in his heart wants—to pay for his passage through this world in good coin.

He shrivelled in his self-contempt. And what of Mrs. Danford? What of the woman who had been so evidently misjudged by him? What would she think, and oh, worse by far, what would she feel, when she learned the awful truth? The superintendent's light shone like a pantomine star at the head of the ladder again. Sliding down like a lamp-lighter, he turned to his constable.

"The Yard," was all he said. Then he spoke to Marjoribanks. "The chief constable has put the inquiry at once into the hands of New Scotland Yard. One of their detective officers is coming here as soon as possible."

"Do you know which one?" Marjoribanks asked. "I know most of the men there."

"Indeed, sir?" The superintendent's voice sounded less coldly aloof. "No, we don't know yet who's coming. But I'll venture to say that he'll find his work cut out when he does get here, I don't care who he is. But I want Mr. Cox now. He's not inside. Every room's empty, though another bedroom has been occupied, bed slept in, and so on. You say you're staying at the land agent's cottage, sir? I think we'll go round there first. This Mr. Cox may have gone for him—for help, I mean. He evidently hasn't roused anyone at the big house, by the look of it."

Around to the cottage they hurried. Marjoribanks had closed the self-latching door behind him, and they had to have recourse to gravel flung at the window panes.

In an instant two heads popped out some distance apart. One Marjoribanks recognized as Rivers, the other was that of a stranger. Probably the friend with whom he had heard. Rivers talking as he had left the cottage. The stranger had a clever-looking face tanned to the color of teak. He ,had dark eyes, large, very penetrating, and very bright. Dancing eyes they were, that flickered as though lit by an inward, light.

"Anything wrong?" the man called down before Rivers spoke.

"Yes. Let us in as quickly as possible, please. I must have a word with both you gentlemen." It was the superintendent speaking.

On that the two heads withdrew as though pulled by the same string. A movement later and the door swung open. The police officer and Marjoribanks entered. Rivers stood in the hall, his friend had let them in.

"Is this gentleman Mr. Cox?" the superintendent began eagerly.

"No, this is Mr. Jackson-Gupp. But what's wrong?" Both men stared intently from Marjoribanks to the police officer and back again. Rivers with his quiet, rather sad gaze, Mr. Jackson-Gupp with the ripple of light, or was it the flicker of steel, showing in his eyes. Marjoribanks knew the name of course. Marjoribanks knew the names of all eminent men, and Jackson-Gupp, was England's greatest expert on everything to do with wireless and wave lengths. He was, among many other things, a civilian member of the Air Ministry. He was a shining member of the Society of Electrical Engineers. He was an honorary member of the Royal Society.. He had worked for years in a cabin high up on Snowdon at all sorts of problems, abstruse and practical, connected with his enormous field.

"Well, gentlemen," the superintendent replied. "Mr. Danford has been murdered in his bedroom at the Chantry, and a Mr. Cox—"

"But how—how—" broke in the land agent.

"I've no time to tell you anything for the moment, sir. Who's Mr. Cox? That's what I want to know. And where is he?"

"Cox is Danford's partner. He dined last night at Farthing I believe. I haven't seen him. I only know of him by name."

"We want him at once. But unless he's already done it, I think you, Mr. Rivers, had better come with me and break the news to Mr. Harold Danford." Rivers and his guest Jackson-Gupp were in pyjamas. They flung on a couple of top coats and hurried out. The superintendent flashed his electric torch along the path. No one spoke. They almost ran up the broad marble steps inside the portico, and the police officer rang a long insisting peal. Instantly the door opened, and a man peered out.

"Has anything happened to Mrs. Danford?" he asked at once, staring at the group.

"Is Mr. Cox staying here, Hindlip?" Rivers said, stepping forward,

"Yes, sir. He's sleeping in the Chantry."

"But is he in the house now, this moment?" asked the superintendent.

"No, sir. He's in the Chantry." The man was puzzled.

"Why are you up and dressed so late?" asked the police officer.

"On the chance that Mrs. Danford might come back after all. She's a lady as generally changes her mind Mr. Super. and—"

"Wake Mr. Harold Danford at once," the police officer interrupted. "Tell him that there's been an accident to Mr. Danford. No, don't stop and ask questions. We'll wait in the hall."

The man hurried off. Rivers led the way in, looking about him as though in a dream.

Jackson-Gupp came up to Marjoribanks.

"We missed each other last evening," he said pleasantly. "Rivers and I were working over an experiment at the tower when your 'phone came on to him, and by the time we returned to his cottage, you were asleep, I fancy. At least I hope."

Marjoribanks made some sort of a reply. He was feeling too utterly heart-sick for talk.

"You're working with the police, aren't you?" Jackson-Gupp went on as one stating a fact, not asking a question.

Marjoribanks explained how he came to be in the company, the close company, of the police officer.

"So you're working for Mrs. Danford? Good! I'd like immensely to help you. After all, Mr. Danford was my host-in-chief, wasn't he, last night? I'd very much like to help you in any way that I can."

Marjoribanks thanked him. The offer of Jackson-Gupp's brains was not to be passed over.

Harold Danford hurried in at that moment. He took the news which the superintendent brought him very quietly, though his face was gray. He asked if he could see the body. He said that he found it impossible to believe that a mistake had not been made.

The superintendent wasted no words on reminding him that he too knew Mr. Danford very well, but led the group to the ladder propped against the open window, and motioned to him to mount.

"Stand aside, Tompkins. But prepare yourself for a dreadful sight, sir. I left the light turned on."

Harold Danford gave a clutch at the window ledge as his eyes fell on the bed.

"Is he—are you sure he's—past help?" he gasped.

"Quite sure, sir. The doctor will be here shortly together with the chief constable."

"But where's Cox?" Harold Danford stared down at the officer with distended eyes "What's become of Mr. Cox?"

"That's what I want to know, sir. Who is the gentleman?"

"My brother's partner. He had the spare bedroom, the room next to this. What's happened to him? Cox!" he called loudly, and then again, "Cox!"

"He's not in there, sir. No one's in there. But where he's got to. He telephoned us to hurry here, and then seems to've vanished. But please come down, sir, and tell me what you can of him. Description, I mean. Height—"

Harold Danford came gropingly down the ladder and stood a moment with his face in his hands before he looked up. "Thank God, Mrs. Danford is in town," he said hoarsely. "Is she, sir? Well, that's a blessing!" the superintendent agreed warmly. "And I'm sorry to press, but if you could tell me about this missing gentleman— and perhaps it'll take your mind off for a while."

Harold Danford nodded shakily and after once more covering his eyes as though to shut out the awful sight that met anyone standing on the ladder, filled in accurately the list of personal characteristics fired at him by the police officer.

Finally the superintendent blew his whistle lightly. Another of the men who had been told off to watch the great house hurried up. And to him his superior gave detailed instructions as to what was to be telephoned and wirelessed all over Great Britain before dawn.

So that when Chief Inspector Pointer came down a little later to take over the case, it had been already well started by the local efforts.

Pointer had been staying at the police station of a little town, the town where a mail-bag robbery had occurred as the porter had divined when he called Mrs. Danford's attention to the tall, lithe figure passing by.

A ring on the telephone by his bed roused him. A quick inquiry told the waked that it was the assistant commissioner of New Scotland Yard who spoke.

"That you, Pointer? You know that talk we had day before yesterday about the warning laugh a certain Mrs. Danford told you of?"

Pointer had learned by the simple means of a question to the guard of the train that the lady who had talked to him in his compartment had been Mrs. Danford of Norbury, and had telephoned his talk with her to the chief constable of her part of the world, and later on to the assistant commissioner of New Scotland Yard.

He now murmured that he remembered it perfectly.

"Her husband has just been found murdered. Strangled—apparently. The curious thing is that the police station was notified of it by a telephone message and that the man who telephoned is missing—apparently. His name is Cox, and he's a partner of the murdered man. The chief constable has just asked us if you will take over the case. The murder of Danford of Farthing will make a tremendous stir. Will you go down to Norbury at once? You've practically solved that job you're on, except for some routine work, genuine routine work I mean, not what you call by that name. You can leave it? You're starting at once? Flying over? I'll tell them to rig up a landing signal in the best field, and to be on hand with a car. What's that? Your plane doesn't like cows? Personally mine prefers them to a bull. Good luck!" And the assistant commissioner rang off.

By train it would have taken half a day, by car a good two hours to get across country, to Norbury, but Pointer's Blue Bird flew it in under thirty minutes. The chief constable was waiting in a car on the road, and drove the detective officer out to Farthing while he ran over the case so far.

"'Straordinary story," began Captain Boodle. "Most 'straordinary story I know. The police got a telephone call at a quarter to one o'clock this morning from a little chapel, or Chantry, which adjoins one of the big houses in this part of the world. The one with which that laugh is connected. I wish I hadn't taken that laugh quite so easily . . . however . . . the message was to say, Mr. Cox was speaking, that Mr. Danford was lying dead on his bed in the Chantry and would the police hurry over at once as there had been foul play. The 'phone snapped off there. No ringing got any reply—the voice was artificial and quite patently disguised, but the constable who received the message is certain that it came from a man. The superintendent hurried over on the off-chance that it wasn't a joke, and found Mr. Danford lying on his bed—strangled. The marks of a powerful hand-grip—from the front—two hands—are on his throat. The doctor's examining the body now. But those marks! And that face! There's no doubt of the cause of death. Now it seems that

Cox was Danford's visitor last night, and is a partner in his firm. And he's missing! No one has seen him—apparently—since after dinner when a servant took over some wine. Whether he too was murdered after that message to the police—though there's no sign of such a thing, and how any body could have been hidden in that time—the superintendent and his men rushed up in a car. They weren't fifteen minutes from door to door—"

There was a pause. Pointer made no remark. He was listening intently, and yet with a closed mind to any inferences. Open only to the facts told him.

"You know, chief inspector, all this coming on top of Dame Anne's laugh, which was heard for the third time at Farthing last night by the way, is most amazing! A warning laugh, a murder, a telephone message, and then possible another murder. . ." Captain Boodle shook his head. "That's why I asked for you. I knew you were interested in Mrs. Danford's account of that laugh, and we need Scotland Yard in this case. Most 'straordinary case!"

He went on to give Pointer a summary of the dead man and the people whom he would find at Farthing.

The present owner had bought the estate from its late holder, a distant cousin of his, a Colonel Rivers, some sixteen years ago now. Both Edgar and Harold Danford were very much liked in the country. He spoke of the elder Danford's two marriages, and of Miss Hood. "She gets on capitally with the present Mrs. Danford. Quite like sisters."

"And this brother, Harold Danford, has any gossip ever connected his name with that of his sister-in-law?" asked the man from Scotland Yard.

"Well—they have many interests in common, music—he's a really marvelous musician—and art. She's the daughter of an R.A. Yes, I have heard it said that she should have married the younger brother. And I've heard it hinted that she would choose differently now if it came to marrying one of them. But you know how tongues will wag." He mentioned the ages of the three.

"Were the two brothers good friends?" asked Pointer.

"Used to be. But lately—I've thought there was some coolness between them. Frankly, the idea in my mind was that it was over Mrs. Danford. Harold Danford met me at the Norbury and Saxby cricket match only last week and told me that he was thinking of leaving Farthing. Found life down here without concerts a bit dull he said, but I had an idea, I distinctly had an idea, that it was something between himself and his brother."

He elaborated his idea. Pointer saw that it rested only on fancy. Yet Captain Boodle was a shrewd judge of men and women.

"Then there's Rivers, Beaufoy Rivers," the chief constable went on. "He's the land agent and the son of the late owner. Very keen on wireless. Evolving some kind of a hush-hush patent I understand which Danford is financing. Or rather his firm is. Every one likes Rivers. Thoroughly nice lad. But a bit of a dreamer. Shouldn't wonder myself if he wrote poetry." Captain Boodle mentioned this last in the tone of a man who hides nothing from his helper, however much it may tell against a friend.

"Is Mrs. Danford liked in the county?" Pointer asked suddenly.

"I like her myself. But she doesn't care a hang for the lot of us, and lets it be seen. Thinks hunting cruel, is against preserving, and doesn't play games. I've seen her on the links. Ye Gods! Likewise on the courts. More Gods! The women say she's two-faced and always gives them a dig with her claws. Trouble is she's got brains and no scope to use them."

"And she and her husband? How did they get on? None too well apparently from what you said."

"He was devoted to her I should say," replied Boodle promptly. "But she treated him very coolly lately. Yet my wife was at dinner at Farthing night before last when the laugh was heard for the third time, that amazing and to me most 'straordinary laugh, and she told me that it completely upset Mrs. Danford. That she took it frightfully to heart. The fact is I don't know what to think!" Captain Boodle shook his head.

Pointer asked who was in the house at the moment.

"There are no guests at Farthing this week-end. Usually the house would be full of cricketers, but the weather drove them all away. The house is practically empty. Rivers has a friend, Mr. Jackson-Gupp, staying with him at his cottage. I mean the Mr. Jackson-Gupp who's a Fellow of the Royal Society, and on the board of all the societies that have to do with magnetism and atmospheric electricity and that sort of thing—"

Pointer nodded. He knew the name and what it stood for.

"Rivers also put up a private investigator last night. A Mr. Marjoribanks whom Mrs. Danford apparently had engaged to investigate that warning laugh. She was kept in town last night by the storm. Went up in the morning and couldn't get back. There, was another partner of Miss Danford's staying at Farthing, he's just got engaged to Miss Hood, chap called Ormsby, one of the Derbyshire Ormsby's, but he went up to town yesterday morning too. Cox, Danford, and Ormsby are the three partners. The firm is called Cox and Plumptre."

The car stopped. Superintendent Lang saluted. They had arrived. Harold Danford was waiting to meet the man in charge of the case. He looked very moved, indeed, as he said a welcoming word to the chief inspector who, after replying, turned with a smile to Marjoribanks. The two had worked together on a' case before. Pointer hurried into the Chantry and bent over the body on the bed.

The doctor had not been able to wait for him, but his verdict—a temporary one pending the autopsy, of course, but a very positive one—was that Danford had met his death at the two hands of someone standing in front of him. It was Pointer's belief too, as he studied the body carefully.

According to the medical man, death could not have taken place much more than an hour before he himself had been summoned, if that. Seeing that Mr. Danford was in morning dress, it looked as though the murder might have taken place immediately before the police arrived in answer to the telephone summons of the missing Cox.

The chief inspector straightened the sheet and turned away. This part of his task was always painful. His purpose in life was the prevention of crime, not merely the capturing of the criminal, and every murder meant that the wild beast of the jungle, whom he was trying to rout out of civilization, had scored a success. And in this case there was an added sting. Like Marjoribanks, he wondered whether he could have prevented this man's death had he acted differently. He himself could not have come down, it was true, but he could have asked for some other Scotland Yard man to be sent to Farthing to investigate that odd story of the warning laugh.

Pointer felt conscience-smitten. As for poor Marjoribanks, he turned away from the terrible face before them with a groan.

"I was down here last night—and spent it fast asleep while this was happening! Yet that poor woman came to me. You sent her? I thought it was Rivers. But no matter. She appealed to me and I—" Marjoribanks made a gesture with his arms. "I didn't believe her. I didn't believe her story. I didn't believe in any danger."

Pointer said nothing. His eyes were rapidly roaming the room. For once the murder was not of paramount importance. The whereabouts of the missing man, Mr. Cox, Danford's partner, was the first puzzle to solve. Even the question of his guilt or innocence came second to that. Was he alive or dead? If alive, every passing second might mean life or death to him.

Pointer passed swiftly into the passage. There was only one other bedroom. It too had its own bathroom opening out of it. Lang kept his eyes on the chief inspector. He wondered what the man from Scotland Yard would make of the marks he would find here. They were very odd. On the polished floor of the bedroom, which was of the kind that shows up any spots of wet until rubbed out, were great splotches of mud, and marks as. though someone had stood by the bed in dripping clothes. In the bathroom the white and gray tiles showed the outlines of a pair of muddy shoes. Both must have been sodden. One had a heel, one had none. On the white bath-tub was a black smear where a large, and apparently filthy, hand had clutched at the soap.

Pointer looked at the marks carefully but quickly, and took a scraping from each.

Lang volunteered the information that like the other bedroom, this bathroom and the bedroom beyond had been carefully photographed. He added that measurements of the foot-marks had been taken. Back in the bedroom, Pointer looked at the window sills as he had at those in the other room. There were no marks on any of them. The bed had not been touched. There was no sign of occupancy whatever in the room. Nor of any struggle.

"How about the roof?" Pointer asked. "It's flat, I noticed. And the trap-door, at the end of the passage has a dust-free handle."

Lang had not examined the roof. Pointer made for the trap-door which had its own ladder folded up against it, of the kind that let itself down on opening the door. Pointer had the men wait down below, while he made his investigation. He was back in a moment.

"Someone was up there very recently. Left these matches—" Pointer held out eight.

"Same kind as those in the visitor's bedroom," murmured Lang. "Was he all over the roof, sir, or just in one place?"

"Can't say. The matches were all in one place. A sheltered nook by the chimney, facing away from Farthing. Just above the visitor's bedroom, which may account for its having been chosen."

Lang vanished to have a look for himself. Marjoribanks examined the little black sticks.

"Burned down to the limit? That suggests someone studying something by their light. Watch? Map?"

"Looks like it," Pointer agreed. "There were no signs of ash anywhere about, and seeing how damp everything still is, some would have stuck. Watch I should say, rather than map. There were better places to open one out than the nook where he must have crouched."

He was now examining the downstairs part of the Chantry. The door facing the main house had a Yale lock. There were no bolts. Pointer disliked Yale locks. They helped criminals, affording as they did, no evidence as to whether a door had been last closed from the outside or the inside. He had a look at the little passage, and a very careful one at the gravel path outside and all around the little building. The former showed no footprints, the latter was too marked up with the many feet that had passed to and fro to furnish any clues save negative ones.

But they were important enough in this question of alive or dead, for none of them were deep sunk. No man had walked them carrying any load, let alone a dead body. And there was no way of getting away from the house except along, or across a gravel path, soft from the rains of yesterday.

And there was no means of disposing of a body on the premises. Unless he had walked out therefore, Cox must be still indoors. Hidden? That was impossible too. The Chantry was thin-walled and without cellars. All the floors were smooth and polished. The walls were papered with a patternless paper. The passage, moreover, leading down from the guest-room was exceedingly twisty and narrow. To have got a dead body down would have been a difficult feat; to have got it down without leaving a mark on the velvet grained paper, impossible.

Pointer definitely made up his mind that there had been no second murder in the Chantry; that, whatever might have happened afterwards, Cox had left it as he had entered it, in the usual way, on his own feet. He crossed over to Farthing itself.

He knew that the household had been questioned before he came, with no results, as far as suggesting what could have become of the missing man.

The building had been searched from attic to cellar under the guidance of the chief constable who knew it well, while the police, under the superintendent, had hunted through every out-house and every cottage within the boundary of the first gates. They were positive that Cox was not in any place which they had examined. As to Farthing, it was impossible to speak with the same certainty of such a thick-walled house, but they had come on no trace of a hidden man nor of one in hiding. No marks were found, of disturbances in walls, ceilings, or floors. . .

Moreover, and it was a most important point, the footman who had sat up in case Mrs. Danford should come back unexpectedly, said that he had not left the big hall, and as the early part of the night had been so close, and all the steel shutters were fastened, he had opened every door on the ground floor to get a breeze.

He was certain that no one could have moved about without his being aware of him, let alone no one carrying a dead body. The position of where he sat bore this out. Nor could anyone, he felt sure, have come up or down the main staircase without his hearing them, for both creaked badly.

There were several stone stairs in the building but they were approached by corridors that no stranger could have found in the dark, nor, reached undetected, though he did not pretend that anyone who knew the house could not have slipped out and in unnoticed. The man said that he had not felt at all sleepy, as he had found a book that interested him. He seemed a very reliable witness and was considered a most scrupulously truthful by both butler and housekeeper.

Altogether the police and now Pointer, who rapidly asked a few questions, felt fairly certain that Cox had neither taken refuge in, nor been coerced into Farthing.

CHAPTER FIVE

POINTER asked a few further questions now of the household. The account of Mr. Cox that Mr. Harold Danford had already furnished the police, was duly confirmed and simplified in a few particulars.

Mr. Cox was reported by everyone who had seen him as a tall, red-haired, red-bearded man who wore spectacles and was very sunburnt, and who spoke in a high squeaking voice.

There was one more piece of evidence connected with him that came from a gamekeeper. He heard, he said, on cutting across the garden about half-past twelve last night, Mr. Danford's voice saying sharply—so sharply that it rang through the rain-sodden air—"What are you doing there?"

His voice had sounded amazed and very startled. It had had in it a note so peremptory that the keeper had stopped, thinking his master was speaking to him. He had taken a step towards the Chantry windows but when some distance off, he saw a man, who fitted the description of Cox, come to the window, and stand in it as though listening intently, or as though looking out. He did not put his head out of the window. The keeper had his glasses and had a good look at him. He saw a red-bearded fellow with a gray hat turned down all around his face, and dressed in gray. Then the figure stepped back and he went on about his work.

The chauffeurs were especially questioned. Neither of them had seen or heard a strange car in or around the grounds Though during the violent storms of late afternoon and early evening a bomb might have exploded without their hearing it, they said, and they had kept close to their rooms over the garage. Mr. Danford had driven away in the morning in his Silver Ghost, and had come back in it shortly before dinner. He had picked up Mr. Cox on the way. Mr. Cox had had a breakdown.

Pointer hurried towards the lodge gates. As has been said, there were four in all, one north and south of the gardens, one north and south of the park within which the gardens lay.

Cox had left the Chantry alive, so the chief inspector believed, but what about the gardens?

All four gate-keepers were positive that they had not let out anyone answering to the description of Cox. Two of them had noted his arrival, sitting in the car that their master was driving. They had not paid much attention to the guest. One had a vague idea of a cap and motoring coat, but both had the usual impression of red beard and large spectacles and brown face which Pointer knew by heart now.

It was half-past twelve when the gamekeeper had seen a figure standing at the window that tallied exactly with the description of Cox. At eleven o'clock all the gates of Farthing were locked, and Pointer believed the women when they assured him that this had been the case last night also.

True, such gates are easy to climb over, but by good luck, all had just been newly painted white, and all were quite unmarked and unsmeared, though their last coat was still tacky. No one could have clambered over them. And they creaked when swung like souls in pain. And the click they made in closing reminded one of the snapping of an alligator's jaws. Each lodge was stuffed with children all of whom had been watching the wonderful free fireworks of last night.

There was one other gate out of the gardens into the park, a little wicket gate, to which Mr. Rivers had a key, he was told. It was called "the land agent's gate," and shortened the walk from his cottage to the main drive through the park.

It too had its coat of sticky white to vouch for its not having been scrambled over in the dark of last night by a fleeing man, and along the path leading to it was not a single footprint.

Pointer stood with his back to it and looked the gardens over. No gate could be approached except by a gravel walk. The gardens themselves were very pretty and very old, but small in extent. The turf, beaten by the deluge of last night, ran mostly in unbroken sweeps with very few bushes. There were plenty of these in the park, but around the house were only flowers and grass. The lily pond was a shallow blue-tiled affair. No corpse had been flung in there last night. Altogether, as the chief inspector's eye passed over it very carefully, he gave the stretch of earth before him a clean bill of health as far as hiding dead bodies was concerned. And live ones? The gardens were bounded by a carefully tended holly hedge four feet thick. Farthing stood on a hill, from it, or the terraces around it, the hedge showed only as a line of green, hardly detaining the eye from the sweeps of park beyond, but in reality it rose eight feet from the ground, a formidable, impassible barrier. No where was there a hole in the earth beneath it, nor a break in the shining wall. True, any hedge can be surmounted by ladders, but not without leaving some traces among the branches and in the soft earth. There were no such traces. Besides the land agent's gate, there was another on the opposite side, but it led merely into the wire-screened tennis courts, and though a gate led on through them into the cricket fields, yet, since the covered courts were formerly an orchid house, this further gate was a very high stout door with inside bolts.

Pointer found, as the police had already found, that owing to the paint and the rain both bolts were stuck fast. They could not be drawn now, and certainly had not been drawn last night.

All this meant—to Pointer—that Cox had come, but had not left the gardens. That meant—what? His well-cut jaw set more firmly still. This was going to be a stiff case. Cox had come, there were no traces of a dead body, then where was he? Was he in danger and keeping out of sight to avoid that danger? That telephoned message of his—he had not named the criminal. Supposing he himself were not the murderer, the simplest explanation of that omission was that Cox did not know it. In which ease he might have left the Chantry for some reason, say a stroll in the gardens after the closeness of the storm had passed, and returned to find a dead man.. Then why was he not waiting for the police, to help them with his evidence? Evidence of Danford's words and mood last night?

Pointer returned to the Chantry. The sole fact that had interested him just now was whether Cox was alive or dead. This time he entered it to search for evidence of any kind that it might contain. He found nothing of any interest except a small green-tiled Dutch stove that stood shoulder high on a handsome china stand in one corner of the study. The top was empty, but still faintly warm. From below he raked out a pile of fine ashes which he sealed in a tin and sent to headquarters for analysis. Behind the stove, in a cupboard, stood a large empty bottle of methylated spirit which had lately been used, for the cork was damp, and a small bottle of sulphuric acid quite full.

The chief constable joined him with the superintendent for a moment.

"We're scouring the country for this Mr. Cox, Mr. Danford's partner." Captain Boodle went into details. "It may be a murder or an abduction. Do you think it's a murder, chief inspector, and flight? Or two murders—one hidden, one found out? Or what?"

"So far, it looks to me like 'what,'" Pointer said thoughtfully. "Flight? How did Cox fly? Murdered? Where's his body?"

"It's that warning laugh that I can't understand," murmured the chief constable. "Heard beforehand three times. Ghost or not doesn't affect the point that it was a warning! I confess I find that a most 'straordinary story.'"

"And what about Mr. Cox's message to us?" asked the superintendent, "telling us to hurry! And then, within fifteen minutes to find him disappeared. Now that's what I call odd! I can't think where he's got to."

The superintendent had had a score of workmen at work since dawn, hunting, questioning the railwaymen and every garage-keeper for miles around. No traces of Cox had been found. A flying policeman had circled the park in the 'plane that brought Pointer down to Norbury. He had seen no trace of a man hiding or hidden.

Pointer once more went over to the main house. He had time, now that he felt sure that whatever had happened to him, Cox had neither been murdered nor kidnapped, to ask other, wider questions concerning the man—and the household.

The butler had a most interesting piece of information—startling enough in its own way.

After dinner last night, Mr. Danford had arranged with him that if the bell from the Chantry to his pantry should ring, a bottle of a certain kind of wine was to be sent over. The S. Chantry had its own complete though, small, wine bin, and the soda-water siphon was always kept freshly charged, so that, as a rule, nothing of that kind was ever asked for.

Yes, there was a speaking tube. Evidently his master had not wanted to interrupt whatever he was doing long enough to use it. At any rate, the bell had rung about half-past nine.

The side door was open as usual when anything was ordered. York explained that Mr. Danford by pressing a knob on his desk could slide back the inner bolt. Everything seemed as usual, and he had gone on into the study. At the further end two men sat talking earnestly. He had heard his master saying in a firm and resolute tone, "Don't attempt to threaten me! I have the proofs. I tell you I have them. But I promise that I will take no steps as long as—" Then his master had caught sight of him, and had stopped abruptly, saying, after a second, in a confused, awkward sort of way, "Mr. Cox and I are reading through a play which we're both acting in, York."

He, York, had not believed the explanation, and the mere fact that it was offered was absolutely unlike his master in his experience of him. His master had nothing in his hands, but Mr. Cox had been sitting with a lot of papers in front of him. No, not a book—papers. Mr. Cox had looked up from them, he had his finger at a place, and said, "Shall I read on where it's marked? If so, I reply, 'I shall find means to silence you. Very simple means. Very effective though." His master had said rather nastily, "Will you, by Jove!" And then, as though recollecting himself, the man said, had laughed, and went on, "I forget what I reply to that in the play. Something quite different to what I should say in real life, I fancy."

The butler had gone out and heard no more.

Pointer next questioned the valet about the garments that Mr. Cox had been wearing. The man could not tell him anything about them. He explained that he had asked Mr. Cox if he could do anything to his clothes and that gentleman had replied with a laugh that his clothes needed no seeing to. Cox had not left anything in his room when he changed for dinner. But he had locked the wardrobe and taken the key with him into dinner, a proceeding which the valet evidently considered swept Mr. Cox from among the ranks of the possibles.

After the servants had been heard, Harold Danford— the only Danford now—was once more questioned. He told them that he blamed himself bitterly, now that it was too late, for not having pressed his brother to explain what it was that had been worrying him increasingly this last fortnight. He had put the casual query to him, and Edgar had replied that it was some business complication, trivial yet annoying, of which he would rather not speak.

"And"—Harold Danford bit his lip—"I let the matter drop."

As regards yesterday, he thought that Edgar had been in quite his usual spirits at dinner except that he seemed annoyed at Mrs. Danford's absence.

It was Pippa, who had waked at some stir in the house, and had had the dreadful news broken to her, who now added her account of the reply that her stepfather had asked her to make over the telephone to any inquiry on the part of Cox about a paper, and her account too of her stepfather's intention of driving into town early this very morning to lock that same paper in his office safe. She did not know what paper.

Harold Danford said that he did not either, but his brother, before dinner last night, had told him that he might want him to witness a very important business transaction between himself and Cox later in the evening. This idea had evidently been abandoned by the end of dinner, as Edgar had then spoken as though no business would be discussed by his guest and himself.

"But his words to me in the library a few minutes later didn't sound like that," Pippa reminded him, and Harold only looked bewildered and very troubled.

Pointer hurried into the hall where Rivers was standing staring up into the face over the fireplace. He had been asked to be on hand.

"Mr. Rivers, would you let me look through the safe in your office? In case a paper we want has got locked in there?" Rivers started.

"I don't quite follow? What paper do you mean?"

"A paper of Mr. Danford's."

"It wouldn't be in the estate-office safe," Rivers said sharply.

"Not as a rule. But it's not on Mr. Danford. It's not in the safe in his study in the Chantry, it's not in the safe in the business-room which Mr. Harold Danford has just unlocked for us. There's just a chance that Mr. Danford might have laid it in your safe. He has a key?"

"Yes, he has a key. But I think he keeps that key in town. It's never wanted."

"Very likely. But suppose you left the door open while talking to him, and left him in the room with it, he might have laid it inside and forgotten to speak of it to you. At any rate we must look through it just to make sure."

"Quite true. The keys are at my cottage. I'll get them at once, and meet you here."

Nothing could have been pleasanter than his voice, but Pointer thought that the young man was not at his ease. He hurried away at once, and Pointer too hurried off to where a gardener was working near by.

"Where's the estate-office? Quick! I'm in a hurry to speak to Mr. Rivers who's gone there. Take me to it outside."

The man was young, and with a "this way, sir!" ran around the end of a wing. Then he pointed, "that's the estate-office, sir—where Mr. Rivers is just shutting that window."

Pointer said a forcible monosyllable to himself. He had hoped to be there, if not first, then at the same time. A moment more and he was at the window in question. As he reached it something slammed. It would be the safe, of course. It was. As he tapped on the pane, Rivers hurried across.

"I had my keys on me after all. You startled me so that I slammed the safe shut."

He opened it again and went through all the documents inside. None could have been the paper wanted. The chief inspector thanked Mr. Rivers and asked him about his friend and guest, Mr. Jackson-Gupp. When had he arrived?

Last evening, just around nine. He had meant to come over in time for Rivers's half-past eight dinner, but had got delayed. Had he been to see Mr. Rivers before? No, but as he was in the neighborhood, and as both he and the land agent were working on what amounted to two ends of the same problem, he had walked over to see some of Rivers's work, and have a talk.

Could the chief inspector have a word now with Mr. Jackson-Gupp? Rivers suggested that that famous man was probably snatching a nap in the cottage, and there Pointer found him on a sofa, a dressing gown wrapped around him, and a book on wave-tensions in his hand.

Questioned, Mr. Jackson-Gupp told how he had intended to get to Rivers's in time for dinner, but had been delayed by the storm, and finally reached him about nine. They had gone to the old Roman tower, which the land agent used for his experiments, and had both stayed there until long past midnight. He had not heard or seen anything of any stranger, either on the way from the cottage: to the tower, or when returning.

"You know of nothing, sir, bearing however slightly, or that could bear, on this night's tragedy," Pointer asked finally, as he had asked each of the others.

"If I did," Jackson-Gupp said promptly, "I should wire in myself. I assure you I want to help you in any way I can. There's nothing I'd like better than to catch the man who did that horrible piece of work."

"We're always glad of any help we can get," Pointer assured him.

"Are you?" Jackson-Gupp's tone was sceptical. "I thought the regulars always sneered at the volunteers."

"I don't think anyone would ever sneer at your brains, Mr. Jackson-Gupp," Pointer said with a smile. "Therefore any help you can give us would be most useful."

"Well, what job can you set me on?" the wireless expert promptly asked.

"Anything that occurs to you," Pointer said.

"You've no definite plan in which I can take part?" The brilliant scintillating eyes were fixed on him. Even if Pointer had never heard of the man's name and his position in the world of science, he would have felt something of the power of his intellect.

"I think, where it's a case of help offered us, that the French plan is the best. You know their way in a criminal case? They assemble all the detectives they intend to assign to it, inform each one of the facts and then wash their hands of them. It's a go-as-you-please race. Whoever gets in first with the criminal, gets the prize. Here there's no prize—"

"I should consider catching the murderer a fine prize in itself," the other assured him grimly.

"Then pray compete for it!" Pointer begged. Jackson-Gupp made no reply for the moment. He had rather a sardonic mouth. It parted now in a smile.

"Anything to keep baby occupied," he murmured gently.

Pointer asked him for the name of the people with whom he had been staying when he decided to walk over to Farthing. Jackson-Gupp gave it at once.

Pointer asked a few more questions, and then finished up with the request that he might have a look at the shoes that he—Jackson-Gupp—had been wearing yesterday night. The chief inspector explained that they had come on some footprints, and wished to eliminate all people staying in the house.

"Why so?" Jackson-Gupp asked with a lightning glance. "Why not concentrate on them?"

"The footprints don't seem to fit anyone found here, so far." Pointer thought of the strange mark in the guest's bathroom at the Chantry, of the two shoes, one, sprung at one side, one with a heel off.

"Seem to—if things were what they seem, we wouldn't need detectives," Jackson-Gupp said sharply.

Pointer agreed with him, but repeated his request for a glance at the shoes that Mr. Jackson-Gupp had worn last night.

The other waved a hand to the wardrobe by a window. "You'll find my modest outfit in there—barring what I'm wearing," he said a trifle dryly. "Please don't hesitate to take any casts you would like, or measurements."

Pointer gave one swift, seemingly casual glance at the shoes and the blue suit hanging up. Then he put them back again, thanked Mr. Jackson-Gupp, and left him to glance over the other rooms of the cottage.

There was only one thing that interested Pointer in Rivers's boot cupboard were several pairs of shoes, all of which showed one place on the left heel where the rubber top-lift had been worn a trifle.

It was but the merest rub on each, but the odd thing was that the pair in the wardrobe which Jackson-Gupp had claimed as his, had an exactly similar mark in an exactly similar place.

But marks on shoes, interesting though they were, did not link up with Cox. Where was he? Why could he not be found? The police were still hard at work hunting through every nook and cranny. To make extra sure, the gamekeepers were examining every hollow tree. The gardeners had been told to hunt for any freshly disturbed earth. All had reported, and were reporting, nothing but a series of blanks. Yet Pointer refused to alter his belief that the man had not left Farthing. Once taken, Pointer held to his convictions. They were never based on anything but bed-rock.

Yet there remained the knowledge, the self-evident fact, that, by hiding, or spiriting away Cox, the murderer of Danford, supposing he were not Cox, was providing himself with a scapegoat. The mere fact that Cox was missing would have been enough under certain circumstances to throw suspicion on him. Only his own telephone call to the police could be brought as a proof of innocence. For even if he were hidden, it might be with his own connivance. Judging indeed by the absence of all marks, it looked to Pointer as though—supposing him to be hidden in any room of Farthing—the latter idea would prove the true one. He now got Rivers to show him some modern and some old plans of the house and he too studied them closely. Then he investigated the concealed rooms—priests' rooms under Elizabeth, but built for Bible rooms, under her terrible sister. He opened old powder closets, he searched the bricked-in chimney corners. Like the local police, he came on no traces of recent occupancy—the cellars, vast and spreading, were not charted. When Farthing had been partly dismantled in the Civil War they had never been entirely repaired. There was a tradition, Rivers told him, that there was a concealed suite under one wing, built by an owner as late as the early years of Victoria's reign, who believed in black magic and practised necromancy there. But here again, though Pointer scanned the dusty passages from end to end, there were no marks of recent disturbances, except in such as were beyond suspicion and open to his inspection.

Thanking Rivers, who had helped his search with apparent zeal, the chief inspector took a turn through the grounds and revolved in his mind all the points. They led to no conclusion that seemed tenable. So he meditated awhile, equally unprofitably, on the mud smears in guest's room and bathroom of the Chantry.

There was one other point that became obscure too when probed into. Danford had said that Cox had had a breakdown, or at least an accident, and that he had had to fit him out with evening things. No trace of any car that could have been Cox's was found, unless he had returned to it in some mysterious way and gone on in it. But all the roads to Norbury are main ones. A car left from before dinner—before eight that is—until past midnight would certainly have attracted notice. Unless some motor thieves, had made off with it. But no notice of such a breakdown had been reported by any A.A. scout.

Back at the house, Pointer found Marjoribanks finishing a further, very detailed, questioning of the inmates. He had learned nothing that cleared up any of the puzzling points. Pointer joined in the desultory talk that followed for a moment, then he turned to Pippa.

"What did you think of Mr. Cox when you met him at dinner?" he asked her.

"I thought him a very odd man. But it's difficult to say why. He seemed to be laughing inwardly at something all the time. I can't explain it"—she made a helpless gesture—"if Mrs. Danford had seen him, she would know what I meant. He seemed to pay no attention at all to what was said to him by me, though he listened sharply enough to whatever my stepfather said."

Harold Danford, questioned on this point, agreed with her. He too had thought Mr. Cox distrait, though he had not noticed that inward laughter of which Pippa spoke.

Pippa went on to say that she was certain that her stepfather had rather an objection to introducing Cox to his wife, or to herself, or they would have met earlier. She believed that, deep down in his heart, her stepfather had had a rooted distrust of Digby Cox, though he laughed at her opinion of the man, an opinion which she now believed was a woman's intuition. She too had felt that her stepfather was in trouble lately, and she spoke of the newspaper yesterday morning which had seemed to upset him. But the trouble was with Cox, of that she felt sure.

"I always felt that he was dangerous," she said now, her eyes red with the tears that they had shed, her face still pale and drawn with shock.

"There was something so unbalanced about Mr. Cox's notes, short though they were, they were never twice the same.

"I can't explain"—again she wrinkled her forehead in the useless effort—"but I used to feel it very strongly as I read them."

The superintendent and his men now came in. Again they had nothing to report but failure.

The investigators decided to allow the household time for breakfast. Pointer declined anything at Farthing, and walked to the inn with Marjoribanks, the superintendent dashing off to continue his telephone inquiries for Cox at the Brighton hotels.

Marjoribanks overflowed on the walk with Pointer. He poured out a little of what was burning inside him,—regret and remorse. And then he discussed the murder itself.

"To my mind the strangler's is the most horrible of crimes. In any other form one might think, hope, that compunction, though belated, stirred in the heart of the criminal, but the strangler can feel the breath leaving his victim's body and yet does not relax his grip, and from in front too where he could see—ugh!"

"It simplifies the search in one way," Pointer thought. "At least women are ruled out of the list of possible suspects. I am glad of that. For every reason it goes against the grain when a woman's the criminal."

"Yes, no woman killed Danford," Marjoribanks agreed.

"And no man of weak physique. Though taken unawares—Danford was taken unawares, don't you think?"

"I do. I think he was killed by someone who, after that first exclamation of surprise, which the gamekeeper heard from Danford, had some reason to come into his room and come up to him."

"Cox?"

Pointer was not ready to say yet. Marjoribanks went on.

"You know my way of solving problems? I rely on instinct. It invariably points out the guilty from the innocent to me."

"I've heard you say so," Pointer assented with a faint grin. He liked Marjoribanks, but he by no means followed him.

"A guilty man can never be himself—or he would betray himself," Marjoribanks went on thoughtfully. "He must for ever wear a mask. I think I feel that mask even before I see it. How those rooks are calling!"

Pointer, who was country born, suppressed an inclination to ask whether Marjoribanks also relied on his instinct to tell him what the bird was, for the sound that they heard was the screaming of new-fledged sparrow-hawks.

It was the "top of the morning," with the warm beauty of a perfect July day caressing them as though trying to make them forget the bad deeds of yesterday. In the park, though the bluebells had gone with the nightingale's songs, the harebells were lying in broad drifts of azure. The stubble of cut grass on a distant slope glittered like brass in the light. Such of the ripening crops as had withstood the storms of yesterday, were beginning to define themselves from their neighbors, wheat from barley, and barley from oats. The damage done was very great, but pimpernel and sow-thistle, poppy and corn marigold, cornflower and corncockle had shot up overnight, and swayed and bloomed in the very heart of some swathe ploughed by the storm. The smell of mown hay and of fresh stacks rose in the air, rooks and starlings were foraging busily, while the sparrows rose in swarms and settled again in the stricken wheat-fields, insatiable vermin as ever.

"You know," Marjoribanks went on dreamily, "I ought to have known that tragedy was close upon us, for I felt it brush me yesterday in the great hall of Farthing. Above all, when I saw that picture there of Dame Anne's husband, I sensed the weight of an active, malevolent intelligence oppressing me." He paused. "I suppose you don't believe in such things?" he said shortly.

"What things?"

"The doom that lies in old houses. Sometimes it is a blessing, but more often a curse. And mark you, chief inspector, whichever it is, it is of deadly potency. Whatever else may be in this terrible tragedy, I know one thing, Farthing will be in it."

"It's a wonderful old place," Pointer murmured.

"It has an awful power." Marjoribanks spoke with a shiver. "I felt it as soon as I stepped inside. An obsessing power, a suffocating grip that seemed to squeeze out everything but itself. You evidently think Cox, the partner, the missing man, has something to do with the crime?"

"Don't you? At least to the extent that his disappearance voluntary or involuntary is extraordinarily odd."

"To me there is but one criminal here—Farthing. And Farthing's instrument, who is certainly not a visitor."

"Meaning?" Pointer asked.

"Harold Danford, Edgar Danford's brother."

"He may be the criminal. But I confess I don't quite see how you arrive at his guilt." Pointer succeeded in keeping his face straight.

"He is, by blood, most open to the deadly influence of the place or that evil picture. Oh, I know he acts sorrow convincingly enough, and has a gentle and kindly face, but those facts are nothing."

"Nothing at all," Pointer agreed. "But the motive?"

"Farthing, of course. He will inherit. He's the only Danford left."

"It must simplify your work a lot, Marjoribanks, to get a leading so early in a case," Pointer could not help saying. Marjoribanks nodded.

"It does. Instinct is to me what the compass is to the mariner, what his twig is to the water-diviner. But I'll tell you one thing—apart from my instinct—did you notice the extraordinary likeness between him and that portrait over the fireplace in the big hall, the portrait of Dame Anne's husband, his direct ancestor? Really, it was Jackson-Gupp who pointed it out to me, but while you and Miss Hood were talking, just at the end, Harold Danford stood looking across at it, and by Jove, for an instant it was like seeing a man look at his own reflection in a mirror. It was positively uncanny. Under the circumstances."

"That portrait?" The chief inspector lit his pipe. "And you and Mr. Jackson-Gupp saw a resemblance between it and Mr. Harold Danford? Now, I was struck by the—to me—amazing likeness to the dead man, to Edgar Danford. I didn't notice it when I looked closer, but when I first stepped into that hall, I thought it was his portrait.

Frankly, I can't see the slightest resemblance between Harold Danford and it."

"Nor I to Edgar Danford. Whereas—for the moment only, I grant you—it seemed a replica of Harold."

"The murderer, according to you?"

"And according to you I feel sure, in the end. He has no alibi—" Then catching the twinkle in the chief inspector's eye he added grudgingly, "Of course no one has an alibi in this case. Everyone says they were in their rooms asleep, and no one can prove it. But still in this case—"

"And was it he who kindly arranged that those warning laughs should be heard? Like Captain Boodle, I find them very odd," Pointer was not laughing now. "Very odd!"

"Ah, those laughs! They, or rather the way Mrs. Danford spoke of them, made me distrust the whole affair."

"No, no, that was instinct surely!" grinned the chief inspector.

"Here's the inn and breakfast," Marjoribanks said hurriedly.

The news of the murder had reached here already. Curious eyes were on them as they entered.

"The other partner, Mr. Ormsby, may be able to throw some light on the affair," Pointer said when they had finished. "He's up in town unfortunately for the moment, and not at his flat or his club."

"I'm off for another talk with Jackson-Gupp," Marjoribanks rose. "His brains should help to bring this affair home to the brother."

"Does he share your certainty as to Mr. Harold Danford's guilt?"

"Between ourselves he does. I think he was rather agreeably surprised to find me already in complete agreement with his own conjectures. Of course they can only be that as yet, with him."

"You discussed the matter?"

"Well, naturally we talked of the criminal. What else can one think of."

"Has he also a conjecture as to what has become of Cox?" Pointer asked.

"Cox doesn't seem to interest Jackson-Gupp. Well, I'll push along. He's really exceedingly keen on assisting us."

"Very good of him," Pointer said with no hint of sarcasm in his voice. "You might also ask him—" Pointer began, then he shook his head. "But better not."

"Mysteries!" Marjoribanks made a. grimace. "Why not put your cards on the table? If you hold the winning ones, you'll win."

"Think so?" Pointer asked with his imperturbable and exasperating good temper.

"Don't you?"

The chief inspector shook his head.

"You can't speak of cards where the values change from minute to minute," he said.

"Call your factors x and y then," suggested Marjoribanks. "And do your sums in the open."

"In mathematics x and y are imaginary quantities and can be made to keep the same values throughout the sum," the chief inspector pointed out. "But what about it when x and y come to life, and change under your hand? Working with ideas means you're working with live things—much more complicated than working with names or labels."

"There's something in what you say," Marjoribanks agreed, a little more uncertain. "But I intend to put my suspicions before Jackson-Gupp and see if I he can help me to clothe them with life. You won't. Oh, I know you of old. You go your own way. You even make your own trail most of the time. All I object to is that it's never an open trail."

"You mean I don't give the criminal enough warning that I'm after him?" Pointer asked. "I've thought myself that perhaps I don't."

Marjoribanks laughed.

"I've told you frankly what I think about this crime," he said turning off from the main road. "But I don't for a moment expect any frankness from you in return."

"Not if you're going to talk things over with other people," Pointer agreed heartily.

"Well I certainly intend to profit by the presence among us of a really brilliant brain. But I think you know me well enough, Pointer, to feel sure that I should never—under any circumstances—betray anything that you told me. I may talk over my own theories with carefully selected people, but never those of others."

Pointer knew that this was so, and hastened to assure the other of his implicit confidence in Marjoribanks's trustworthiness. The waiter came up to them.

"There's a gentleman here, sir, a Mr. Ormsby, who is staying at Farthing—only he couldn't make it last night in the storm. He asks if he might speak to you at once. He's just heard of the—the—whatever has happened up at the house," the man finished discreetly.

Ormsby looked very shocked at what he had heard, as he came into the private room where the two men waited for him.

Questioned by Pointer, he went into what seemed full details concerning the absent Cox.

"By the will of the original partner and founder of the company, his nephew and sole heir, sole relative in fact, Digby Cox, inherited all his rights in the firm, except that of directing or controlling the actions of the other partners. This meant the continuance of the interest on the original capital of forty thousand pounds, which was being paid, when the elder Cox died—fifty-six per cent.

"But about a month or two after he came into it, he discovered, or let us say he produced, a paper by which his uncle, and he therefore in his turn, was entitled, besides, to an annuity of a thousand a year from the firm.

"This paper purported to be one of the original agreements between Cox the elder, and a man called Gresham, who was his partner at the time, and who died shortly after. The paper seemed in order. There was nothing to do but pay. Digby Cox's explanation was that his uncle, who had other means as well, had not troubled to collect the one thousand, but he, the younger than, thought it would round things off nicely, bringing, as it did, his income from the firm to something over twenty-two thousand a year.

"That all clear?"

He was told that it was, and duly docketed, mentally, and in notebooks.

"Then, three years after his uncle's death, Cox found another paper. It too purported to be an agreement between the original Cox and the dead Gresham—who, if he really signed it must have died of senile decay. By it, the annuity could at any time be communed into a sum calculated on the holder's living to the age of seventy. As a matter, of fact, the older Cox lived to over ninety. This too seemed all in order. Danford told me that he boggled a bit, but finally the firm had no option but to pay young Digby Cox a sum of thirty thousand pounds. That clear?"

Again he was assured that it was.

"Well, all this about the papers found, and the paying out of first an annuity and then commuting it, is an old story. But just lately Danford has been very mysterious over something to do with Cox. Friday night—night before last, he went into details. He in his turn has made a find in an old portfolio of the elder Cox's. He has found a paper, genuinely, by the original Cox, enumerating very precisely what right and privileges the nephew was to inherit under the will, and expressly stipulating that only those on this list are to be considered valid. The paper was signed and witnessed and was evidently, intended to be attached to the will. It was dated shortly before Cox died, and more than a year after the conversion paper that the nephew had produced. It absolutely cancelled the annuity, let alone any conversion right, because it did not refer to it.

"Danford believes now, so he said to me, that the other papers were clever forgeries. Not done by Digby Cox he thinks, but forgeries none the less.

"He intended to have us three meet to-morrow in the offices of the firm's solicitors and there thrash the matter out. But he had wanted first to sound Digby Cox a bit. He wasn't so sure as he wanted to be, I fancy, that the latter knew nothing of any forgery—supposing, of course, that the papers were forged—the elder Cox might merely have changed his mind. If Danford wasn't satisfied that Digby Cox acted in perfect good faith, he intended to threaten him with an action for obtaining money under false pretences, unless he allowed the deed of partnership to be dissolved—apart from restoring the moneys received. I thought it doubtful if he could get young Cox to do this, but of course, if he could pull it off, it would tremendously benefit the firm to be free of a partner whose only interest was the collection of his dividends. Now it's only too clear what happened last night when Digby Cox arrived after all."

"You think so?" Pointer asked, with an irony lost on the speaker.

"Don't you?" Ormsby looked surprised. "He wouldn't intend to refer to it under his own roof I take it, but I fancy that one word led to another and that the two had it out. Danford told me that he always carried the important paper, the list in the elder Cox's writing, on him. I protested against the danger of this. I only thought of accidents of course. But since no such paper was found by you on his body, evidently Cox has taken it by force. It is the only proof in existence as far as I know. As far as Danford knew."

"By Jove!" muttered Marjoribanks. "This certainly sounds like a powerful motive."

"What other motive could there be for murdering Danford!" Ormsby asked almost impatiently. "He was a most popular chap."

"One would say—offhand—" mused the chief inspector, "that Digby Cox must have had some helper to forge those papers, if they were forged."

"They evidently were, or Danford wouldn't have been murdered," came firmly from Ormsby. "Yes, I suppose there must have been someone helping on a share basis. Until this murder, of course, I too thought the mistake might have been made in good faith, but this end to the visit of Digby Cox clears things up rather terribly. And now the paper's gone, and the firm's hands will be tied unless we can find those other notes to which Danford just barely referred. I'm going up to town at once to see if I can find anything, if I can get into touch with the head clerk."

"You've never met Digby Cox yourself?" asked Marjoribanks.

"Never. He was to've come down Friday for the weekend, but put it off, indefinitely, Danford thought. Looks as though he knew there would be trouble, and intended to come to Farthing when there was no one else but the family there. Unless it means that he had planned what happened last night."

"You know nothing about him, his friends, what places he might make for?" pressed Pointer. Ormsby could not help him, he said.

"There's no business deal on between Mr. Danford and this Mr. Cox which must be kept a secret?" Pointer next asked. "Something which would prevent Mr. Cox's coming forward at the moment?"

Ormsby shook his head very decisively. Digby Cox took no part in the business of the firm. And Danford had no private business deal on. He assured the chief inspector that he was certain of this, and was fetched to the telephone. Returning, he said glumly that the head clerk was out of reach until tomorrow morning, so that there was no use in his going up to the office.

As to how he himself came to spend the night at the inn, Ormsby explained that he had gone up to town yesterday morning, and had taken a late train back, to find that it was quite impossible to reach Farthing from the station last night. The wind and rain swept the roads like a sleety whirlwind, so he had stayed the night in the village, and got up this morning, intending to walk to the house, only to learn of the dreadful tragedy.

"Have you any idea who inherits?" Pointer asked finally.

Ormsby said that he had no idea whatever, and excused himself. He wanted to be with Miss Hood—apparently only since he could not be with the head clerk.

Pointer went on to the police station. The superintendent must have some information by this time, gleaned over the telephone, about Digby Cox at Brighton.

CHAPTER SIX

POINTER turned over in his mind what he had just heard. It sounded very circumstantial. Ormsby had provided what, if true, suggested a quick and ready motive for the murder of Edgar Danford. Digby Cox, a forger, or partnered with a forger, and threatened with being unmasked or disgraced, unless he returned a sum that might no longer be in his power. The story too was corroborated by Danford's own words to Miss Hood as to what she was to reply to Cox over the telephone should he speak from the Chantry, and by the object of Danford's proposed early trip to town planned for this very morning. But other facts might fit those remarks of Danford's too. Ormsby's story did not explain why Cox should have telephoned to the police. Nor the warning laugh heard at Farthing. Yet it was so complete that it hardly seemed as though these two points could be incorporated with it.

Digby Cox was a strange problem. Apart altogether from the crime, where was he? How had he vanished so completely without passing outside Farthing's gardens?

At the police station, Pointer learned that Mr. Digby Cox had left a Brighton hotel yesterday morning early, going up to town by one of the trains that business men used. He had stayed at the hotel twice before within the last month. Each time arriving late in the evening and leaving early next morning. He always came alone. He took one of their best rooms and generally had a bottle of wine—Montepulciano of a certain specified year —sent to his room. He came too late for dinner. Yes, there were generally letters waiting for him. He had left orders yesterday morning as usual that any correspondence arriving after his departure should be sent on to his club in Piccadilly. In appearance—the description given by the hotel clerk was the same as that already heard so many times by the police. As for the club in town, it was an expensive enough caravanserai, but a "pot-house" pure and simple. Telephoning to it, the superintendent had only learned that Mr. Digby Cox had been a foreign member for some five years. He had been in lately once or twice for letters. They described him. It was always the same story. Cox's appearance was remembered, but the man himself seemed to have made no impression. Who was his sponsor originally? Mr. Plumptre.

"That's a former partner of Mr. Danford's," the superintendent muttered. "He's retired and gone into politics." A specimen of Mr. Cox's signature was asked for in both places, and the name of his bank was obtained from the club. He paid by cheque. The bank manager when summoned—though it was the sabbath—to the telephone, was inclined to be reticent until told "frankly" that Mr. Digby Cox was missing, and that foul play was feared. Upon which he slipped down into the bank below his flat, and over his ledgers gave all possible information. Cox always invested all cheques paid into his account in bearer securities of the best class which were handed over to him himself as soon as possible. The cheques always came from Cox and Plumptrc. At the moment there was only a very small sum standing to Mr. Cox's credit. When had he last been in! As far as the manager knew, about a month ago. That was all.

Pointer next had a rally call sent to the various news-distributing agencies. Any reporters coming down to Norbury and asking for the police superintendent would hear something to their advantage.

Meanwhile he telephoned to Mr. Plumptre who lived the other side of London and by good luck found him in. He was given an immediate appointment and the chief inspector flew across at once. He found a clever-looking, keen-faced man who seemed hardly able to credit the news when told him.

"Danford murdered and Digby Cox there at the time, and now missing—" he murmured to himself as though trying to accustom his thoughts to the facts. He had seen very little of Danford lately. And as for Digby Cox, though he had known him well as a lad, during his uncle's lifetime, he had not seen nor heard anything of him for years. His description of Cox as a young man fitted well enough with the one which the police had.

As to any plan of Edgar Danford's which might have meant trouble between himself and Digby Cox, Plumptre had no notion, he said. He repeated that he saw very little indeed of Danford nowadays, but that the dead man had loved making plans.

"He was a clever chap—" Plumptre said thoughtfully. "But too confident in his own wits. As we see here—it would never occur to Edgar Danford that he could blunder or be taken in—he had an immense amount of self-confidence."

Pointer learned nothing from Mr. Plumptre which in his opinion bore on the mystery, and hurried back to Norbury. Before he left Farthing, Pointer had asked Harold Danford, though it was Sunday, to try and get hold of his brother's will. Mr. Quintin, the family solicitor lived in Norbury, and a fast car had whizzed him up to town and rushed him back with it in his possession, just before the chief inspector hurried in after his needless visit to Plumptre.

Rivers had been invited to be present at the reading, but at the last moment he had sent in word that some imperative business called him elsewhere. So the party who finally seated themselves opposite Mr. Quintin in the business-room consisted of Harold Danford, Pippa, Ormsby, the chief inspector, and Marjoribanks.

The will referred first of all to the money in Edgar Danford's firm which on his death reverted to his wife. Then came a few trifling bequests. Barring them, he left the whole of his property, real and personal, to his stepdaughter, Phillippa Hood, "whom I regard in all respects as though she were my own child." Danford had then proceeded to so tie up the property that Pippa only enjoyed actually the same rights in it that her husband would, should she marry. In fact, if not in wording, it was left as much to whoever she should marry, as to her herself.

Pippa was very pale. Harold Danford smiled encouragingly at her.

Marjoribanks, in spite of what Ormsby had told of Cox and Danford, looked very keenly at Harold Danford, but there was no mistaking—or faking—his air of tranquillity. Very evidently he had known of his brother's intention. He said, with his quiet smile, that he and his brother had talked it over many times.

Pointer asked if this was Edgar Danford's only will? No, Mr. Quintin told him there had been others. "The one made after his last marriage for instance. That was the one before this."

"And how did Mr. Danford dispose of his property in that will?" the chief inspector wanted to know.

"Except for a yearly annuity, and a bequest to Mr. Harold Danford, everything was left to Mrs. Danford."

"Including Farthing?"

"Everything was left to Mrs. Danford," replied the solicitor. "Real and personal."

"And when was this will that we are now reading made?" He was told that the solicitor had drawn it up about a month ago. Just over three weeks to be exact.

"Did Mrs. Danford know of this new will?" was Pointer's next question. Mr. Quintin said that he had no idea. Mr. Danford had sent in a draft of his intentions, and arranged to call in and sign on some convenient date.

"I feel quite sure that my sister-in-law knew, and approved of this will," Harold said earnestly. "My brother would never dream of altering it without consulting her. Seeing that he discussed it even with me, to whom it made no change. Mrs. Danford disliked Farthing very much indeed. More than I do even. She thought it had a baleful power over those who lived here. A sort of survival of Sir Amyas Rivers's strong spirit."

"Nevertheless, you cannot be certain that Mrs. Danford knew of this fresh will," Pointer persisted. "She might have been unaware of it?"

"I consider such a possibility highly improbable—in fact, out of the question." But that did not impress the chief inspector. Crimes were improbable, and often seemed out of the question.

Pippa said nothing until Mr. Quintin had removed his chilly presence, then she turned impulsively to Harold Danford, the sole executor.

"I can't accept Farthing, Uncle Harold. I can't!" He stared at her.

"My dear Pippa! Why, it was Edgar's wish!"

"But I can't take it! I can't let the will stand!" She seemed to choke.

Shocked disapproval showed in every line of Harold Danford's face. "The wishes of a dead man, Pippa, are sacred," he said almost sternly. "Unalterable. Even if you disliked Farthing—"

"Oh, no!" she said quickly. "It's not that! But—" her eyes filled. She did not finish.

"I see," he murmured sympathetically. "Yes, yes, of course! Very natural that you should feel like that. But, as I was going to say, feelings have no place when the dead speak. It has always seemed to me the least the living can do is to hear—and carry out implicitly—their words, words that come from the tomb. Spoken by voices that will never speak again."

Pippa did not trust herself to answer. It was all so sad. To have Farthing come to her like this! Farthing which only yesterday had seemed slipping away, sliding away. She left the others together. Ormsby followed her. Pippa turned to him in the gardens.

"I wish he hadn't done it," she said suddenly, drawing her hand from his. "Oh, I wish he hadn't! It—it ties one. I don't agree with Uncle Harold. The dead are dead.

However much we loved them, they're gone. I think the feeling that you're held by something you can't argue with, can't explain things to—"

Following the direction of her eyes, Ormsby saw Rivers coming towards them.

The land agent gave Pippa's disturbed face a look of inquiry.

"Anything wrong? I mean anything fresh?" he asked at once.

"My stepfather has left Farthing to me," she said, her eyes traveling over the lovely gardens, and something of pleasure creeping into her voice.

Rivers said nothing. He looked at her with a new expression, a sort of speculative, watching eye.

"That's unexpected," he said finally. "Are you quite sure?"

"How do you mean quite sure?" Ormsby asked a trifle curtly.

"Well—for instance, are you sure it's the latest will? Mr. Danford drew one up just lately."

"Oh, yes, it's his last." Pippa spoke almost wearily. "My dear stepfather has left me—me—Farthing, and somehow—oh, I can't describe it, I feel as if he had left me a prison for life."

"Pippa!" Rivers's tone was so aghast that Ormsby in his turn stared hard at him. Very hard.

"You can't mean that! That you don't want Farthing!" The young man spoke in a tone of horror, absolute and stark.

"I don't suppose I do," she said grudgingly. "I suppose it's just the shock of the way it's come to me. Of his death—his murder!"

"It's a wonderful place," Ormsby said heartily, and as Rivers nodded and left them hurriedly, he went on, "and a wonderful home. Eh, Pippa? You mustn't let this fearful tragedy make you morbid, dearest. After all it would have come to you anyway."

"You didn't know that?" she suddenly flashed at him.

"How could I dream of such a thing!" he said promptly. "But it is a wonderful possession."

She only nodded, with her eyes downcast.

"Pippa, you're unhappy, you're wretched! And no wonder! My mother wants you to come and stay with her, and get away from all this grief and suspense. I've been talking to her over the telephone. She's writing, of course, but you'll go to my old home, won't you? It's a dear place. Nothing compared with Farthing, but very pretty in a quiet, simple way. And we could be married up there," he went on, "and you needn't return here until we both came back together when things have quieted down."

"Married? Not for ever so long," she said briefly. A shadow passed over his face. She saw it.

"Don't count on me," she said suddenly.

"But I do!" he retorted with something at once more and less than lover-like in his look and tone. "Of course I count on your promise, my dear girl."

"A promise to marry isn't like any other promise in the world," she said at once.

"It's more sacred than any other, except a marriage vow," he returned almost sharply, "and I hold yours. Otherwise—why, Pippa, if I didn't know you so well, I should imagine that because you had come into Farthing you didn't think me a good enough match."

He looked at her with something very forbidding and lowering in his face. "You can't play fast and loose with a man like that," he said as she flushed, but did not reply. "Of course I know that's not your reason, but that's what it would look like. In justice to yourself, you must be true to yourself. I didn't ask you to marry me because of Farthing. I had no idea that Farthing would ever be yours. So why should your inheritance separate us? Why, my dear girl, it's impossible!"

"Nothing's impossible!" she said desperately.

Ormsby looked at her with a dull flush in his face.

"You know that I'm hard hit by this Fairbairn matter, the sham suicide that didn't come off, and you take this moment to turn me down? I refuse to let you do it," he said crisply.

A servant appeared at that moment. Would Mr. Ormsby come indoors for a moment.

Rivers seemed only to have been waiting for him to go. He appeared again on the path. Pippa was pulling a flower to pieces in the cruel way of the unthinking in a garden. She evidently felt him come close, for with her back to him she burst out:

"It would be like taking an advantage of his murder to keep his gift, such a gift, and do just what he didn't want me to do!"

"Marry me?" Rivers asked with a certain cool detachment. She nodded.

"Still, marry me!" He took both her hands in his, and there was nothing cool in his voice now. "Don't think of Farthing—nor of him—just think of us both. Of you, and me, and life together."

"In the Roman tower?" she asked with a faint smile. "Oh, Beaufoy, I wish I could. But I can't. I meant to tell you so last night if the storm had let me get to the lily pond as we arranged, that I can't."

"Can't what?"

"Let Farthing go. It's no use pretending that I can. I can for a minute, but I know that I should regret it so that it would spoil both our lives. I couldn't help but think of it. No other house would seem to me bearable as a home, once I had had the chance of owning it. Oh, I know it's horrible, and all that! Sometimes I feel as though it were a sort of poison in me, that my years in those walls have rotted something in my heart, but I must be frank with you. I daren't be frank with Mark."

He still held one hand of her, and stood watching her closely, then he looked up at Farthing's great bulk, then at a white peacock that strolled along the Italian balustrade down by the lily pond, its tail trailing like a robe. The sun was warm and bright. Something seemed to catch fire in Rivers. He bent forward swiftly.

"But why should you let Farthing go? My dear girl, you're quixotic! Farthing is yours absolutely. I've just had a glance at the will too. There are no provisos attached to your legacy. No one can prevent your keeping Farthing—nor marrying me."

For a second Pippa looked at him with wide, soft eyes. Then she drew back.

"Oh, no, no! If I keep Farthing I'm in honor bound—after what my stepfather said to me and I to him—to marry Mark Ormsby!"

He was watching her averted face. There was something of calculation now in his own as he said slowly: "I don't see that." He spoke as though thinking hard. "We'll find some way out." There was meaning in his glance.

"It's a horrible position for all of us!" she said almost in tears. "I can't let Farthing go. I simply can't! Yet I don't—I can't—I can't break your heart, Beaufoy! Oh, what am I to do?"

"Nothing," he said promptly. "Do nothing whatever for the time being. I don't mind anything so long as you still want Farthing." He spoke in a voice of passion. "The idea that you didn't want it as I thought you did—I mean—! mean—I couldn't bear you to change all of a sudden. You've always liked the place, always seemed to value it above everything else." He spoke hoarsely, and then with some words about his work hurried off precipitately.

Pippa gave him a puzzled glance. But she was too miserable, too torn by the shock of her stepfather's murder, by her own emotions, to pay much heed to lesser things. What was she to do? If she let Farthing go, it would be forever. Harold Danford would never leave it to her, in his turn, if she went against his brother's wishes. She would have to leave the place on her marriage. It would be an irrevocable surrender. She looked long at the towers. To her they were transparent, and she saw each loved and noble room, each beautiful piece it contained, and closed her eyes in anguish.

She could not give up this. But it was cruel. She had hoped, had her stepfather lived, to have worked on him, she would have tried to do so, and got him still to give her Farthing as a wedding present even if she had married Rivers, but her stepfather was dead. And being dead, yet spoke. So then, it was Ormsby if she kept Farthing. Irrevocably Ormsby. And she knew now that he too counted on Farthing, intended to use his engagement to her to help him out of some financial embarrassment. There was no harm in that, of course, but suddenly the great building passed under a cloud. How black it looked. It seemed to her to be watching her, watching them all, these short-lived creatures that only lived to minister to its needs, as a monster, bloated and misshapen, watches what it feeds on.

She shut her eyes for a second, and looked again. The illusion, the vision, the fancy, was gone. But it left a feeling of still more acute discomfort than before behind it, and for the first time in her life, now that it belonged to her, she walked towards it with unwilling feet.

Meanwhile Pointer had asked whether the contents of the will had been known to any one except the maker and his brother.

Harold Danford made some vague reply. When he was pressed, he explained that by an accident, Mark Ormsby had learned of his brother's intentions just before he proposed to Miss Hood, but in fairness to him—and to her—it had been generally agreed between the three men that she was to believe that Ormsby knew nothing of the matter,

Pressed again, he admitted that there had been some sort of a boy and girl attachment between Pippa and young Rivers. Did Edgar Danford approve of this? Harold grew restive.

"I quite understand that you want to get all the facts clearly in your minds," he said coldly. "But I must really protest against being used, however skilfully, as an informer." And with that, he went out for a talk with the solicitor over a glass of wine.

Marjoribanks gave the chief inspector rather a wry smile.

"I confess that for once instinct has played me false. For once. I mean about Harold Danford. But I still think Farthing is the key to the murder of his brother. Only by some other hand than his. Now, we have two young men here, Mark Ormsby and Beaufoy Rivers, either of whom would come into virtual possession of the place by marrying the heiress designate, provided that Danford had not changed his will at the time of her marriage.

"A very important 'provided that.' And now we know that one of these young men, Ormsby, lied to us when he told us that he had no idea to whom Farthing would go on Danford's death. I don't say that one can't understand the awkwardness of telling us the truth, but the fact remains, he lied. On the other hand, he could count—apparently— on Danford not changing his will should he and Miss Hood marry, whereas we both think that that might not have been the case had she chosen Rivers. And that, of course, throws rather a doubtful light on Rivers. He would gain immensely by Danford's death, provided he could get Miss Hood to marry him after it. By the way, the solicitor says there's a signed copy of the will somewhere on the premises. I wonder where?"

"There's no copy in the safe of the business-room or in the Chantry. We might ask Rivers to open the safe in the estate office. I heard his footstep outside a moment ago." The chief inspector stepped into the corridor. Rivers was just turning a farther end. He at once offered to take them to his safe.

Opening it, he pointed to a drawer. "There's an envelope in there which contains what you want. Mr. Danford gave it to me to put away at the time the will was made."

"You know its contents?" Marjoribanks asked.

"Harold Danford has just told me of them. But I think there's a mistake being made." Rivers spoke with a little trace of hesitation.

"In what way?" both men asked.

Rivers had opened the drawer which he had indicated. Now he pointed to the docketing on a long narrow envelope that lay inside, closed and sealed with Edgar Danford's seal.

"Do you notice that Mr. Danford has only written on it 'Copy of my will'?"

"Well?" Marjoribanks asked.

"I shouldn't be surprised at all if there's another will in existence—a later will. Or rather, I shall be surprised if a later one doesn't turn up."

"Did Mr. Danford ever speak as though this were not his last will?" Pointer asked, scrutinizing the writing on the envelope. It appeared to be that of Edgar Danford.

Rivers could not—or would not—say that he had, yet after the date of this, Mr. Danford had come into the estate office where he, Rivers, was transacting some business with the tenant of the home farm, a Mr. Frost and his son, and had asked them to witness his signature.

"What makes you think it was a will they were to witness?"

Again Rivers could not, or would not say. But from some phrase or turn of a sentence, he had an idea that Edgar Danford had changed his will only this last week. He refused to be more explicit.

"Since you weren't asked to sign as a witness, any later will might have included you among the beneficiaries?" Marjoribanks pressed.

"It might have," Rivers agreed.

"To any large extent?"

Rivers tapped his strong, knotted fingers, the fingers of an engineer, on the table. He seemed to hesitate.

"Edgar Danford once spoke of leaving the place to me." He said it quickly, almost furtively, almost as though ashamed of the words. "It was my father's you know, and barring Harold Danford, I was his only living kin. I only mean that I don't feel satisfied in my own mind as to that will you have just heard, standing."

On the way out, the chief inspector and Marjoribanks met Harold Danford. Marjoribanks mentioned the talk they had just had with the land agent. Harold Danford was obviously surprised.

"That's rather an unsettling thought," he murmured, "and I very much dislike to be unsettled unnecessarily. Mr. Quintin feels quite sure that it was my poor brother's last will that he just read us. And speaking for myself, I can hardly think that my brother would have altered it to any great extent without telling me of the fact. Though I don't say that would be impossible. The matter, of course, seemed a very far-off contingency. But of one thing I do feel absolutely convinced, my brother would not have left Beaufoy Rivers anything of any importance. Rivers makes a mistake there. You see, my brother felt that Rivers's electrical discoveries are bound to assure him a very large income in time. He had the greatest belief in those experiments. As you know his firm was backing Rivers financially."

"Supposing he had made another later will, who would be the chief legatee, do you suppose?" Pointer asked.

"Mrs. Danford. Quite obviously, Mrs. Danford. My brother may have thought that Farthing as a gift to Miss Hood might attract fortune-hunters. Though as I say, personally, I am convinced that he has made no later will, nor intended to alter the leaving of his estate to his stepdaughter."

Marjoribanks said nothing for a few minutes when they had left the house, then he murmured:

"Rather a clever idea! I mean on Rivers's part. To suggest that Miss Hood is not an heiress. So that one cannot be accused of fortune-hunting if one makes love to her, or gets her to break her engagement to another man. Why does Rivers contest that will? He looked to me, he 'felt' to me, like a man determined to block it if that can be done. I had an idea that he was not really half as doubtful as he strove to seem. Which reminds me of Mrs. Danford—" he went on with a jump that was clear enough to his listener. "She's expected down by the last train. Heaven help the poor soul to bear the news that's waiting for her! I confess I funk meeting her. So Farthing is to go to Miss Pippa . . . and to whomever marries her. Except that you can see in the wording of the will, that it must be some one of whom Edgar Danford approved. Yes, I shouldn't wonder if after all, in another form, Farthing was to prove the kernel of the crime. Ormsby's account of a quarrel and a powerful motive is of course interesting, but if that laugh means anything, in the crime it means premeditation. Of course that doesn't rule out Digby Cox. But still—" He stopped. "I'll just cut across this lawn and let Jackson-Gupp know of this will. You've no objections?"

"None whatever. There's nothing private about the contents of the will."

"I confess, Harold Danford's whole attitude has cleared him far more than any reasoning could do. Yes, I—for once—was a bit hasty. But so was Jackson-Gupp, and his is not a brain that easily goes wrong. I sinned in good company."

"Ah, yes, Jackson-Gupp!" Pointer did not tell Marjoribanks beforehand, but the morning train from town, which though it did not bring Mrs. Danford—to every one's surprise —had brought down a member of the Royal Society who very kindly dropped in to see Jackson-Gupp. On leaving, the chief inspector happened to meet him in a lonely part of a lane, and signaled to the car that was taking the savant to the station, to stop.

"Perhaps you would permit me to drive on with you?" he said civilly. "I'm on my way to the station, and recognized one of the Farthing cars."

Then, as they drove on, he said quickly.

"Well, sir?"

"It's *the* Jackson-Gupp all right."

And on that, Pointer's desire to reach the railway seemed to leave him. He "changed his mind" at the next corner, and got out after thanking the man inside most warmly.

So Jackson-Gupp was vouched for. And yet—.

One of the friends with whom the electrical engineer had been staying before he walked over—according to his own account—to stay the night with Rivers, had motored past Farthing an hour or so ago and left a suit case for him. Pointer had had a look at it. It contained only some clothing. Just the sort of things that a man, detained longer than he expected would have telephoned to be sent him. Nevertheless, Pointer lifted out a pair of walking shoes and a pair of slippers. Much used, both of them. Neither of their heels showed the slightest sign of having been worn down unevenly. Pointer rubbed the soles of the outdoor shoes with a rag which he took from a tin box before he wrapped them in their coverings of paper again, and had the suit case sent on to the land agent's cottage. Marjoribanks came in when he had finished and the two had tea together. The private investigator was very pleased with himself. He had come upon something unexpected. He had found someone who reported a car with lights out, waiting at a point where you have a good look into the grounds of Farthing if you stand on a seat, and this spectator had seen someone taking a great interest in the lily pond, which was a pretty sight just now it was true, but not on a day like yesterday. With his glasses out, Mr. Ormsby, the man was certain that it was he—had been watching the grounds intently for some time before he drove back to the inn.

"Now you know my way of cards on the table," Marjoribanks went on. "So as this is my own discovery, and as you refuse to take the slightest interest in anyone beyond the missing gent, Cox, I had a chat with Ormsby and told him what I had heard."

"Yes?" Pointer asked.

"Well, he looked very awkward and then said that—this is in confidence, mind!—that he had an idea that Miss Hood was going to meet Mr. Rivers down by the lily pond at nine and so he had arranged to be where he could see them. Nice sort of thing to have to own to! And what I want to know is, is his explanation true? Especially coming after what he told us of Cox and Danford, a lot hangs on that."

"Ah! That's where your instinct comes in!" Pointer said enviously, and dodged the scone that was flung at him.

"I've said already that I confess to my having been a bit hasty in—well—in reading the compass where Harold Danford was concerned," Marjoribanks murmured. "And possibly Ormsby is all right. But that will of Danford's leaving Farthing to be competed for, as it were. By the way, I have something very odd about Rivers to tell you. Just now I dashed back for something I had forgotten, and there, in Farthing's big hall, was the land agent, standing in front of that accursed picture, for it is that, mind you—and actually lifting his cap to it. Quite solemnly. Not as though he liked doing it, but as you might thank someone for a kindness done you. Yes," he went on ruminatingly, "there's something very, very odd about the land agent. I've been delicately talking him over with Jackson-Gupp." Though they were alone and in a distant corner of a private sitting room, Marjoribanks lowered his voice still more.

"I think he's beginning to distrust Rivers too. In fact, it was he who rather gave me the idea that there was something odd about him. Oh, not intentionally! Not at all! But I can read between the lines as well as any man. And my sober judgment is that Jackson-Gupp distrusts Rivers. By the way, he sent you a message. Said he much enjoyed Crossly's visit, and hopes that your mind is at rest now. Crossly is the big-wig on air-whorls, and hurricanes, and that sort of thing isn't he? What's he to do with your mind?"

Pointer only laughed and went off to hear whether anything further had been learned about Mrs. Danford or the many, threads that the superintendent was spinning over his telephone. So Jackson-Gupp knew why the Royal Society Fellow had happened in. Clever chap, Jackson-Gupp. He puzzled Pointer, for no gatekeeper had seen Mr. Jackson-Gupp arrive. Though each ran over the lists of goings and comings with that accuracy that all lack of outside interests generally insures. Questioned, Mr. Jackson-Gupp carelessly said that he had walked in during one of the downpours. Yes, he had duly passed both cottages. Pretty cottages, weren't they, with their thatch and flowering creepers? No, he did not think that he had seen anyone about, but really in that downpour— he had been only intent on reaching the land agent's cottage. Had he been to Farthing before, then? No, but he knew that Mr. Rivers worked in the Roman tower and made for that. The cottage was near it, as he had found. Jackson-Gupp acknowledged a dislike to asking his way. A foible of course, but a very strong one with him, and the tower was certainly an easy landmark, even in a storm.

All this was quite true, but there were other odd little points about the man.

He looked to Pointer—a good judge if ever there was one —like a man who had just come through a very severe physical and nervous strain. Yet he had only walked over to Farthing from some ten miles distant, and he could have come by car had he chosen. Then the shoes in the wardrobe to which he had pointed as those he had been wearing last night—Pointer had made a long scratch down each wood heel as he replaced them, and not half an hour ago, Rivers, not Jackson-Gupp, had passed him, wearing shoes so marked.

As soon as he had looked into the land agent's boot cupboard, Pointer had been certain that Rivers's guest— or his accomplice—had palmed off his host's shoes as his own. Why? What had become of the ones in which Jackson-Gupp had walked to Farthing?

Pointer went onto be introduced to Harmony, an old foxhound, past her running days, but who had once been the cleverest in the Norbury pack. She was now lent to Pointer on the chief constable's request, for Pointer had rubbed the soles of the shoes sent to Jackson-Gupp with a rag that had been lain in a fox's earth.

To-night promised to be dry and fine. Though too dark to follow a man easily, nor did Pointer want Jackson-Gupp followed. That distinguished authority on atmospheric electricity was too clever not to notice that he was being trailed—supposing he took it into his head to roam, yet should he stir from the cottage, the chief inspector meant to know where he had gone, if possible. For Pointer did not quite accept Mr. Jackson-Gupp's statement that he was staying on at the cottage merely for the sake of helping to solve the mystery.

It might be so, but like many things that Jackson-Gupp had told the chief inspector, it might not.

Pointer had carefully explained to him that he was quite free to leave at any time, provided he let the police have his address, yet Jackson-Gupp seemed to have promptly arranged for enough things to be sent him to let him stay on almost indefinitely.

CHAPTER SEVEN

EARLY next morning, as soon as a Moslem would have called it day in Ramadan, as soon as one could distinguish a black from a white thread that is, Pointer took Harmony on a leash, and went for a stroll through the gardens, passing by the land agent's cottage. All the blinds were still down, as he expected.

Harmony, suddenly stiffened, and nose to the ground she quivered. Fortunately she always had been a silent girl, too silent for the Master. Now she circled for a moment, and then went off at a great pace towards the Roman tower. There she hauled Pointer up on to a rocky boulder that stood on a little hill reaching nearly half-way up the tower on this side, acting indeed, as a bolster to that older stonework.

In behind some mountain-ash Harmony nosed herself, and then stood looking up at Pointer, who promptly gave her a biscuit. Behind the screen of trunks and branches, and bushes of wild bramble, was a long pipe that seemed to run up to the top, of the tower and curve over its edge. Pointer examined the pipe. No one had, or could, climb up by it. It was a rain pipe not over firmly fastened by string bands and gardener's "mortar tacks." He had noticed that the lower part of the rain pipe was missing from the back of the land agent's cottage as he passed it just now; this seemed to be that one, judging by its measurements and color. The curved end that had led into the rain butt at the cottage, here went over the top of the wall. What became of it then? Pointer could not see.

He patted Harmony, told her how clever she was, and taking her on a short leash again, made for the path that led directly from the land agent's cottage to the wicket gate, to join another straight path that would eventually lead out of the park through one of the ordinary gates.

Pointer had a bicycle, and let Harmony out at full leash's length now. She led him, stern waving, nose down, out through the small gate, of which he had been supplied with a key, the mate to that kept by the land agent, and then, leaving the path, cut across the park to where, under the close-cropped hedge was a hole in the ground, probably burrowed originally by a dog, and enlarged by the torrents of Saturday night's storm. Here she made ready to worm her way through. Pointer checked her, and investigated the place. Clear enough were the marks of someone who had pushed himself through from inside the park, using the toes of his shoes as levers, but there were other marks. Pointer studied the ground carefully, and decided that Jackson-Gupp, supposing him to have been wearing the tainted shoes, had pushed a not very heavy, but bulky parcel wrapped in stiff paper that made marks like tin edges—ahead of him through the opening, and had then scrambled through after it. Also, Pointer found a place where a small electric torch had been stood upright in the ground on the outer side of the hedge, doubtless to light the procedure. And there was a twig on this side of the hedge which showed a scorch mark. Pointer thought from the look of the twig below it, that a still smaller pocket torch had been fastened here, one that would send out a light not much stronger than that made by a large glowworm but probably of a color that would tell the man who had tied it there, what particular part of the hedge to make for. Pointer now let Harmony do as she liked, and she promptly scrambled through the opening. He hoisted his bicycle on to the top of the hedge, crawled through after the hound, and got his machine down. Once out of Farthing's boundaries, Harmony set off down the main road at a fine pace. Pointer was relieved. He had feared that Jackson-Gupp, after he had left the park, might have got a lift last night. But for nearly two miles Harmony trotted on. Then she stopped in front of a pleasant little house set in a pretty garden. On the brass plate was the name of Dr. Burton. The dog nosed under the gate and tried to squeeze beneath the lower bar. Pointer left his bicycle, pulled in Harmony, and opened the gate. She drew him across the little plot of grass to the left and around the side of the house. Here she ran forward on to the gravel path and stood there nosing, then she began to circle over a flower bed close against the wall, then to cast back along the way she had come. She was just going to give tongue, when Pointer caught her head, patted her, and gave her another biscuit.

He looked up at the house. It had only two stories and an attic. All the windows were open. All was still. It was now six o'clock. Everyone seemed to be still asleep. Pointer looked at the blossoming bush in front of him. Some of the flowers hung broken on their stalks. Yet it was a rose bush of a kind whose stems are fairly stout. Against the wall other roses were climbing. The ground around was thick with, their petals, yet the heads from which most of them had fallen were not full blown. Some petals still lingered on the roses below one of the window sills. Nowhere else had the flowers suffered, for those broken by the storm had been trimmed off. Pointer looked up at the sill. There were no marks of a ladder, either in the earth, or against the dark and rather grimy stone. Yet those half or quarter roses below it told their own tale! Something—a cord, or strap, must have been let down and something had been hoisted upon it into the window.

Two leaves—rose leaves—lay on the sill, yet no roses climbed higher than the window opening. And the leaves were still green, though crushed. They had not been there long. Pointer eyed the remaining portions of flowers thoughtfully. Yes, something bulky, but light, had scraped past them, half through them.

Suddenly a head was poked out of the window that so interested him. A man's shoulders followed, and for a long moment, Pointer looked into as fierce a pair of eyes as he had ever encountered. The man was young, evidently very tall and big of frame, and the hand that grasped the window fitting as he leaned out, was big in proportion.

Also it had a scratch running up the back of it and across the wrist.

"Are you Dr. Burton?" Pointer asked anxiously, in the tone of a man certain of an affirmative. "Can you come with me at once to—"

"I'm not Dr. Burton," the man replied in a harsh voice without shifting his eyes. "I thought you and that foxhound were coming to serenade me. People who want the doctor go to the front door."

He stared at Pointer with black suspicion in his face. And it was a face that showed it up well. So might Paul Jones have gazed down on to an enemy's deck, or Captain Kidd eyed a king's officer.

"Sorry!" Pointer said pleasantly. "There's been an accident on the road. Child injured. I went to an open window thinking I could make someone hear quicker." He strode back to the front door, with Harmony held close against him, and rang the bell hard. After the third effort, another head came out, this time from another window above, and a young man leaned out sleepily.

"Child's been run over," Pointer called up. "If you're Dr. Burton, can you come with me at once?"

He was sorry for the doctor, but that glowering face at the side window had to be placated.

"Passing on my bicycle I saw the car knock the kid down and then whizz on," he continued.

The doctor said something warm and sincere about road hogs, and something regretful about people's fussiness over lynching, and in a few minutes was out beside the chief inspector. He patted Harmony and followed Pointer, who trundled his bicycle with him, around the first corner.

Pointer liked the look of the doctor. Like most people, the detective officer had a very warm spot in his heart for a country practitioner, and a tremendous respect for the men, who, year out, year in, toil for their fellows, but he could not take him into his confidence. Friends of criminals have very pleasant faces too, sometimes, move in pleasant circles, are pleasant people to meet—outwardly.

He gave an exclamation of dismay.

"Why! The child's gone!" He gaped about him, the picture of amazement.

"The kid was lying on the off-side there—about where those bushes are. And the car—a Vauxhall two-seater—'

"There's no sign of any accident except these swirling marks here." The doctor stared at the road. Pointer, promptly insisted on paying him his fee, a night fee, which little act of common decency relieved the young man of a vague suspicion of a hoax.

He insisted on walking with Pointer part of the way on to the police station, where the latter said that he would give full particulars.

"I'm afraid I woke up someone in your house." Pointer went on chattily as the two lit up. "He wanted to know if I and the hound had come to serenade him," Pointer laughed.

"That's a patient. He was badly man-handled a couple of nights ago. Attacked by some tramps on the road. I'll bet he gave them what for, but he says he'd had a glass more than he should, which made him keep hitting the ones that weren't there. Certainly he was pretty well done in when we found him on my doorstep to which he had managed to crawl. Broken arm—bashed in rib, among other things."

"Hope the police got the chaps."

"He wouldn't hear of my reporting it, Ashamed of not having been able to hold his own end up better."

"Well, of course a chap like Windermere wouldn't enjoy such a story being told against him."

"Windermere? Who's Windermere?"

"Surely that's Windermere, the South African cricketer!" Pointer spoke with a certainty that seemed to puzzle the doctor.

"He told me his name was Hatter. Windermere! Never heard the name."

"Kenya Colony," Pointer said hastily.

"Well, he told me his name was Hatter, and I don't see why he should lie about it. This part of the world is getting dangerous. There's a man who owns one of the show places not far off who was murdered—*murdered*, mind you the same Sunday night!"

"Sunday night—" muttered Pointer. "Why, I wonder if I passed the poor chap and took him for a tramp? I saw one pitching about the road. Just before your house it would have been too. I thought he was blind drunk. He was mud from head to foot!"

"He was," agreed the doctor. "And pretty well done for too."

"I had no idea of that!" Pointer spoke as though naturally shocked at the mistake that he had made. "I'd have offered to help him had I had an idea. As it was I pedaled past at top speed. I particularly remember noticing his shoes. One heel was clean off, the other had the seam busted."

The doctor said that he hadn't noticed the shoes, but that nothing in the description just given by his companion would have been out of keeping with the appearance poor Hatter presented when he came on him unconscious on the doorstep next morning.

"But here's the police station," the medico went on. "Lucky you remember the number of the car. Though apparently they had turned back and carried off the kid to the hospital after all." Pointer bustled into the station with the air of a man bursting to get some information off his chest, no suspicions must be raised in the host of the fierce-eyed stranger. He made his complaint—the doctor might ask them some time whether they had found the car—but Pointer could no longer remember its number, nor was he quite sure now of its make, and even its color seemed to have become an uncertain quantity.

But his complaint made, he and Harmony went home together, very pleased with each other. By the time Pointer had returned her to Captain Boodle, he thought that he might drop in at the land agent's cottage. As he hoped, he found Rivers at breakfast.

Could he be permitted to see into the Roman tower he asked? Cox being still missing, of course, every possible and impossible hiding place must be gone over carefully every day, if merely as a matter of routine.

Rivers took him at once inside. The place was always kept locked. Ship's ladders led up mast-like poles to cross-struts on which were strange implements and boxes.

Standing on the stone floor, Pointer could just make out, under some feathery mountain-ash tips, the curved end of a rain-water pipe. Even his keen eyes might not have noticed it had he not been looking for it.

"Are you doing very important work just now?" he asked Rivers.

Rivers in general terms told him that he was working at various problems, one of them being an effort to invent a device that would really prevent aeroplanes from stalling. Jackson-Gupp was keen on the same idea he added, but he approached the problem by different methods.

"I suppose he's a rival of yours then?" Pointer said lightly, apparently pacing the ground so as to be certain of the size of one curve.

"Partner rather," Rivers said equally lightly, and then his face changed. He turned his back for a second When he looked around again he seemed to be graver than ordinary.

Pointer thanked him, and left him at his work, while he himself stepped up on to the boulder where the trees grew, and inspected the rain pipe by means of a mirror held below its straight end. (The end so well concealed behind the trees.) As he expected, since he had seen inside the tower, the rain pipe had been turned into a periscope. Mirrors had been wired into place at the other end and at the bend, mirrors that reflected into the piece of glass that Pointer held, everything that Rivers was doing. He could see the whole of the interior by a little twist this way and that of his hand. At night Rivers worked, he knew, by the aid of a very powerful red arc-light. So Jackson-Gupp had gone to some trouble to spy on the other man. Humph. . . . Some of Rivers's work was expected to be of immense importance commercially. Danford's firm had been, and was, backing him very heavily. Jackson-Gupp was working at the same idea but by different methods. . . . Like a contrapuntist trying to find some common chord which will let him weave one aria with another, Pointer was groping among these facts. He felt that they belonged together in some way, yet, if so, it was a long way.

And where did Mr. Hatter come in? Mr. Hatter who, on the morning after Edgar Danford had been found murdered, had collapsed on Doctor Burton's doorstep not more than two miles off, badly mauled, with a broken arm and a crushed in rib, and muddy from head to foot?

Pointer thought of the immaculate appearance of the room where the murdered man had been found, of the neat gray suit that he had been wearing, of the absence of any marks therefore on his antagonist, one would have said. He thought of the filthy hand on the bath tub, of the footprints on the bathroom floor, and shook his head. This case was one that was going to tax his brains to solve. He might have wondered whether another man had worn Jackson Gupp's shoes, but for the fact that the man in question had been seen to leave the cottage at precisely one o'clock last night. Pointer had set watchers inside and outside Farthing itself, and front and back of the land agent's cottage. But as to why an eminent wireless expert should crawl through hedges with a parcel at dead of night, and take it two miles in order to, presumably, hand it over to a battered man, was beyond the chief inspector. At the moment, only Marjoribanks's intuition could be expected to solve this, he reflected with a smile. The answer to a guarded question put to Rivers assured him that nothing whatever was missing from the tower or the cottage. A police inquiry of Mr. Harold Danford and the butler was receiving the same answer at Farthing itself. Nothing whatever was missing. Yet, if Pointer was right, something light and bulky had been hoisted up to the room of Mr. Hatter. It might still be there. Though Pointer doubted this. Being Sunday, no parcel post left to-day, but what about cars and friends as carriers?

The local police inspector of Compton Bury—the village where Dr. Burton lived—called on the medical man very shortly after Pointer and Harmony had arrived home. He explained that the doctor's patient resembled 'a man who was wanted in Norwich for burglary.

The doctor was impatient at the idea. "Mr. Hatter is certainly no burglar," he said almost angrily, "he's a gentleman."

"He may be that, sir," the inspector agreed, "but nowadays, gentlemen too, take to crime. Has he by any chance sent off a parcel from here to-day? He couldn't by post, we know, but what about any friends of his calling in a car to see him?"

Dr. Burton started. "Well, in point of fact a friend did call round this morning early to hear how he was getting on. Hoped to be able to take him off with him, but Hatter very sensibly declined to go yet."

"When was this?"

"Well, about five. The man was going on to Dover to catch the first boat." .

"And Mr. Hatter hadn't telephoned before the car arrived?" Dr. Burton almost bit his cigarette in half. His face answered the policeman.

"When did he telephone, sir?"

"As a matter of fact he telephoned earlier in the day—"

"Before five in the morning?" The. inspector's tone showed his interest in this early riser.

"Well—yes. It was about—well around two o'clock. The telephone is in the hall you know, and I have an extension by my bed. When he rang up his friend, he woke me. But I can assure you that his message had nothing to do with burglaries."

"What was it?"

"I think you had better ask Mr. Hatter that, inspector." The doctor said crisply. "Though I must ask you to remember that he's had a very bad shock. Those tramps pretty well finished him Sunday night. I hope you're on their tracks?"

"I'm sorry to say we're not, sir. Not a sign of them. And it's just because I don't want to worry Mr. Hatter, if he's all right, as you think he is, that I hoped you would be able to set my mind at rest. I don't deny that I'm a bit worried. I'm sure you don't want to aid and abet a criminal to escape, and I'm sure I don't want to let him slip away from here, either, if he really is the man wanted at Norwich. So I should be much obliged if you'd let me know what Mr. Hatter telephoned about so early in the morning. If it was something innocent, why not let me know, it? And if it wasn't—well, sir, I really can't think you'd be willing to hide it from us."

The doctor was young, very young, and a newcomer to Compton Bury. The inspector was none of these things. After a second's delay the doctor gave in.

"Certainly Hatter is in no state yet to be badgered. And his message over the telephone was certainly nothing private.. He merely told some man at the other end that he'd been pretty badly mauled by some tramps the night before, and had got into a comfortable haven— he was kind enough to put it like that—with a doctor, and would like the man he was talking to to drop in as soon as he could. Oh yes, and he asked him at the same time to bring him down a complete outfit, as his own was, pretty well done for. It certainly was!"

"He didn't mention any other name? Any third party?" The inspector pressed. "It certainly sounds all right . . . I don't want to blunder over the job, and yet one has to keep one's eyes and ears open."

"He mentioned nothing else but what I have told you," the, doctor assured him.

"I suppose you haven't had any sort of reference, or heard him refer to anyone one could use as a reference," the inspector said next.

"I have. He gave me three names as soon as I had patched him up. Said I might think him escaped from Dartmoor otherwise." The doctor laughed. "And I'll get the names for you. They'll set your mind at rest."

They certainly were names of the kind to satisfy the most suspicious. Even the inspector of Compton Bury had heard of them. At that moment a bell rang, a short touch.

"He's ready for his bath." The doctor rose. "I act as his bathman. His balance is precarious, of course, with an arm in plaster strapped to his side, and a rib bandaged too."

"I'll just finish my notes, if I may, sir, and then be off." The doctor had no objections, and left him writing laboriously.

The inspector sat with his ear cocked to upstairs sounds. As soon as he heard a door shut, the bathroom door he guessed, he slipped up into the room of the injured man. Apparently he had been told what to do, for, after a quick glance around, he stepped to the wardrobe. He found a complete suit of clothes inside, bought so said their tag, ready-made at a large shop in town that goes in for that sort of thing. The shoes and the hat bore the same name in them. On the floor of the wardrobe he found some rose petals, and a good deal of earth, plain common earth, judging by its look The inspector—acting on instructions—scooped all he could into an envelope. Then he felt the top of the wardrobe, then he had another glance around the room, and then he made his way noiselessly out of the house and mounting his bicycle pedaled off for Norbury and Chief Inspector Pointer, where he handed in notes and envelope. The earth was to be sent off to be analyzed, and Pointer filed the notes. So the Jackson-Gupp and Hatter path looked like being a cul-de-sac. If it were not one, if it lead anywhere in the problem, then he would assuredly find himself on it again. After all, it was Cox whom he was trying to trace. It was still only something that might lead to, or connect with him, that the chief, inspector was after for the moment, and that being so, he decided to have another talk with Miss Hood. The pretext would be a word as to Mrs. Danford's absence. She had not come by that only other Sunday train that could bring her to Norbury, supposing she were coming by train to-morrow—the morning papers would be full of the murder of her husband. Then only, would they know whether her absence were due to a most unfortunate chance, or meant another problem. Her maid was not certain what her mistress had taken with her. Mrs. Danford kept so many things in town. Her jewelry she certainly had not taken. Most of it was in the safe of the Chantry, the remainder locked in her room And it was very beautiful jewelry too. Not the kind that most women would leave behind them during any prolonged absence. Nor had he any reason whatever to think that Mrs. Danford's absence was other than due to chance. However, she was but of secondary importance for the moment.

Marjoribanks and he walked up to the house together. They found Pippa alone in the great hall. She turned with a look of relief as they were announced.

"I'm so glad you've prevented me," she said simply. They promptly inquired what plan they were spoiling.

"It's only that I—as Farthing's new owner—must bob to the portrait," she said soberly. "Tradition demands it. Anyone who owns, or even who expects to own the place, is supposed to bob to the monster or raise your hat to him. That puts you under his protection as it were. Mr. Danford had never done it. I used to chaff him about it, and prophesy all sorts of dreadful ends to him. But never one so dreadful as the reality. Never half so dreadful!"

Marjoribanks eyes positively glittered.

"Forgive me, but this sort of thing always interests me, do you mean that anyone who owns, or who intends to own Farthing must—"

"Curtsey, or take his hat off, according as it's a lady or gentleman," she finished. "Alone in this hall. As the clock strikes midday. It would be much more to the point to do it to Dame Anne's picture, I think it's she whose curse rests on the house, not his. But that's the tradition." She stopped and stared again at the painting.

"I'm very much tempted to have it removed," she said finally, "it seems vandalism. But somehow—"

Marjoribanks was thinking of Rivers. Rivers whom he had seen lift his hat yesterday, to the portrait. Yes, it had been exactly at noon.

"I've grown to positively loathe the picture," she finished abruptly. "Don't you think his smile is too gloating for words?" she asked Marjoribanks.

"It seems to vary with the lighting," he suggested, and then excused himself. He decided to see if he could find Rivers; Sunday was a more or less free day with the land agent.

Pointer asked whether Mrs. Danford had telephoned to say when she was coming down. No, Pippa had not heard from her. Her faced clouded as she spoke of the dreadful shock that awaited the woman who must still be all unconscious that she was a widow. Pointer made some appropriate sound of sympathy. Then, as though on a sudden impulse, he said:

"By the way, Miss Hood, what did Mr. Cox seem most interested in on Saturday night at dinner? I mean, what subject of conversation, or what object in your wonderful collections here did he speak of?"

Pippa turned away from the portrait.

"I don't know . . ." she said slowly, evidently thinking back. "I know that I had the feeling that he was very keenly interested in something all during dinner, but it wasn't anything we talked about. Nor was it anything in our collections. It sounds incredible"—she flushed a little—"but when I showed him the buttons that we believe were cut from the coats of the two little princes that were murdered in the tower, and certainly they are of that date, and are engraved with the royal arms of England as then worn, he barely glanced at them and said, absent-mindedly, 'taken from their clothes because silver was valuable in those days, I suppose. Well, why not?"

" Why not?" Pippa repeated almost shrilly, "Can you imagine a more inept remark!"

Certainly it did not sound like the comment of a fellow collector, Pointer agreed, with some inward amusement at Pippa's expression of disgust.

"I should have thought him interested in masonry," she said again, "because of the way his eyes kept roaming over the walls when we stood for a moment before dinner out on the terrace. Yet when I pointed out some Saxon 'long and short' quoins—the only Saxon ones still left in this part of England, chief inspector—I don't think, from his face, that he knew what I meant, or cared to find out."

Neither did the chief inspector, but evidently as an amateur of old buildings, Cox was as unsatisfactory as a collector.

But Pippa had given him something to think over. The fact that Cox had impressed her as keenly interested in something at Farthing, something apparently to do with its outside walls

In this case, more than in most, Pointer had to grope his way inch by inch.

Monday morning, the papers extended themselves over *The Danford Murder and the Cox Mystery* as was expected of them. Pointer hoped for much from the garrulity of the press. He was most exceedingly anxious to get on to Mr. Cox's past or present tracks, and, as the reports stated at great length, hoped greatly that any people who had ever met the missing man, or who believed that they had seen him, or had even heard of him, would pass on all information to Scotland Yard.

This would mean a sheaf of spurious trails, but some might lead home. The Monday morning post brought, among others, a letter for Edgar Danford in Mrs. Danford's writing. Pointer opened it with a wonder as to what he should find, It was not dated and was without a heading. It ran:

"You pretended that Dame Anne's warning laugh meant nothing to you. How brave of you. Yet foolhardy surely. At any rate it has frightened timid me away, yes, quite away to where no report of the sad fate that is about to overtake you can reach me. By the way, in case before you pass away, as of course you must, or Anne would not have obliged us all with a warning, you pick on the wrong man as my companion—you'd be sure to do that—let me confess that I have run away off with your partner Digby Cox, the man whom you offered to introduce to me this week-end!

"I'm afraid I showed that the idea amused me, you looked at me so searchingly. Do not be too hard on us. You said yourself, when you met him in April, that he could be very fascinating. You never suspected us? You are too trusting, Edgar, and too apt to think that others are as trusting as yourself. By the way, so long as you do not take any steps to find out where we are, I waive all my rights under my marriage settlements, both as to the allowance from you and as to my share of the interest in the money invested in your firm. Though, obviously, there is only a very short time left for you either to investigate or to pay. Poor, poor, doomed Edgar!

"For the last time I sign myself
IVORY DANFORD."

Captain Boodle had dropped in for a word with the chief inspector about the inquest which would he held this afternoon. He read and re-read the extraordinary note.

"It's the letter of a—well, I don't know what!" Captain Boodle said finally, "the woman must dope! Nothing else would explain the whole tone of this. The whole monstrous tone! So, she's gone! And Cox with her. Cox! Then was she the motive for Danford's murder? Mrs. Danford was a wealthy girl, I understood, at the time of the marriage. As we know, whatever money she refers to as having been put into Danford's firm comes back to her on his death."

"Or do you think it's an attempt to locate Cox where we can't find him, and will give up looking for him? Do you think she's trying to throw us off the track about Cox being with her now?" Marjoribanks wondered.

"It's one of the oddest letters I ever read," Pointer said slowly, "but as to what it means. . . . Dope? Sounds like that. Or else—"

"Yes?" But Pointer did not finish his sentence. He was frowning down at the tips of his shoes, as, hands in pockets, he stood with head bent in reverie.

"Either it means nothing, or it means the deuce of a lot," Marjoribanks said slowly. "The deuce of a lot . . . Mrs. Danford and Cox is a new combination! And yet . . . and yet..." He too ended off vaguely, thinking, instead of speaking.

"I think I must show this to Mr. Harold Danford and Miss Hood," Pointer said finally. "It's not a pleasant thing to do with a letter written by his wife to a dead man. But under the circumstances—"

"Quite so," agreed Captain Boodle. "Most 'straordinary story!"

Pointer asked for Harold Danford and showed him his sister-in-law's startling epistle.

When he had read it, Harold Danford stared at the paper, and eyed the envelope, as though wondering whether he were in a dream. . .

"I can't understand it!" he muttered finally, "I simply can't understand it! But she evidently knows nothing of Edgar's terrible end. And Cox . . . It doesn't seem possible that I had no idea that she knew the fellow. Why, Cox dined with us only that same night, Saturday night. They must have left immediately after—but, good heaven, surely that's impossible? Yet, what is one to think? Does this mean that Cox was the murderer? That it was a *crime passionel*? Over my sister-in-law?"

Pointer asked for the name of Mrs. Danford's solicitors, and then, very reluctantly, showed the letter to Pippa. She gaped in effect, if not actually, as she finished it.

"It can't be true! She's just saying it to hurt. I mean about Mr. Cox! She wouldn't write like that if it were true. She couldn't!" She read it through again.

"Oh, chief inspector, how horrible! This letter to a man who's been murdered. Poor Mrs. Danford! Whatever she's done, such a punishment seems awful. She'll never get over it."

She read it a third time.

"I don't believe it's from Mrs. Danford at all," she said finally. Pointer did. The writing was hurried and swiftly, carelessly done, but to his eye, quite unmistakably hers. That would, however, be tested by handwriting experts.

"Why should she write like this?" Pippa went on. "And gone off with Mr. Cox! Why, it's a nightmare. And no wife would write like that about his—his dying. Or—Dame Anne's warning did frighten her tremendously, as it did me—she has gone off her head? That letter isn't the letter of a sane woman." Pippa looked quite alarmed at the thought.

"It's a very peculiar letter," Pointer, agreed, "and, I should say, could only have been written by a very peculiar woman. Is Mrs. Danford peculiar?"

"She is," Pippa agreed hesitatingly. "Yes, she is. But still—"

"In what way is she peculiar?"

"She doesn't come straight out with things," Pippa said, thinking hard, "you might think she hadn't noticed or felt, or seen anything. Then perhaps soon afterwards, perhaps long afterwards, she'll say something that tells you she knew all along."

"And bore a grudge?" Marjoribanks asked, who had joined them.

"No, I don't think Mrs. Danford ever bore a grudge against anyone. Not to my knowledge. No, what she didn't like was that you should think she had been taken in. I think she couldn't bear you to think her anything but what she is, frightfully clever and quick."

There was a silence.

"Now, Miss Hood," Pointer said slowly, "it's no use saying that that letter is the letter of a woman who loves her husband. It isn't. Whatever it may mean, it doesn't—to my thinking—stand for affection. What was the real state of things between the two? I really must press you to be frank with me. I've let it slide up till now,. thinking that it didn't concern the kernel, the death of Mr. Danford, but that note—well, of course, I must look into things a bit deeper."

"They weren't happy," she said very unwillingly, "at least, Mrs. Danford wasn't happy, all this last year. I thought it was just that she didn't like Farthing—that she wanted to be more in town—just vague things of that kind. I never dreamed—and I can't believe it of her! Her of all women" She looked almost helplessly at Pointer.

"You know, Mrs. Danford always seemed a little—not scornful—amused is a better word—at anything sentimental—" Pippa flushed—"and now she says—oh, I simply can't think it's true. I believe she wrote it to annoy my stepfather. Never dreaming that he would be gone—dead—when it would reach Farthing. Thank heaven he never got it! At least he was spared reading it."

"Miss Hood," Pointer said after looking at his shoes very closely, his way when he was deep in thought, "do you know of any definite complaint Mrs. Danford made against her husband, any one grievance, definite grievance, however mistaken it might have been?"

Pippa looked so unhappy, that he saw that there was something definite to be learned from her—at last.

"Oh, Mrs. Danford was very trying in some ways," she began hotly, "charming though she was in others. But she's so illogical. For instance, she always has spoken as though she rather despised people who think of money, yet all this last year, but especially latterly she was always talking to me about it. About my little sum that was left me by my father. Saying that I ought to ask my stepfather for details about it, what it amounted to now, and all that sort of thing, and that I ought to have a yearly statement from him."

"She wasn't content with Mr. Danford's management of affairs, you think?"

"I don't know. She used to talk a lot about having perfect faith in my stepfather's business ability, but that he was too trusting. She thought, she said then, that Digby Cox had a bad influence on him. I can't make it rhyme with her having gone away with the man!" Pippa broke out.

"Perhaps she fell in love with him only very recently," Marjoribanks suggested.

"But it was only last month that she and I quarreled over it all. I—" Here Harold Danford stepped in for another word with Pointer. He would have left the three alone, but Pippa signed to him to stay.

"She said that Mr. Cox was making my stepfather do all sorts of unwise things, and that I really ought to see to it that my money—she called it that—didn't get swept away, in some mad scheme. She kept on about my stepfather being so trusting, believing all Mr. Cox's fine promises of future profits and all that sort of thing—"

"I think you ought to have told me about this," Harold put in. He looked a little startled. "I had no idea—I mean, she may have been right—My brother may have been too much under Cox's influence. You should have told me this before, Pippa! Ivory never mentioned her fears to me. At

least, I don't think she did . . . I don't always listen closely
. . ."

"Why should I tell you something that I thought, and
still think, nonsense, Uncle Harold? My stepfather was
awfully clever, and not at all the kind of man to be
anyone's dupe, as you know. She's right in saying that
because he was so straight himself, he couldn't be
suspicious of others, but that's the only, true thing she
said. The rest was just bunkum. But this letter—I think
she's really gone out of her mind. And it's a dreadful
thought. Ivory off to heaven knows where, alone, and not
in her right senses! It's a ghastly fear." She looked at
Harold, who nodded pityingly.

"Can you suggest anyplace she especially liked
abroad?" Pointer asked.

"She liked the East. But you wouldn't go to Egypt or
Morocco in July, would you? She liked Spain, the same
thing's true of Spain. And of Rome which she loved. No, I
can't think where she's gone if she's left England. South
Africa never seemed to interest her. She likes old places
with old associations."

"The Lido?" suggested Marjoribanks hopefully.

"She loathes the place."

"Is she fond of mountain climbing, or swimming?" .

"She is not."

"Golf, I suppose?" came from Marjoribanks.

"She generally goes round in a little over nine
hundred," Pippa said scathingly, "and she never looks at
a racquet."

Apparently, too, Mrs. Danford detested the sea, except
as a means of getting to land.

Pointer left them after a little more desultory
conversation. There might be some difficulty in locating
this lady, he thought. He had a word with Ormsby before
he left. From him he obtained an account of the odd
undercurrent that had seemed to the new partner, to run
beneath the married life of Edgar Danford. Something
there had been, though just what, Ormsby, could not say.

"Dislike on her part, masquerading as affection, it seemed to me at one moment," he said finally, "though just a while before, I had thought her very devoted. Just as I fancied at first that she was very worried about that extraordinary warning laugh, and yet after it, I had an idea that she was only pretending to be frightened. There was something very, odd about Mrs. Danford, I thought, though I have only met her the once—Friday evening. But why do you ask, chief inspector?"

Pointer made some general, non-committal reply. Ormsby hurried out to his car. He was off to town.

Jackson-Gupp strolled past Pointer.

"Well, chief inspector, the usual thing, I suppose? The police are in possession of clues which will lead to the arrest of the murderer very shortly?" He asked, with that dance of his eyes that Pippa had noticed.

"I hope to heaven they are!" Harold Danford said fervently. He came out of a long window and joined the two. "I confess I hoped that—but of course"—he gave a little sigh—"outsiders are always impatient. And now this idea of Cox—"

"Cox?" Jackson-Gupp repeated. "He's not the murderer, I feel sure. He called up the police."

"Then where is he?" Danford asked, "why doesn't he come forward? We don't know the reason for that summons. Personally, I can't pretend to explain it?" He looked interrogatively at the chief inspector who only nodded.

"In my belief," Jackson-Gupp said in his incisive, clipped tones, "the investigation is losing time in laying so much stress on Cox. I think his presence here at Farthing is a side-issue. It stands to reason that he would know that suspicion would attach itself to him at once, and would have waited for some other, some more general time, if one can put it like that, before carrying out any plan of murder."

"Plan of murder, possibly," Harold Danford agreed, "but I don't think it was a plan. I begin to think Ormsby is right. That it was a quarrel, a desperate quarrel, caused by Cox's sudden realization of where he had landed himself and of what my brother might be going to do. And only my brother. I don't think Cox had an idea that anyone else yet knew of the paper. He didn't telephone to Miss Hood, we know."

"Onlookers are supposed to see most of the game," Pointer now said, "what is your idea of what happened, Mr. Jackson-Gupp?"

"I think someone murdered Mr. Danford who knew that Cox would have left Farthing, and also knew, and knows, that for some reason Cox won't or can't come forward—so that he is certain that suspicion will fall on the dead man's missing partner?" Jackson-Gupp spoke with every appearance of deep thought "I think the murder must have been committed after Cox had left the Chantry. Then, I think, Cox returned for some thing that he had forgotten and found Mr. Danford dead, and at once telephoned to the police. The doctor thinks Mr. Danford was dead before the summons was sent to the police station. And after telephoning, I think Cox hurried off, and for some reason daren't, or can't, come forward."

"Of course, you may be right," Harold Danford said a little wearily, "I confess the whole thing is inexplicable and very terrible But Cox seems to be becoming the only possible solution."

Pointer agreed that he certainly stood for something in the mystery. Marjoribanks, who had stayed for another word with Pippa, now came out, and soon wandered off with Jackson-Gupp

Pointer and Harold Danford were left alone.

"Forgive the question," Pointer said, when he was sure they were safe from eavesdroppers, "but were you and your brother on good terms?"

"Fairly good," Harold Danford said with a sigh. "We were fond of each other, but we had nothing in common."

"And he and his wife?"

Harold Danford hesitated Then he said, with every appearance of frankness "I think they were approaching the trying years that come in every marriage. My sister-in-law, especially, felt a little cabined and confined down here at Farthing, and lately, as you must have learned, my brother's means did not permit of their doing much entertaining in town. He had had to sell a pretty little place he had up in Yorkshire. But I know of nothing that would account for that most amazing letter of hers," he wound up, "nothing whatever."

"You and she were on good terms?" Pointer asked casually.

"Very," was the instant reply.

"She is a charming lady, I understand?"

"Very," Harold agreed as promptly as before, "but not an easy one to live with."

Pointer was watching him keenly, though apparently merely glancing at him in the casual way one glances at the person to whom one is talking. He felt fairly sure that the man speaking was not in love with the woman of whom he was talking. The eyes were as indifferent as the voice. And with a few more questions concerning the state of affairs between the dead man and his wife, questions that brought out nothing helpful, Pointer took his leave. At the police station he learned that the medical certificate as to the cause of death had been, handed in. Edgar Danford had, as was thought, died from strangulation. There were no signs of a struggle, nor of any other attempts at murder, such as poisoning.

CHAPTER EIGHT

THE chief inspector flew up to town and made for Danford's offices in Fenchurch Street. Apparently Danford's terrible death had momentarily disorganized the office routine, or, perhaps it was the rumor that the newly joined partner, Mark Ormsby, was trying to get his partnership canceled, alleging, so one whisper ran, that Edgar Danford had promised him the return of the twenty thousand which he had just put into the business.

It was said that he had a line or two to the effect written shortly before the murder.

Pointer sat in the office waiting for Mr. Ormsby. Apparently he had forgotten that Ormsby had mentioned, as he drove off, that he was not going to the office before midday. Finally, Pointer asked a few casual questions himself, and learned that Mr. Cox had last been at the office on Thursday, and had had a short interview with Edgar Danford, an apparently ordinary interview. Though he tried his best, the clerk who had ushered him in, was unable to add anything to the description of Cox that might now be called official.

The chief inspector next paid a brief call on Mrs. Danford's family solicitors. They claimed to have no idea of her whereabouts, but he learned from them that the sum which now, on her husband's death, passed into her keeping absolutely, was close on thirty thousand pounds.

The chief Inspector and Marjoribanks dined with Captain Boodle on Monday evening, and as soon as they were alone over the cigars, they plunged at once into the various aspects of the baffling case. It was of the murdered man's wife, of Mrs. Danford, that the chief constable began to speak.

"We've learned that she left Dover by air for Calais on Saturday noon. Visas for France, Switzerland, Germany and Italy. Comprehensive little tour. Cox must have followed next day, or by a night boat. I never would have believed it! My wife doesn't like the woman, but only because she thinks her—well —intellectually contemptuous of the things we like, comfort and sport, and so on. No, I wouldn't have believed it of her! I thought her a woman temperamentally only too cold. She and Cox have evidently been seeing each other all the time, while we understood that she was constantly up at concerts and oratorios, and off at the Four Choirs and that sort of thing . Women are extraordinary creatures. By all accounts Cox was the last sort of chap to attract Mrs. Danford, I should have thought."

"Jackson-Gupp insists that Cox is a detail," Marjoribanks threw in, "and that chimes in with my own fixed conviction, that Farthing—not any partner—is the real crux here. The real motive. In some involved way, probably. Do you remember my telling you about seeing Rivers lift his hat to the portrait in the great hall? Well, Miss Hood's story of a family tradition throws a lurid light on that little scene, eh?"

"It certainly was odd," Pointer agreed, "very."

Marjoribanks told the chief constable of what he had seen, and of what Miss Hood had told them. Captain Boodle pursed his lips thoughtfully.

"And I hear he maintains that there's another, later will somewhere. Odd, as you say, Pointer. Almost as odd as that warning laugh . . ."

"I asked him this morning," Marjoribanks said thoughtfully, "why he had seemed so certain, when he met me at the station on my arrival, that the laugh was not genuine. Well, after a little hesitation, I got this out of him. He had once heard Dame Anne's laugh. Before his father died. So he says. And hearing it on Friday evening brought that horrible time back, and so perturbed him that he did not notice the difference in the laugh itself.

But, so he says, on thinking it over Friday night, he is certain, and has remained so, that this laugh—the laugh which has been heard three times before Danford's murder—was totally unlike the laugh heard before his father's suicide. He tells me that this one struck him as a gramophone laugh. He maintains that there are many cupboards and drawers in any of the rooms at Farthing where a small hand gramophone could be hidden and set going by a touch."

"That's what we all think," the chief constable said a little dryly, "the point is, who set it going, and why? But as to Rivers having heard the laugh before, that's interesting. Very."

"So is the fact that his father's end might have been self-inflicted and might not." It was Marjoribanks's turn to speak dryly now. "I've glanced over the account. There seemed no earthly reason for anyone to have shot Colonel Rivers but himself, and every reason why he should have done so, seeing his character and situation. But what strikes me is, that here is a young man who was in the house when that warning laugh was heard before, and a death follows—it may have been suicide, I'm not disputing that—all I say is, that Beaufoy Rivers was there. And is here again, when, in the same house, the warning comes again, and is again followed by a death. One that cannot be a suicide, it's true. But one in which he does not seem implicated—yet."

"That's rather a staggering thought," Captain Boodle said very slowly, "what do you say, chief inspector?"

"I see no explanation of that warning laugh except one that won't fit in here," Pointer said honestly. "This case is very puzzling," and he fell into a brown study.

"About Cox," the chief constable finally roused himself from his own revery to ask, "I understand you've had Lang getting together quite a hatful of facts bearing on him?"

Pointer ran them over now.

Cox had crossed this last March from Mexico. This they knew already, but Pointer got into touch with the officers and stewards of the boat in question. The crossing had been smooth, but Mr. Cox had kept to his very comfortable deck cabin all the time. He had injured his foot just before coming on board which hindered him getting about the boat. Pointer had had a talk with the steward who looked after him. Was Mr. Cox's beard genuine, did he think? The steward was certain that it was, and as he had shaved Cox just before landing, shaved the small patch of face not covered with hair that is to say, his assurance was absolutely conclusive.

What had the man thought of Cox? Nice, quiet gent, was what he had thought, though he looked as though he might have a nasty temper if crossed. Very nasty. His account of Cox's appearance tallied with the usual one, and furnished nothing fresh. Nor did the few other officers of the ship who had come in contact with Cox add anything to this.

The man had in no way roused any comment. His quarters had been among the best in the ship. He had been traveling alone. His things seemed all quite new, the steward had told Pointer in answer to a question on that point, but that was usual in the case of men coming home from the colonies. They usually re-fitted for the occasion.

Pointer had pressed the steward to remember any conversation which he had had with Cox. The man could not seem to recollect anything helpful. Where had Mr. Cox's interest lain, the persistent Pointer then wanted to know. In a general way. What had seemed to attract his notice in the daily wireless bulletin, say?

"Races," the man said immediately, "horses." The day before he shaved him, the Lincolnshire Handicap was won by Warrior, and Cox had spoken as though he had quite a tidy bit on Union Jack. Mr. Cox spoke as though he had lost a pile of money over horses in his time. Pointer had pressed for further details but had got none. He tried the chief steward, and questioned him as to the man's tastes in food and wine. What sort of meals had he ordered? Especially what wines? None. No spirits either. Doctor's orders he had said, and something in the way he said it made the steward think that Mr. Cox would have liked a bottle of the best as much as anyone. And something in his face too. Nothing of the teetotaler about his complexion, for instance. What did he mean by that? Well, just a general effect of elbow-crooking, difficult to say more, clearly. But appearances are deceptive. At any rate on this voyage Mr. Cox had touched nothing but long drinks. His favorite was a lemon squash with a squeeze of pomegranate in it. He was very partial to pomegranates anyway.

"Dress?" Pointer pressed.

Good and plain. But a "diamond" ring of the kind the head steward associated with steerage, rather than cabin, passengers.

"We know that Cox came to London at once and stayed at the Royalty," Pointer now went on. "There he took the *table d'hôte* and again ordered lemon squash and a dash of pomegranate in it—Grenadine syrup from the bar was added as the best equivalent. The next two recorded stays in hotels of his are at intervals during April. He stopped then at the Savoy and chose a very well selected dinner on each occasion, the dinner of an epicure, and some good wines. Even the *maitre d'hôtel* spoke of him as a man who knew his vintages. He had a penchant for Montepulciano of a certain excellent year and had a bottle on each occasion sent to his room."

"It was a bottle of that wine and year that Danford had sent in to the Chantry," murmured the chief constable.

"Next," Pointer went, on, glancing at his and Lang's notes, "come a couple of stops in an hotel towards the end of April. It's the Langham hotel now, and Cox seems to have returned to his lemonade and pomegranate beverage."

"Gone back to his doctor's orders," Marjoribanks said with a smile, "like me and salads. I love 'em, but can't stand 'em. So I keep off them for a few weeks till I'm all right again, and then have one, and repent in sackcloth and ashes in a Harley street waiting-room."

"Y—yes," Pointer collected his papers together again, "y—yes, but you don't combine a liking for salad with the wearing of a glass diamond ring and a fondness for racing tips, do you? The odd thing is that this man does. Or did."

"I don't follow?" Captain Boodle and Marjoribanks leaned forward together, as though bent by the same wind.

"Well," Pointer was speaking, as he felt, like a man groping his way, "when he has wine with his meals, Mr. Cox stays barely overnight. Arrives about eight in the evening. Sometimes changes, sometimes doesn't, in which case he dines in his rooms. Orders a really well-thought-out meal, after discussing it carefully, and knows what years of which wines to avoid, and what ones to order; leaves before breakfast next morning, generally around seven; says no idle word to any member of the staff; is very quietly dressed; wears no jewelry, except some pearl studs if he changes, and, though he was being taken up in a lift on the night when Reindeer won the Grand National, and a couple of men were chatting with the lift man as to what they had backed and what they wished they had, looked as though he hadn't the faintest idea of what they were all talking about, and when the lift man ventured on a feeble pun with him, it was a wet evening, he stared at the man blankly, and on being reminded of the race and the winner, only stared more blankly still. As though, the lift man told me, as though he had never heard of the race nor the day. On the other hand, when Mr. Cox refuses wine and chooses lemonade and pomegranate juice as a drink, he gives the *maitre d'hôtel* the idea that he has no notion of even ordinary restaurant-French. Asks once what *pré-salé* means, and another time what a *canneton* is. Wears a glass bulb on his little finger, and spends half-hours discussing racing tips with the hall porter. He arrives too on these occasions, much earlier, and leaves next morning nearer midday than breakfast time."

He paused a moment. Neither of the men staring at him intently, spoke. Pointer went on, still at the same slow pace, as though feeling his way.

"Now Digby Cox was at Rugby and Oxford, where he certainly took no honors, but where he must have learned enough French to know mutton and duckling when he sees them on a menu. And he certainly was fond of racing. He rode in the Grand National himself the last year he was at the university, and finally got sent down because of some extra rag to celebrate backing the Derby winner. Yet we learn that this last April he seems to have no knowledge of, or interest in, a race in which he had once ridden?"

"Impossible!" came fervently from Captain Boodle.

"You've noticed, of course, that Mr. Cox never seems to go to the same hotel when he orders wine and a good dinner, that he chooses when he takes what's put before him and drinks lemonade and pomegranate juice? They're both good hotels, and he's been twice to the one, and seven times to the other in all, besides one down at Brighton, but he never mixes his styles. He's one thing at the Savoy and at Brighton, and quite another when he stayed—twice—at the Langham."

"Creating two personalities, you think?" Marjoribanks looked muddled and doubtful.

Pointer shook his head.

"He would alter his appearance in that case, surely."

"Ah, you think we have here a case of impersonation!" Boodle was an enthralled listener.

"Of course!" ejaculated Marjoribanks, "of course!"

"It looks that way," Pointer agreed with a little wrinkle of his straight forehead, "or at least it doesn't look any other way. Though, strictly speaking, perhaps, nothing 'looks' in this case. Everything has to be looked at."

"And for?" breathed Marjoribanks.

"Nothing is clear and definite," Pointer went on thoughtfully, "but we seem to have a man here copying the appearance of another man to the best of his ideas of copying, yet blundering in such little things as continuing to wear a pseudo-diamond ring, and betraying an interest in horses. A man who, because he knows his head won't stand them, refuses to touch spirits of any kind, and has the sense to stick to soft drinks, but without reflecting that a taste for pomegranates is a peculiar one in England. There's one thing certain. The impersonator not only knows the real Cox, that, of course, but must be able to keep track of his movements, for the two Coxes never seem to meet or overlap. We've not found one occasion of both being in town together. But there's one odd thing"— Pointer went on, staring at his shoe-tips, he had a corner seat—"that applies to Cox as a whole, to the two of him. He seems not to have looked up any of his old friends. He must have some. He's never done anything, as far as we can find out, to forfeit them, yet no one has come forward who has seen anything of him for years. Not since he entered his uncle's firm as partner and legatee."

Captain Boodle had noticed this. So had the private investigator.

"All but Danford," Pointer went on, "all but Edgar Danford!"

"Can you keep the two Coxes apart?" asked Boodle, "which was the Simon Pure, do you think? The gentleman, I suppose, the *gourmet?*"

"Apparently. For, apart from probability, Mr. Danford dined with him at least three times we have found out, and he seems to've called at the office last Thursday. A bottle of Montepulciano was sent in on that occasion too. Whereas there's no record of Mr. Danford ever having dined with, or met, the other. By the way, Miss Hood commented on the odd character of the letters, as though they were not written by one person."

"Woman's intuition is a wonderful thing!" agreed Boodle.

"Any intuition is a wonderful thing!" corrected Marjoribanks.

"Handwriting?" asked the chief constable.

"Entries in the hotel registers are very similar. Now, as I say, apparently Mr. Danford never met this temperance Mr. Cox on the occasions of which we have any record of him. Unless—"

"Unless?"

"—It was he who came to Farthing this last Saturday night." There followed a profound silence.

"Good God!" muttered the chief constable, "this sham Cox? True, he took lemonade and refused anything stronger. But the bottle of wine—the wine he, or the other, always liked?"

"Danford ordered that brought in," Pointer went on slowly, "Which suggests that he expected the other, the one we think was the real Cox."

"What makes you incline to think it was the racing teetotaler, the sham Cox who came this last Saturday night?" Captain Boodle asked cautiously.

"I don't go so far as 'incline to think,' sir," Pointer demurred, "the only thing I stand firm on is that there were two Coxes. What that means is still to find out, but now supposing the sham one came to Farthing . . . Mr. Danford met him on a very dark day, a day of artificial light all afternoon . . . then too, he was driving himself, that means that, especially on Saturday last, his attention would have had to be centered on the road, on his driving. Mr. Danford spoke of having picked Cox up after a car smash. Seemed very vague about it."

"As though he had taken Cox's word for it," nodded Marjoribanks.

"And that would explain to him, to everybody, why Cox had nothing with him. He said his bag was under the car, you know, and would be retrieved and sent on later by an A.A. scout. As we know, we can't get anything bearing out that yarn. At dinner there are very few people at Farthing. Unusually few. It looks as though this Cox, always supposing he isn't the real one, knew that that would be the case. Altogether, he seems a really well-informed man . . . at any rate, he only finds, besides Mr. Danford his host, who is still, Miss Hood thinks, very much engrossed with some disagreeable news that he had found in the morning's paper, Mr. Harold Danford who had only met Cox once, very briefly he says, and Miss Hood, who had only caught hurried glimpses of him once or twice, going or coming from her stepfather's room down at Fenchurch Street. Miss Hood, last Saturday night, seemed to have something on her mind too."

Pointer had noticed her faint flush as she confessed that she had paid very little attention to the visitor.

"The two, Danford and his guest whom he called Cox, went off almost immediately dinner was over. We know that on bringing in the wine that was ordered into the Chantry, the servant overheard what sounded like a threatening talk which, he was told, were lines in a play—"

"And which be very sensibly refused to believe. I never heard of Danford acting. At least not since we were all young fellows together," the chief constable threw in.

"And then, what happened?" Marjoribanks wanted to know.

"Then, apparently, the sham was detected, and the impersonator murdered Mr. Danford to avoid the consequences of his detection, or to obtain whatever it was that he was after—"

"The real Cox's money?" Boodle wondered.

"By George!" Marjoribanks was on his feet, "and the other Cox, the real one, arrived and found Danford murdered and telephoned for the police."

"If you're going to give me *two* missing men, as well as a possible tramp who left those mud marks, to hunt for, I throw up the case," Pointer said fiercely.

The three laughed.

"I put that telephone message and the warning laugh on one side for the moment," the chief inspector continued, "all I am suggesting is that we may have here a murder motive of quite a different character from the one we should be looking or if we were sure that it was the real Cox who came Saturday tight. The sham Cox would not have worried over the other's forgery, certainly he would not have committed a murder because of it. At least, that's how it seems to me. I think he would have refused to discuss it."

"Possibly that very refusal, or some blunder he made when speaking of it, roused Danford's suspicions," suggested Marjoribanks, half to himself.

"But, you know, Pointer," it was the chief constable now who was speaking, "it seems to me a most difficult and dangerous undertaking for the false Cox to have come down to Farthing. A man visiting his partner, mind, would—must—expect to have all sorts of business things crop up, where he would be sure to blunder."

"But that's what it looks as if he had done!" threw in Majoribhanks.

"I quite agree," Pointer nodded to the chief constable, "my theory is full of improbabilities. I only mention it because as I said, it suggests a quite different line of reasoning. To me here's only one simple solution of Mr. Danford's murder, relatively simple that is, but it's impossible. But it's just possible that the impersonator, supposing it was he who came down, had some reason for refusing to discuss business matters . . . Mr. Danford's words to Mr. Harold Danford rather suggest that . . ."

"The absence of Ormsby the newly joined partner, might have done," suggested Majoribanks.

Pointer thought that it might have. He agreed that it was a desperate game to play without being found out, and therefore must have been played for high stakes.

"Important papers. Or securities of some kind."

"Ah!" the two men listening intently, nodded their heads. "Just so!" murmured the chief constable.

"Of course, even supposing it was the sham Cox who came down here, he might not have gone to any such length. The murder might have been totally unconnected with his impersonation of Cox, or its reason."

"Then why did he disappear?" cut in Captain Boodle.

"If you could tell me how he disappeared, sir, I'd give my next month's pay to your favorite charity. Or who left those marks of wet mud on the polished boards of the Chantry guest-room. Who gripped that bath-tub with a black and filthy paw? Mud from some beechwood, says our analyst, not surface mud either, but such as someone might have got on his hands and feet who had been digging about five feet down—"

"Good Gad," goggled Boodle, "the depth of a grave!" In his interest he tried to light his finger instead of a cigar.

Suddenly, Marjoribanks who had been sitting thinking deeply, looked up.

"By George, Pointer, that idea of yours—or rather that discovery—about the two Coxes explains Mrs. Danford's letter. She's off with the real Cox while the sham one is dining at Farthing and murdering her husband. And that suggests, as does the fact that they never overlap, the idea that the two may be working hand in hand, eh?"

Pointer said nothing.

"Don't you think there may be something in Marjoribanks's idea?" The chief constable did.

"I can't understand Mrs. Danford's letter at all, sir," Pointer said slowly.

"Ah, if you're speaking of it psychologically, neither can I," confessed the private investigator. "I was concerned for the moment only with the bare facts."

"No facts I've found out explain that letter," Pointer stared at his shoe-tips with a steely glare.

"But, at any rate, it, your discovery of the two Coxes, might explain how she could have left with Cox and yet he have, apparently come down here after it. We were taking it for granted that he must have crossed later. He may have gone on earlier on the contrary. Quite unaware that he was being duplicated."

"Mrs. Danford holds some clue," Pointer said, looking up from his inspection.

"And to the laugh too," Marjoribanks said firmly. Pointer nodded.

"I'm off to see if I can find her. After that letter, she must be found—if possible. I have an idea where I might run across her. It's quickly tried out. Successful or not, I shall be back here before any fresh developments are likely."

"Any expected?" Captain Boodle promptly wanted to know.

"Unfortunately no," Pointer had to say.

"No idea as to what has become of Cox?"

Just for a second the chief inspector hesitated.

"I've found no clues," he said finally, and the other nodded.

"That means there are none to be found. Well, the inquest is to-morrow. We'll get it adjourned for a fortnight."

"Personally, I think a couple of years would give us more chance of unraveling this tangle. But we might begin with two weeks," Marjoribanks said, as he took his leave. He had an appointment, with a former client. Pointer and the chief constable went over to the police station, and discussed the handling of the, case during the absence of the Scotland Yard officer with Superintendent Lang.

Pointer's hopes of finding Mrs. Danford were based on that love of music which he had learned was one of her passions.

He had asked a musical critic of a big London paper whether anything was now "on," or had been, in the last couple of days, of sufficient importance in France, Germany or Italy to attract an amateur of the art that was in the world before man knew himself as man.

The critic suggested two events as likely to draw any music lover who was free. The first was just over in Germany, the other was to take place in a couple of days at Riva, where Oblowsky, the new Polish operatic tenor, was to sing for the first time at a concert. Then the critic had added:

"And isn't next Sunday the third in July? I thought so. Then if I were at Riva I'd be sure and cut across to Venice for the Saturday night, the Eve of the Redentore festival, and listen to the popular music on the canals. It's a quite unforgettable and very exquisite experience"

Pointer tried Riva—the pearl of Lake Garda—as some of the advertisements call it. The chief inspector intended, some day, to write a guide-book on *Where Not to Go. What Not to See.* He decided that he would star Riva in it, with the note. "Whatever else you can't miss, be sure and miss Riva." It seemed to him one of the most desolate holes into which he had ever stumbled.

True, there is Lake Garda, which, from the other, the Peschiera end, can show itself blue as a Reckit's bag, but which from Riva is only blue on a fine day, when all lakes are sky color. There are no walks in Riva. Behind it rises Monte Baldo, a name which is singularly appropriate to English eyes. Pointer did not consider it a mountain but a lump. A mountain has contours, has grandeur. This hard-fought position of the war has neither. But just now Riva was flagged and crowded. Just for the once Italians were here. Italians, as a rule, are far too knowing to come to Riva, or to near by Arco, with its decrepid palms, and general air of trying to be what it is not—a health resort. The concert was a great affair. Was not that first class advertiser and publicity expert, D'Annunzio arranging it, were not his poems to be sung at it?

Pointer read through the list of visitors in the hotels; there was no sign of either name he wanted, Danford or Cox. Nor was she at the concert as far as the keenest scrutiny could tell.

Next day was the Saturday of which the critic had spoken; so for Venice Pointer left—his last cast for the moment. As he neared the city, the train seemed to turn into a steamer, and run on the face of the waters, with boats sailing along both sides of the windows, so narrow is the built-up causeway on which the lines run. He arrived none too soon. The preparations were finished, the last nail driven into the pontoon bridges, over the Grand Canal and the Giudecca Canal, so that for this one time in the year Venetians have the—to them—singular joy of walking where the rest of the time they must go in boats.

He got into a gondola.

A July evening in Venice going east. There is nothing in the world quite like it. To float along lanes of silver sheen into a sea of crimson and gold that meets the gold and crimson sky, out of which—whether sky or sea is hard to tell—rise islands, themselves all shades of heliotrope and lilac. Time is not. Life is not. You float, as might an atom, in palpitating color. But to-night was different. The ceremonies begin with a great service in the Redentore Church, on the Island of Giudecca, the church which the Senate built as a fulfillment of their vow when the pestilence of 1536 was stayed in answer to their prayers.

To one standing inside, the church seemed built of blossoming, sweet-smelling flowers. Tier on tier into the highest point of the big dome they rise, not cut, but growing, and nodding down to the people below them as to their friends.

Hundreds of great candles turned the high altar into a dazzling glitter, so bright that the eye could not stare at it long, a glitter that fell sharply on the brilliant folds of the velvet draping the pillars, and softly brought out the tints of the flower walls.

Pointer only stood a moment to enjoy the scene. All around him thronging dark-eyed men and women, the latter, high and low, swathed in black fringed shawls worn tight around their lithesome bodies. He had been warned that no musician would consider the service in the church anything remarkable. Mrs. Danford was not a Roman Catholic. Nor was she particularly given to church services of any kind, as far as he knew. He left the building, and stepped out into the Venice of the Middle Ages which, on this one night, comes to life again.

Since the days of The Plague, supper is taken on the eve of the Redentore in gondolas out on the canals to the sound of music. A white tablecloth, a bunch of flowers in the center, with shining Venetian glass and wine and fruit, and—always—one or two musicians in the stern with their tireless mandolins.

Rocking, dipping, swinging, swaying, they pass. Everywhere there is music, and the water reflects it like the lights. Fireworks begin at ten, and for once they do not jar. The network of canals, the old palaces on their banks show like colored lantern slides out of the darkness as the Roman candles burst; and when the rockets fall in showers, they are reflected in the still waters until the gondolas seem to pass through spinning circles of colored stars. Everywhere are lights, soft music, and the singing of the old folk-songs of Venetia. It is a pageant that is unique. A memory and a picture. When midnight is past, and the last fireworks has spluttered down, comes the final procession of the gondolas led by the Gallegiante, the modern representative of the old Bucintoro.

Pointer stepped out onto the pretty little Bridge of Sighs, and leaned over the old, old parapet, watching the boats file below him.

Suddenly he saw a woman—alone in a gondola— whom he recognized from her photograph. It was Mrs.

Danford. A word to his gondolier and they kept her in sight as she made her way to the Lido.

Old custom demands that the people watch the sunrise from there, and then, after a great Sunday service of thanksgiving in the church the duties of the festival are over.

Pointer could not get near enough to Mrs. Danford to speak to her privately. Her gondoliers beside her, she sat on the sands with brown-faced peasants for the most part as her companions. It is no longer smart to fulfill the old regulations.

When the sun was well up, came another procession of the boats going to Giudecca.

A July morning in Venice going west. Who can forget any one of them? All around you shifting patches of every color in the rainbow, but chiefly rose, and gold, and azure, and sea. green, rise and fall, translucent and shining.

The boatman is behind. Nothing impedes the view. No sound of an oar comes to your ear. His call, when he turns a bend, is like the call of the curlew, long-drawn and melodious. Nothing is heard but the lisping waters against the sides of the most comfortable boat in the world, and across the liquid floor rise churches and palaces and arched bridges and cypresses and down hanging willows. The air is light and invigorating and vital.

Mrs. Danford got out at Giudecca. But she paid off her gondola, and Pointer, who told his to wait for him, followed her at a distance past the church, and down to a house almost buried in orange trees. There, as he stood apparently loitering like any tourist, he saw her seat herself at a table in a shady loggia.

Pointer went around to another side of the villa. He found a gate out of sight, and passed up to the front door, also out of sight of the woman in the veranda room.

He was looking for a lady, an acquaintance, who might be stopping here, he told the maid, could he glance at the visitors' book, he did not know where the Signora in question was staying.

The book was promptly fetched. There a few lines back he read Mrs. Danford's name and the particulars concerning her arrival accurately filled out.

"This is the name," he said, handing the book back. "But it may not be the same lady. Is she alone, this one?"

"Quite alone. She is breakfasting in the loggia if the signore would care to step this way—"

Pointer presented himself at the door. Mrs. Danford recognized him on the instant.

"The chief inspector from Scotland Yard whom I talked to in the train—" Her eyes asked a dozen questions. Excitement showed in them, and dread. It was gone in a second, that last swift gleam, but it had been noted. "How in the world did you find me?" she asked in bewilderment.

"Routine," Pointer said vaguely. "Just a bit of routine work did it. But, Mrs. Danford, I'm the bearer of bad news. Very bad news. An accident has happened to Mr. Danford. A serious accident."

She sat back, or rather she fell back into her chair. "Oh, tell me quickly!" she implored.

"I'm sorry to say that Mr. Danford is dead," Pointer went on simply and very gently.

"Dead!" she whispered under her breath. She had turned very white. For a moment she seemed stunned. Then: "But why hasn't my brother-in-law come? There's been something wrong?"

Evidently her brain was working again.

"As you say, there has been something wrong about his death, and that is why I am here. In my official capacity. Mr. Danford, I am sorry to say, was found murdered a week ago to-day, in his bedroom in the Chantry—"

She sat staring at him. Her mouth a little parted. Her eyes wide.

"—After putting Mr. Cox up for the night. Mr. Cox has not yet been found. It is to have an interview with him—as well as with you, Mrs. Danford—that I'm here."

"Mr. Cox!" She was incapable of further speech for a moment, then she said again in a tone of one who is sure that some mistake has been made. "Did you say that Mr. Cox was at Farthing at the time?"

"He dined there and spent the early part of the night there. When did he join you?"

She jumped from her seat. "Oh, but how awful! That dreadful letter! I've been all wrong. I thought—" She seemed to reel a little where she stood.

"Dreadful letter?" Pointer repeated inquiringly.

"A letter in which I said—oh, anything, anything that came into my head. I never guessed that things were as they must have been—" She fell back rather than sat in her chair again, and covered her face with hands that trembled.

"I am in charge of the inquiry into the cause of his death," the chief inspector reminded her—or warned her. "And I take it for granted that you want to help us catch his murderer—"

"How was he killed?" she asked suddenly, still with her face hidden. He told her. She went whiter yet.

"Any help that you can give—" he began again.

"But I can't help you!" she almost sobbed. "I—I—oh, it doesn't seem possible!"

He assured her that it was true.

"I want to speak to Mr. Cox," Pointer went on.

She stared at him.

"He's not here. I don't know where he is. I've never seen the man in my life. Did you say, that he was at Farthing Saturday night?"

Again there was stark amazement in her voice.

"Yes. He dined at Farthing and spent part of the night there, but he has disappeared. He was not to be found on Sunday morning when the police got there, and has not been seen since."

"Please tell me everything." She spoke calmly now, and motioned him to a chair. "I haven't looked at an English paper, nor written home to any friends yet. What exactly happened? Please begin with my leaving Farthing on Saturday morning for town—and, though no one knew it, for abroad."

Pointer went over the facts—as far as they were known to the household at Farthing. She listened with a breathless, repressed avidity, that was both natural and unnatural. Pointer would have liked to take her into his confidence. But he did not dare.

"And now you ask me to believe that you don't know this Mr. Cox?" he finished finally, looking very bewildered.

"I assure you that I have never met him, or even seen him," she said earnestly.

"But—you told Mr. Danford that you knew him!"

"No, no! That too was only a joke. Just to tease him. You see I thought then—" she paused, and went on hurriedly, "that I should not be likely to meet Mr. Cox for some time, so it would be perfectly safe to bring is name in as a very poor joke."

She did not look to the chief inspector, like a woman with such an odd sense of humor.

"You haven't met Mr. Cox?" Pointer was all at sea.

"Don't you see that it's because I knew that my husband knew that I hadn't met him that I wrote as I did!" she burst out. Then she seemed to choke back something more. Her face flushed, then paled.

"How could Mr. Danford know that you hadn't met Mr. Cox," persisted the puzzled chief inspector.

"Oh—why—I should have told him if I had, shouldn't I?" she said with a white smile and jumped to her feet.

But Pointer had an impression of much more than she said being dammed back, of only a very few words being allowed through, words which she was certain could not drag others with them. Why this caution? She burst out suddenly: "I don't understand it at all. I mean—why should Mr. Cox . . . how could Mr. Cox . . . I mean why should Mr. Cox . . . have harmed my husband. He, he is— was—his partner!" But this last sentence Pointer thought was merely a rudder hitched on at the last moment to prevent the boat drifting on to quicksands.

"But you foresaw some danger threatening Mr. Danford, you know," Pointer reminded her.

"I?" She stared at him.

"When you asked me to investigate the warning laugh that had been heard twice at Farthing."

A look of something like alarm or even fear, shot across her expressive eyes.

"Oh, yes, yes, of course! I asked you to investigate that because it worried me. Just as a warning portent, you know. A family warning. I had no idea, of course, that it meant anything like this. Or indeed anything at all. I cannot understand this awful tragedy!"

"Nor Mr. Cox having been there at the time?" Pointer asked casually.

She gave him a sudden, swift, suspicious look.

"Because he is my late husband's partner, and therefore I fancied there could be no reason for him to harm my husband," she said now smoothly.

"Perhaps he hasn't harmed him," Pointer said quietly, watching her closely without seeming to do so. "And if he hasn't; we may be wasting very precious time investigating his presence last Saturday night at Farthing. That warning now, if you have any idea about it, or any fancy, however far-fetched it would seem, it might help us a lot, if you would talk it over with me."

She looked at him. with inscrutable eyes.

"But I turned to you for help, chief inspector," she said a little ironically. "That proved how puzzled I was, how unable myself to fathom it, or to suggest anything that might help you now." Her gaze did not falter.

Her face alone, its unreadability, told Pointer that she had lived long among people for whom she did not care, in whom she did not confide. It was the face of a woman who for years had kept her inner thoughts, her deepest emotions, to herself.

But of one thing there seemed no doubt as she now talked on, more easily, and that was that she appeared to be genuinely glad that the chief inspector had found her in time, thanks to airships, for her to be back at Farthing for her husband's funeral, and so avoid the endless gossip that her absence would have caused.

She did not put it on the score of her own feelings, Pointer noticed. She at no time pretended that her heart was broken, or even bruised. She did not again sound the note of the loving wife, as she had during that short talk in the train. Pointer tried to use her relief at his having found her, to get some definite information out of her about Cox. He felt that she was holding back many things about that missing man. Why? And what could she have told him, if she spoke? Pointer had a belief that they were important things. He tried to surprise them out of her. She refused to be startled. He endeavored to draw them out casually, she evaded all his efforts. Finally he fished for more general information, if not about facts, at least about her own thoughts.

"Mrs. Danford, what possible motive could there be for your husband's murder, do you think?"   .

"I haven't an idea. You see I knew so little of his business, and of course, if—since—Mr. Cox is concerned it must have been business."

"But if it has nothing to do with business or with Mr. Cox?" he pressed.

"Well, of course, the first thing one thinks of is someone who wanted to get hold of Farthing," she murmured.

"Do you know how your husband disposed of his property?" he asked.

"Most of it comes to me, I suppose," she said after a moment.

"Including Farthing?"

"I suppose so. Though I'm not sure. He knew that I dislike the place."

"Why? I mean why do you dislike it?" Pointer asked. "It's a very wonderful place to look at."

"Just so!" She caught him up quickly. "But not to live in. I liked it once—at first. My father, you know, claimed to be psychic, I don't, but there's something about Farthing—and about that picture of the man over the fireplace in the big hall that—well—that oppresses me more and more. I'm never in self when I'm there. I have a feeling sometimes as though the very thoughts I think were being suggested to me, and such horrid thoughts too!" She flushed. For once she had spoken unguardedly.

"As a matter of fact, Mrs. Danford," Pointer now said, "we found that he had made a very recent will leaving practically everything—except your own fortune, of course—to Miss Hood."

"Not Farthing!" she said swiftly, and in spite of what she had just said, something showed in her face for a second. Was it anger?

"Certainly. He has left the place to her and practically to her husband, if she marries."

She said nothing. She only studied the nails on her ungloved hand.

"Of course the will might be contested by you," Pointer put out as a feeler. She swept him with blank eyes and nodded.

"That would depend, wouldn't it?" was her only reply.

"On?"

"On what the lawyers think," was her evasive answer. She did not finish her sandwich he noticed. After a while she came and sat beside him.

"What do the police think was the motive?" she said finally.

"Well, like you, with the owner of such a place as Farthing, the first thought is a speculation as to whether the property might be in some distant way the reason . . . but it passed to Miss Hood—"

"You say that Miss Hood's future husband shares in it," she broke in. "Mind you, chief inspector, this is merely talk. I haven't the slightest reason for saying such a thing, but of course anyone who was going to marry her, would be able, I suppose, as future co-owner of Farthing to borrow money and that sort of thing? Supposing his engagement were well-known, duly announced?"

"That's true!" Pointer seemed struck by this thought. "I understand that Mr. Rivers expected to be Miss Hood's husband?"

She started.

"Oh, but Mr. Rivers is quite out of it," she said warmly. "Mr. Rivers is the last man in the world to commit a crime. He's cursed with far too stiff-necked a conscience, I assure you. He's been our, or rather my husband's land agent for five years and more. I know him thoroughly. Nothing would make him a criminal. And as for money—he's only too little use for it—which is lucky."

Pointer nodded his head gravely as though what she had to say quite settled matters.

"Speaking, as you yourself put it, without any reason to go on, what about Mr. Harold Danford? He might have expected to benefit under a wealthy brother's will?"

Ivory Danford laughed outright.

"Oh, no, chief inspector, neither Beaufoy Rivers nor Harold Danford is the criminal. Mr. Harold has all the money he wants, and, as it happens he too dislikes Farthing. It is only the fact that the music room has remarkable acoustics that induced him to come to us at all."

"But—well, there remains the fact that he and his brother weren't always on the best of terms with each other," Pointer mentioned.

Mrs. Danford opened her eyes. There was genuine amazement and nothing else in them.

"My husband and his brother were the best of friends. Always!" And her reply settled another question besides the one that it was supposed to answer. She was not in love with Harold Danford. Her tone, her face, was too casual, too indifferent.

She turned to the chief inspector after another long silence and began to question him about the people who had been at Farthing at the time of the murder.

"Did you know that Mr. Rivers was expecting a visitor for the week-end?" Pointer finished.

She shook her head negligently. "Mr. Rivers often has people down to see his experiments, his wireless work. So Mr. Ormsby spent the night at the inn" . . . and on that she seemed to fall into a puzzled reverie.

"You suspect Mr. Ormsby?" Pointer asked, as though casting about for help.

She did not reply directly. Then:

"I don't, can't, suspect anyone. It's all too horrible and too utterly unexpected, this whole tragedy. But—" she broke off and looked out of the window at the land far below them. "You told me just now that Mr. Ormsby claims that Mr. Danford was going to return him the money that he had invested in the partnership?"

"He say so, yes. I understand that Mr. Harold Danford quite agrees to that, though Mr. Ormsby has no written proof of his statement."

"Harold is always generous. But Edgar Danford? . . ." She paused.

"You doubt Mr. Danford's having agreed to do that?"

"It would be unlike him. Very unlike him," she said coldly. "Forgive me, Mrs. Danford, but the question may be relevant to the mystery. Was Mr. Danford a generous man, or the reverse."

"He could be, or no, he could seem generous," she said after a moment's silence. "But I, personally, have never known him to spend money without getting a return for it. And that promise to free Mr. Ormsby, to return him the money invested in the firm, would bring nothing to Mr. Danford, so I—frankly—doubt this ever having made it."

Pointer was listening very closely. Something was trying to slip past Mrs. Danford's caution. Would it succeed?

"You don't like Mr. Ormsby?" he asked tentatively.

"No, I don't," she said with seeming frankness. "He struck me as the type that's all out for money." Again there was a little silence, then she asked.

"Do you think that Mr. Ormsby and Mr. Danford had known each other longer than the time he tells you?"

Pointer said that the police had no reason to doubt Ormsby's word on this point.

She nodded moodily at his reply. Pointer pressed her, to explain her question.

"Well, as you know I was—afraid—uneasy—at that laugh which. meant some bad luck, if not worse, to my husband. Oh, I know that in that letter I chose to write of it as though—please forget that stupid letter, it was meant for fun, just for a silly piece of fun! But I really was worried."

"You mean before you left for abroad?" Pointer asked innocently.

She bit her lip.

"By that time Mr. Danford had reassured me, you see, with his certainty that there was no laugh, no ghost's laugh that is, and therefore no calamity coming to him. But before that time I spoke to you in the train, I had an idea—that my husband was being led into deep water financially."

"Ah, by Digby Cox!" Pointer nodded.

"I may have been wrong as to the person," she said hesitatingly, her eyes on her gloves. "I'm wondering now whether it might not have been Mr. Ormsby. I had an idea that Mr. Danford was—well getting out of his depths—"

"Nothing of that sort has been discovered," Pointer assured her truthfully. "All his affairs seem in perfect order."

Without seeming to do so, he was studying her carefully. She looked honestly perplexed at that, and fell again into silence.

Pointer too had plenty to occupy his mind. He was exceedingly disappointed at the little, the nothing, that he had been able to learn from the widow. The more so, as he was absolutely certain that she could tell him much more if she chose. Why did she lead the talk away from Digby Cox—the man who most of all interested Pointer, or at least refuse to discuss him as the probable murderer.

"Do you know if Mr. Danford had ever met Mr. Digby Cox, before the latter joined the firm as his uncle's heir?" he asked now suddenly.

Mrs. Danford seemed to take some time before replying, but she had done that more than once.

"As far as I know, he had never met him." She did not look up, and seemed half asleep.

Pointer's thoughts passed Digby Cox, the mysterious missing man, the partner who seemed to have vanished after that message to the police, and thought over Ormsby, and Mrs. Danford's evident suspicions of him.

Pointer knew that Ormsby was in a tight place financially, and that he had been so by the Saturday, evening of the murder. The sham suicide, and absconding of Fairbairn, the inability of his firm to pay their debtors, after Ormsby had just tied up a large part of his money as Danford's new partner, had crippled him greatly in some of his other financial activities, and he had many. Ormsby was all out for money as Mrs. Danford had guessed, or felt. The police, for instance, knew that he had got a loan on the production of a certified copy of Edgar Danford's will, and a statement by the solicitor that he was engaged to Miss Hood. Also, supposing that Edgar Danford had not promised to refund the sum which Ormsby had just tied up in his firm, then Danford's death might have been the only means that would have enabled Ormsby to get the money returned to him.

CHAPTER NINE

AT the same moment, Ormsby was occupying Pippa's thoughts, too.

He and Rivers had just had a most unpleasant scene of which she had come on the end.

"What do you mean by offering a reward for the production of a later will of Danford's than this one we intend to probate," Ormsby had fairly stormed at the land agent.

"Why shouldn't I?" was the off-hand reply.

"It upsets Pippa," Ormsby said still angrily, much more angrily than he imagined showed.

"Do you think so?" was all the reply this received.

"To insert that notice in all the papers—" fumed Ormsby.

"It will be inserted every other day for a week," he was told.

"I shall get Miss Hood to see if she can't make you alter your intention." Ormsby spoke more quietly, but his eyes were furious.

Pippa hearing her name came in as she was passing. She too was indignant at the advertisement which had appeared in all the leading dailies.

"You've no right to do a thing like that without consulting anyone," she protested. "Of course we hold the last will. Why, my stepfather would have had to have made another the very last night, because he told me that Farthing was coming to me. Told me so on Friday."

"I don't pretend to say when he made a later will." Rivers spoke without looking at her. "All I say is, that I feel sure there is a later one."

"Leaving you the property!" sneered Ormsby.

"Perhaps," Rivers said coldly. "You ought to be grateful to me, Ormsby. It would be awkward to—well—make some arrangement on the understanding that Farthing would be more or less yours, and then find you hadn't a look-in wouldn't it."

Ormsby's face was positively dangerous.

"What do you mean?" Pippa demanded.

"Ask him," Rivers said coldly.

"Certainly not!" said Pippa with her head up, privately intending to do so at the first opportunity. "You're always hinting that Mark cares more for Farthing than he does for me—" Rivers had not yet done as much but he did not deny it, he only lit a cigarette nonchalantly, though his face was flushed.

"Mark had no idea that I should ever be the owner of Farthing until we both heard the will read," Pippa said hotly.

"Rubbish!" Rivers retorted rudely.

"What do you mean?" flamed Pippa.

But Ormsby interposed. "Your stepfather trusted me, Pippa, don't you think he was a better judge of me than this—this meddler?"

"Indeed he was!" Pippa said passionately. "I can't think what has changed you so, Beaufoy, lately. And you're letting things slide terribly. I saw a notification from the Royal Fire Insurance only this morning on your desk reminding you that the insurance had lapsed last week. Well—that isn't right!"

"Farthing's too solid for a fire," Rivers said casually. "Though of course I shall see about its renewal."

"Swelled head, that's what's the matter with him!" Ormsby said as he and she finally left a most unsatisfactory young man behind in the business-room and walked out into the grounds.

"I can't think why he's so utterly horrid!" Pippa looked worried. Rivers had always up till now been her sure and certain stand-by.

"He must go, of course," Ormsby threw in, but watching her keenly.

"Go? Beaufoy? He's not a servant, Mark, to be discharged. Beaufoy has done wonders for the place. Besides, what about his experiments?" Then her voice changed. "But what does he mean by your being grateful to him because he's claiming that there's another will leaving the property differently?"

"Sure I can't say!" Ormsby nicked the head off a rose with a vindictive switch. "Doesn't know himself probably!" Then he went on hurriedly: "What he's trying to do—obviously—is to separate us. To sow suspicion between us. But he won't succeed!"

"Of course not," she assented after an infinitesimal pause. "No, of course not!" she repeated briskly.

"Any more than he can frighten you with his tale of a later will. Ridiculous yarn! As you say yourself, it would have had to be drawn up and witnessed on Saturday! Preposterous."

"Quite!" she assented, and a listener might have noticed that her assent to this last speech was much more hearty than to the previous one. "Now I'm off to the station to meet Ivory. Poor Ivory! She'll be broken-hearted!"

"Think so?" Ormsby asked caustically.

"And I want to hear what she meant by that letter," Pippa went on in a tone of frank curiosity, as she hurried off without replying to his query.

Something in the way she and Mrs. Danford met, told the chief inspector who was in another compartment of the same train, of some unpleasantness in the past now tacitly forgiven and forgotten.

The funeral was the same day, and in the evening the widow left for a sister's house in the Cotswolds.

When it was over, the chief inspector found a pile of papers and reports ready for him, bearing on the activities of Cox—or rather the two Coxes—but nothing that altered the aspect of the case, nothing that suggested a solution of the mystery.

Not though a plain-clothes man from the Yard, an expert carpenter, working together with the superintendent, had discovered the cause of the warning laugh. They had found a small occasional table on which an electric lamp stood against the wall. The table had an openwork gilt border which concealed a four-inch deep drawer. The knob of the drawer had been taken off, the spot touched with gilt paint, the back pried away, and the drawer itself then screwed into place with gilt screws, so that even to a searching eye it gave no sign of its presence.

Taking the table to pieces, as he had taken several others in his hunt, the detective had found a small gramophone inside, which just fitted the ten-inch square top. There was only one disc, and it, when played, gave the wild, unhuman laugh which the guests had heard that last dinner party, and which the police believed had been heard twice before. A musical expert had placed the laugh as occurring in a South American version of Lucia di Lammer Moor. The little gramophone was electrical, a short gilt flex fitting into the lamp plug would play it, but once played, once the laugh had sounded, the disc was stopped by a simple device which held it until released, by hand, while the needle arm was raised at the same time. The little machine bore the name of a Mexican firm; a wireless inquiry brought the answer back that the disc and special mechanism had been ordered by a Mr. Cox some weeks before the date on which the police knew that "Mr. Cox" had sailed for England.

But only someone in Farthing itself could have fitted the case into the drawer, and when wanted connected it by a mere touch while apparently fiddling with the lamp, and then duly disconnected it during the search for just some such hidden piece of mechanism.

Who that someone was, remained, as much a puzzle as ever.

As to Mr. Jackson-Gupp, and Mr. Hatter, the closest watch had not shown any further meetings or correspondence between the two men, and Mr. Hatter had now left the doctor's care for after treatment in an institute in town. Moreover the wireless expert had slackened in his attendance at the periscope He had not been near the tower, except openly.

"That seems to end the incident," the chief constable thought.

"But the explanation, sir?" asked the superintendent. No one answered him.

"So Mrs. Danford says she put in her letter that she was off with Cox because she knew that Danford wouldn't believe it—" ruminated Marjoribanks "That seems to me rather far-fetched. Besides she says the letter was a sort of jest—a decidedly ill tempered one to my mind. There's something very odd about Mrs. Danford having chanced to pick on Cox as her companion—if her story's true—"

"Well, of course, it's not odd if it's not true" Captain Boodle pointed out, in the tone of a man on firm ground.

Pointer did not seem to be listening He was staring at his shoes' tips, hands clasped behind him, head bent forward. He was very perplexed.

"I never knew anything so baffling!" he confessed.

"'Straordinary case!" agreed Boodle.

"Because Mrs. Danford's whole manner, what she said, and what she doesn't say, fits—but what's the use!"

"Of what?" asked Marjoribanks with interest.

"I could explain many of the difficulties in this case by one simple explanation," Pointer said thoughtfully. "Only it—well, it apparently is an impossible one."

"You may take it from a man who has lived a rough, a very rough life, that it is the subtleties of personalities, and contacts, and events, that count for interest and memory—and pretty well nothing else," murmured Marjoribanks half to himself.

The chief constable, who did not recognize the speech as a quotation, looked impressed, and also surprised. He had an idea that Marjoribanks's life at Harrow, and afterwards at New, and then for some years in a civil service post, had been distinctly easy-going and pleasant.

"I'm quoting from Conrad," Marjoribanks explained, as he caught the speculative gaze on him, trying to guess where the "very rough life" had come in.

"Oh!" Captain Boodle now understood. "Conrad—deep thinker at times. 'Straordinary things about his books is when he has one chap talk to another for a steady month on end, telling him some yarn or other, and the listening chap never once faints or calls for help. But he's right about subtleties counting for interest. Mrs. Danford, for instance."

"It's possible," Marjoribanks suggested, "that she thinks there's but the one, and that she knows where he was on Saturday night. A place nowhere near Farthing. Do you think she knows or suspects that there are two Coxes?"

"I couldn't say what she knows or suspects," Pointer assured him dryly. "Except that it is far more than she's willing to tell. As for two Coxes, I couldn't let her guess that idea as ours."

"Mrs. Danford was alone at all the stops on her journey—" ruminated the chief constable.

Pointer nodded his assent.

"Jackson-Gupp is positive that Cox left Farthing after telephoning to the police," Marjoribanks put in. "I rather agree. You know, I have an idea that he too suspects that there may have been two Coxes. Naturally I also gave him no hint that such a thought had entered our minds."

"What did he say?" Pointer asked curiously.

"Well, he said that Cox having been seen by the gamekeeper didn't mean much to him, that anyone knowing Cox was coming to dinner and the peculiarities of his appearance, red beard and hair, glasses, and brown skin, might very easily make up sufficiently to be mistaken for him by a man glancing up in the moonlight."

Pointer said nothing.

"I thought it a feasible idea," Marjoribanks said looking inquiringly at him. "Don't you?"

"Certainly, if anyone happened to have a red wig and a red beard in his possession," Pointer agreed. "Not otherwise."

"You think?" probed the chief constable.

"That if anyone made up as the guest of the evening he must have been prepared to do so, and had his make-up ready to his hand."

"True," muttered Marjoribanks. "That does rather scorch that notion."

He and Pointer walked over to Farthing together.

"I have an idea you don't trust Jackson-Gupp?" the private investigator said finally, after they had chatted of Pointer's journey. "It seems a ridiculous notion—"

"He doesn't strike me as exactly a trusting person himself," was the only answer.

Marjoribanks shook his head firmly.

"He's straight. I feel that. He's very anxious to solve the mystery."

At the house, Pointer and he had a talk with Mr. Harold Danford as to the case. The great difficulty was that of no one could the chief inspector ask those leading questions which he would have liked to put, for they were questions which would have suggested the idea of the existence of two Coxes. He had to content himself with general talk about the missing partner.

"Mr. Rivers has just had a letter from a former clerk of my brother's," Harold Danford said casually, as his two visitors were leaving. "He was in the office before my brother joined the firm, in the days of the uncle—the original Cox. He writes how very shocked he is by the terrible news. My brother was liked by all who came into contact with him. It's a most perplexing riddle. I begin to believe that Cox must have lost his mind, and that that's

why we can't find him. That he's wandering around the
country as some derelict somewhere after having
committed that awful crime here."

"Can I see the letter?" Pointer asked.

"Certainly. I'll ring and ask Mr. Rivers to hand it over
to you at once. It only arrived an hour or two ago. The
writer was off on a coastal trip and hadn't looked at a
paper for a week."

Harold Danford rang and was told that Mr. Rivers
was not in the estate office as he thought. He seemed to
be out.

"Perhaps it's on his table," suggested the chief
inspector. "I would very much like to see it if merely in
the way of routine."

The three made for the office. It was unlocked. Mr.
Harold Danford turned over some papers on the table,
papers which seemed to have been hurriedly left. He
lifted the blotting pad. A slip tucked away underneath it
caught his eye. He bent over it. 'Private Memoranda of
Estate Estimates for Present Year,' he read out.

"Oh, the letter—" He looked up hastily at Pointer's
reminder of the reason for their visit to Rivers's office.
"No, I don't see it anywhere." He cast a rather hurried
glance over the table top, and was about to bury himself
again in the slip of paper which apparently interested
him much more than did the missing letter.

"He has it on him, evidently," he said casually.

"Could you give me some idea of the contents,
something of the letter itself?" Pointer pressed.

Harold Danford looked a little impatient.

"It was just a very kind and decent letter of
sympathy," he said vaguely, his eyes straying to the
paper before him. "Winding up with some reference to a
pleasant memory he still cherishes of having gone over a
machinery exhibition once with my brother, the original
Cox, and young Digby Cox. That sort of thing—"

He was speaking absent-mindedly, his thoughts, like
his glance, were on the slip that he had found under the

blotting pad, a paper on which Rivers had apparently been working, for the ink was hardly dry yet.

Marjoribanks was looking down at it too.

"Estate accounts!" he read out.

"Y—yes, estate accounts," agreed Harold Danford frowning a little. "I don't pretend to be up in such things, but surely there should be some reference to death duties . . . this is apparently a rough estimate of what will be the ingoings and outgoings of Farthing for the present half year—the death duties will cripple the place frightfully. Ormsby and I were only discussing them last night. . . . Strange that Rivers has not allowed anything whatever for them . . . yet he's put down even the sale of the willow withes—" His voice trailed off. He was really talking to himself.

Marjoribanks was keenly interested. Pointer and he bent over the sheet too and glanced down the double columns. Pointer had always his flat folding pocket camera with him. He quickly stood the paper up and took a photograph of it, to be later enlarged.

"I suppose no one comes in here as a rule, unless Rivers is in the room?" he asked, though he knew the answer.

"No one. As a rule Rivers locks the door when he's out for any length of time. There is a typist and accountant who comes in once a week, but I don't think they have keys. I suppose, strictly speaking, I shouldn't have read that paper, doubtless it's just part of the usual way of doing these things. Only, unfortunately, I'm supposed to be more or less in charge just now. Ormsby is going to relieve me of the burden next month. At the moment he's too busy straightening out things in town. Miss Hood is quite wonderful, but she too has had no training in estate work. Well, I take it there's nothing to detain us here?" He laid a hand on the door knob.

"Just a moment, sir," Pointer's voice was casual but business-like. "About that letter Mr. Rivers received— apparently, after all, Mr. Edgar Danford *had* met young

Cox before the latter's first arrival in England after his uncle's death some five years ago?"

Harold Danford looked inquiringly at him for a moment with the look of one whose mind is only half on the conversation. Then it focussed.

"Quite—true!" he said slowly. "Now, do you know, I hadn't noticed that when I read the letter. Quite true! You wanted to know more than once whether my brother had met young Cox before then. I don't know what difference that makes?"

"It settles the question of any imposture."

"And I have always thought that Edgar first met him after his uncle's death," went on Harold Danford thoughtfully, "from things my brother said, or things I took for granted, as one does. Ormsby too is under the same impression."

"So is Mr. Plumptre," Pointer replied. "And Mrs. Danford too. Well, there's one thing, this clerk may be able to furnish us with still another description of Mr. Digby Cox as he was as a young man. Do you remember his name?"

Harold Danford thought a moment.

"Ripon, I think. Yes, Ripon. He wrote from Yorkshire. That helped me to remember it. But I'll have Rivers send you on the letter at once as soon as I see him."

Pointer thanked him, asked that it be handed in at the police station, and then turned away with Marjoribanks, after a few inquiries as to Mrs. Danford.

"Danford had met Cox before," Marjoribanks said as soon as they were free of the gardens and in their car. "That rather damages our beautiful theory of impersonation doesn't it?"

Pointer said nothing. At the police station they found the chief constable once more. He had come over on the chance of meeting Pointer and discussing with him, or rather listening to his opinion of, a piece of news that had just come in. One of the men working in town had discovered that Edgar Danford had lunched once with the lemonade and pomegranate, the glass-bulb, Cox, at a place close to the docks. A clean, but not very smart hostelry.

"Then he had met him—supposing it was he who dined here at Farthing the night of the murder." Marjoribanks looked. puzzled. "This last touch, added to the fact we learned a moment ago, that Danford knew Digby Cox of old, has fogged the plate entirely for us, just when there seemed a chance of it being developed into something comprehensible!"

"On the contrary!" Pointer said in a quiet, but oddly ringing voice. Deep down in his steady, pleasant gray eyes there was a glow for a moment. "It's cleared the plate, Marjoribanks! It all fits in now. Oh, I don't mean who killed Danford. No, though that too is narrowed down by this total change of front."

The chief inspector began to walk up and down the room with long measured strides, his pipe well lit, his hands clasped. behind his back. "Yes, Mr. Harold Danford has given me the key at last! The knowledge that his brother did know—had met—the authentic Digby Cox. I felt it! Oh, I don't mean by intuition"—in answer to a look of interest in Marjoribanks's eyes. "but that fact was the one thing that alone would solve the conundrum, as far as I could see. But each person denied it. And so I had to grope in the fog."

"But can you explain how it was that Danford didn't notice the difference in the Coxes?" pressed Captain Boodle doubtfully.

"Because he knew that they weren't the same person," was the reply which he had not expected. Nor had Marjoribanks.

"As far as I see it," Pointer went on in a level tone, the tone of a man following a path in his mind, "there are two ways of looking at Mr. Danford's murder. He was either deceived, plotted against, and killed—perhaps because he saw through, or was suspected of seeing through, or might see through the imposture—"

Lang from force of habit reached for his note-book, then he recollected himself, and nodded eagerly.

"—or he was himself the real plotter."

Captain Boodle gave a sharp exclamation. Marjoribanks drew in his breath.

"As long as it seemed that he had not met both Coxes, but, above all, as long as we were assured that he had never met Digby Cox, at a time and in a place, when there could be no mistake about that young man's identity," Pointer went on, "Danford could be supposed to be deceived, though it was difficult to see quite how that was possible—still, it was possible. And in murder cases difficult and improbable things are always cropping up."

"And in other cases too! muttered the chief constable feelingly.

"But not impossible things. No, not impossible things," Pointer went on. "And it is impossible, as you say, that he should meet two Coxes and not know them apart, not know one of them as an impostor. But if he is not deceived? Why, the case becomes simple!"

"Does it, by Jove!" muttered Marjoribanks with a short laugh.

"That was what I meant when I said that I had an idea that everything fitted, but which was impossible—according to what I was told."

"Everything fits? By Jove!" Marjoribanks scratched his chin.

"Let's try it out together and see," the Scotland Yard man went on "Danford was once an artist, fond of painting, disliking office routine. But he always seems to have liked money. Soon after his marriage with a wealthy brewer's daughter, the first Mrs. Danford, he threw himself into business. I am told that his pictures were good, but not fortune-bringers. I think that at heart he still kept his love of open air, and sunshine and ease. I think he must have only taken to business as a means to obtain these things. Then, suppose the time begins to seem over long to him. Suppose he sees his chance at last, to quickly—comparatively—amass a fortune and leave the old life behind him, and make for the one of his dreams? I think that happened when Cox, the elder, left that will. We'll suppose a theory and see if it works, or if it breaks down. It was Edgar Danford who got into touch with the nephew remember—or who said that he had. Suppose, instead, that he had found that the nephew was dead, suppose nevertheless he pays, year by year, into Digby Cox's account the sums from the firm due to that young man. Suppose—as Digby Cox—that Edgar Danford claims the redemption of his annuity into a sum down. It's possible of course that Digby Cox is alive somewhere, but quite unaware of his uncle's death and will."

"That wouldn't alter your argument, do go on!" begged Marjoribanks.

"He gets yearly a man to appear for a short time at his office, and at an hotel, who passes himself off as Cox. This imitation Cox would have to be someone 'in' with him, of course. A partner in the thieving that was going on."

"But why were there two Coxes?" Boodle burst in.

"I'll come to the second Cox and why he may have been chosen later on, sir." Pointer was keeping to one thread just now. "In the beginning we can only trace the Montepulciano drinking, gentlemanly, quiet one."

Superintendent Lang nodded.

"Three summers running, sir, he turns up in London."

"All the letters received from Cox," Pointer went on, "are written by Danford, who has Cox's few letters to his uncle to go by. Then, when the time seems ripe—for you can't play such a game indefinitely—Danford decides to leave the scene, and apparently this life. He has quite a nice little sum—of Cox's amassed in five years."

"Little sum!" Captain Boodle muttered, casting up his eyes.

"He decides to disappear. I think—yes—I think, from the fact that Cox is seen at Brighton last week, that Danford may have had in mind a disappearance over a cliff, pushed over by Cox would be the idea, after he had paid him the money—the ostensible reason for his murder by 'Cox' would be to wipe out the holder of the paper that could ruin 'Cox,' the paper which Danford has claimed to everyone who would be called on afterwards to give evidence, will prove 'Cox' to be implicated in a swindle if not actually the swindler himself. Of course, 'original paper,' and proof of its being a forgery, will both turn out to be Mr. Danford's own work, if my theory is right. His talk to Ormsby about them serves the further good purpose of preventing Mr. Ormsby suspecting the reason why Danford paid over the earlier claims so easily and promptly. As for the instructions to Miss Hood as to what to telephone back to the Chantry after dinner in reply to any questions about a paper, that was, as I see it, to rivet 'Cox' on his guest. At any rate, Mr. Danford carefully spreads about the idea of this paper and the coming trouble over it with Cox as a reason— retrospectively, seen—for his death. He arranges for a warning laugh to be heard at Farthing, which foretells a violent end to himself as Farthing's owner—"

"Gad!" burst from Marjoribanks. "That laugh—?"

"From the first, it seemed to me that that laugh—if a fake as we all believed it—could only have come from the intended victim," Pointer said slowly. "But we'll suppose on, and see if we get stuck, or if my theory clears all the obstacles—"

"So far nothing has stopped her, sir!" Lang said enthusiastically.

"But this plan—the cliffs and Cox pushing him over— where does that come in? I haven't heard of any such attempt, or faked attempt—" Captain Boodle was trying to grasp the new idea of things.

"No, sir, because that idea was wiped off the slate. Something makes Mr. Danford find that that brain-wave won't do. I think—mind you, I only think, of course—that it was the news item which Ormsby pointed out to him at breakfast on Saturday morning about the fall over the cliffs at Eastborne of a Mr. Fairbairn, with the report that it was believed to be a put-up job, and no death but a disappearance. The item did concern Mr. Ormsby immensely as we know, and Miss Hood told us that it seemed to affect her stepfather very greatly, though no effort on our part has been able to find any financial connection whatever between him and Fairbairn.

"But if we're right, Danford might well have been disturbed when he read it, supposing he had laid all his plans for a similar affair. The laugh had been heard the third time the night before, which looks as though he were near the time limit."

"By Jove, yes, coming after Fairbairn's little effort, his own would be foredoomed to be a wash out," muttered Marjoribanks. "Even the idea of a shove over by a wicked Cox, about to be unmasked in all his villainy, would not be a good card to play after that."

"I take it Danford knows that the ground is quaking under his feet. Ormsby will turn a keen eye on future matters in the office. Ormsby, whose engagement to his stepdaughter—a young lady who is very fond of Danford—he has just announced to practically all the county, so that Ormsby's tongue, should he find anything odd in the past records, will be more or less tied. Though Mr. Danford was clever enough to leave all Danford's affairs in perfect order. Anything else would, of course, throw suspicion on his fall over the cliff."

"Why didn't he intend to have it look like an accident, a slip of his own?" murmured Captain Boodle "Why hazard all the fuss that always surrounds a murder?"

"I think Mr. Danford wanted a reason for 'Cox' never to be seen or heard of again, sir. That's at least how I read the tale. But going back a bit, as the end came in view, it seems to me that the sham 'Cox' grew restive. He hasn't minded sharing the loot, and playing a part a short part each time in hotels and at the office, but not in disappearances.

"There, I think, he stood firm. So Danford has to get hold of a second 'Cox' to mingle with the first impersonator, one who will take part in the final, the dangerous scene. That, at least is how one could explain things so far, supposing my theory continues to work out. At first I thought it was Danford himself who was the second 'Cox,' but, apart from other things that wouldn't fit, the 'Cox' who crossed over this last April from Mexico really had red hair and a growing red beard. But Mr. Danford went around the world a year ago, you may remember. He came back saying that he had not been able to arrange a meeting with Digby Cox in Mexico, yet a few months later 'Mr. Cox' of the red beard and diamond ring and temperance drinks duly sails, and makes his first appearance in England in this tale. I don't know what odds you would be willing to lay that Mr. Danford found some red-haired Englishman on his beam-ends in Mexico, and arranged to give him a free passage home, and a pleasant stay in England of some three months, in return for just calling himself Digby Cox, never touching wine or spirits, mixing very little with the passengers, and carefully carrying out a few directions when he gets back! We may hear from this Cox in time, but I doubt it. Apart from —well, other possibilities, I fancy he would have been chosen from among those who have to keep their suspicions of their masters to themselves, lest some old trouble be raked up against them."

"And of course Mr. Danford bought that midget gramophone in Mexico himself, and arranged for the mechanical stopper," nodded the superintendent.

"I fancy so. After hearing the laugh in the opera and thinking how well it might be fitted in. It was being played the season he was there," Pointer agreed.

Marjoribanks gave an exclamation.

"Mrs. Danford's letter! And her whole attitude of insincerity when she talked over that warning laugh. By Jove, but it fits! She knew the truth! Or at least suspected it."

Pointer nodded.

"Yes, I think she felt sure, was sure, until she heard of the tragedy that there was no such person in existence nowadays as Digby Cox. No wonder, if so, that her husband's murder connected with a real, but missing Cox should have staggered her. I think it was for her benefit that Mr. Danford brought in the warning laugh. I think he expected it to affect the former Miss Beardsley tremendously, and quite lull any suspicions she might otherwise entertain as to his 'death,' when that sad event should be reported to her. Yes . . . the theory works so far," he murmured, "that letter of her's sounded all mockery even to an outsider, and would seem far more so to the man for whom it was intended, the man who would know that there was no Cox for her to run off with."

"That being so"—Captain Boodle thought—"and given Mrs. Danford, it's just the sort of letter she would enjoy leaving behind her."

"And I suppose she won't come forward now with the truth because she doesn't want to incriminate a dead man—and her husband." Superintendent Lang thought all the pieces fitted very nicely, so far.

Pointer and Marjoribanks exchanged a glance.

"We can imagine now why she was so keen on having some one investigate the warning—which she did not believe in as a warning, but which she felt sure meant trickery of some sort on her husband's part," the chief, inspector said with a faint smile. "I think she must have overheard something that made her suspect that a fraud of some kind, an impersonation of Cox connected with some money transactions was on foot."

"She tried to stir Miss Hood up to make some inquiries about her money." Captain Boodle was looking over the notes.

"And when Miss Hood is provided for by a wealthy match, Mrs. Danford washed her hands of her," Marjoribanks finished.

"There are many gaps," Pointer said thoughtfully, "many gaps, but on the whole the theory fits most of the riddle. It was always in the back of my mind, that— granted that Danford was himself at the root of things— the tangle seemed solvable. Only everyone assured me that he had never met Digby Cox, the real article, before the uncle died, and therefore I had no right to assume Danford to be the deceiver instead of the deceived."

"And the Cox who came to Farthing the night Danford was murdered was the teetotal one?" mused Captain Boodle.

"And that's where Danford tripped up, eh?" Marjoribanks said, looking at the ceiling for inspiration, "that's where and when Danford met his match, or his superior. A thief met a murderer, in other words. His accomplice decided to become the sole owner of the brilliant idea of Cox, and of the loot accumulated in Cox's name. Was that how the cards fell out?"

"I wonder . . ." Pointer resumed his pacing up and down the room, "I wonder . . ."

"You don't think so?" Marjoribanks cocked an eye at him.

"I should be more inclined, after the shock of the Fairbairn fiasco, to speculate . . ."

"On?" burst from Captain Boodle.

"On whether one murder wasn't forestalled by another. Whether 'Cox' wasn't intended to be the victim, the real victim, and to be taken for Danford. Whether a murder, and a fire after it, might not have been Danford's new idea. It would be easy enough for him to carry a couple of tins of petrol over from the garage. We found a bottle of acid beside the bottle of methylated, acid that would prevent any certainty, or so he would think, of proving that the body he might have meant us to find was not his own."

"By Jove," muttered Marjoribanks, "thorough-going chap."

"And now the decks are more or less cleared to find out who played Cox that last Saturday. Whether he had ever played him before. Probably he had, of course, but it might lead us wrong to assume that . . ." Pointer's eyes were alight.

"Stop! Help!" wailed Captain Boodle, "you're muddling me, Pointer! If there's a third Cox in the offing—oh, help!"

"Yet none the less I think a third man was called in to help Mr. Danford out in a difficulty. For, in that same paper that recorded the accident to Mr. Fairbairn, on the same page, though in a corner, is a paragraph telling of the finding of the body of a man floating in the India docks. He had been dead some days, and was identified by a letter in a waterproof letter-case as a man called Williams, who put up at a small hotel close to the docks, and who had been seen, half drunk, by a sailor, walking perilously near the water's edge. Well, we've found that Williams' was red-haired, that he seemed to have a fair amount of money, was keenly interested in racing tips, wore a 'diamond' ring of unusual size on his little finger, and never touched anything but soft drinks, except on this one occasion when he got drunk. This letter in his pocket which gave the river police his address and name was unsigned, but it's in Mr. Danford's handwriting, on his paper, and is merely a curt line giving the man an hour at which to be at a certain telephone."

"By Jove!" murmured the fascinated Marjoribanks.

"'Straordinary story!" came heartily from Captain Boodle.

"Now if Mr. Danford came on that little piece of news on Saturday morning, and saw that for once his necessary accomplice had taken too much to drink, and had promptly got drowned, he might well have been disturbed. Even more than by the Fairbairn forestalling of his own idea, though that was a severe blow."

"I'm dazed," came abjectly from the chief constable, "I feel giddy."

"I'm taking you along the road I'm traveling myself, sir," Pointer said a trifle grimly, "and a more puzzling one, with more twists and turns that lead just to the last place you would expect to find yourself, I don't think I ever walked."

"Where does it lead you?" Boodle wanted to know on the instant.

"Somewhere not far from Mr. Jackson-Gupp, sir," was the quiet reply.

"Jackson-Gupp!" Captain Boodle actually jumped, "but Jackson-Gupp is—"

"Here is his record, sir," Pointer picked it out of some papers with a faint smile.

The chief constable read it out as though it were one of the lessons.

"Henry Seaton Jackson-Gupp, only son of Charles Jackson-Gupp, Professor of physics at Kings College. Born . . . educated . . . graduated as fourth wrangler in . . . being also placed in the first class in part II of the Natural Science Tripos ... Fellow of Kings College . . . Research Fellow . . . Fellow of the Royal Society . . . President of the International Geodesy Commission . . . President of the . . .'" the names rolled on. When he had finished, Captain Boodle handed back the paper with a stare of reproach.

"That's just what I always come up against," Pointer agreed with a faint grin, "yet we have a man called Cox whom everyone saw arrive, but who was not seen to leave, and who, according to the best of my belief, had not left Farthing when I arrived. I saw no sign of his having been hidden or hiding himself away. Which meant that he must have turned into someone present. Among these few people was a man who was only seen after the other man had disappeared, except for the evidence of Mr. Rivers, whom no one had seen arriving, and that man is Mr. Jackson-Gupp!"

"Mr. Jackson-Gupp does only drink lemonade," breathed Lang, "I happen to have learned only yesterday that he's a teetotaler. He hasn't asked for pomegranate juice yet, though."

"Nor does he wear a glass diamond ring. Nor has he worn a beard lately, and so on . . ." agreed Pointer. "That Cox is dead remember, but there are a few odd points about Mr. Jackson-Gupp, apart from his unnoticed arrival."

"That would account for his maintaining from the first that Cox stood for nothing in the murder," put in the superintendent, thoughtfully.

"It's not possible!" Marjoribanks suddenly pulled himself together. "Simply not possible! I mean that I shouldn't have felt his guilt if he were really guilty, in all my many talks with him. Yet it is odd. But what about Rivers?" Marjoribanks's face brightened. "Now Rivers is quite another pair of shoes! Rivers, who tells us that Jackson-Gupp arrived about nine on Saturday evening. I shouldn't be at all surprised if we haven't got the cart before the horse, and that it's Rivers who's guilty, and Jackson-Gupp who, mistakenly thinking him innocent, is trying to help him out of what has been represented to him as some awkward position. Ormsby, you remember, said that he came down to Norbury on Saturday night because he feared that Miss Hood and Rivers were going to have a clandestine meeting. Suppose Rivers told Jackson-Gupp that they, he and she, had had a meeting just at the fatal time, and begged him to help him out with an alibi. Jackson-Gupp yields—By Jove, yes, I heard him saying something about 'seeing that they were partners in a way' on that very night as I left the cottage. I take it he was then yielding to Rivers's request."

"No yielding to Rivers's request would explain how he came to get into the grounds of Farthing," Pointer said with a shake of his head.

"Oh, damn circumstantial evidence!" burst out Marjoribanks.

"Not unless it's twisted," the other replied.

"You think"—the chief constable was deep in thought—"that it was the gentleman 'Cox' who had to come down after all, when the other was drowned? . . . and you think that he was Jackson-Gupp . . . ?"

"But the motive!" expostulated Marjoribanks.

"Well, where's the motive in Beaufoy Rivers's case?" Captain Boodle demanded. He spoke rather stiffly. He liked Rivers.

"Farthing," was Marjoribanks's instant retort. "Nothing will shake me in my conviction—"

"Intuition," corrected Pointer under his breath.

"—that Farthing is at the bottom of this tragedy. Now Farthing means nothing to Jackson-Gupp. The notion is ridiculous."

"Edgar Danford was financially interested in some wireless work of Rivers's," Captain Boodle was speaking. "We know that Mr. Jackson-Gupp was for a time, or may be still, a sort of honorary assistant director of Scientific Research for the Air Ministry. He lectures now and then at the flying training school at Spittlegate. Quite lately he did some testing for Bulman's new machines. He's connected in some secret way with the new plane that Airco's are bringing out shortly. That we only found out with the greatest difficulty. It's a profound secret. Suppose in some way the motive lies there, though, I grant you, murder seems absolutely ridiculous to connect with his name."

"What about," put in the police superintendent, "what about the money Danford had got together for himself as Cox? No trace of 'Cox' fortune has been found. We know that 'Cox' took the money in bearer bonds. What about Mr. Danford having had the lot with him the night he was murdered, in a suit case, say. And that there lies the reason for his murder. Now we know that Mr. Ormsby was in a tight place. Suppose Mr. Ormsby slipped across to the Chantry and killed Mr. Danford. I can't forget that it was Cox who telephoned me to hurry along to Farthing."

"Miss Hood would like to speak to the chief inspector;" announced a constable, saluting. "It's urgent, she says."

"Show her in!" was the instant order, and on the man's heels came Pippa. Her face white and tense.

"Captain Boodle" she turned to the old friend, "Beaufoy is missing. He's been missing for hours now— since around three. No one can find him. Yet, he hasn't left Farthing. And it's now close on seven!"

"How do you know he hasn't left Farthing?" the chief constable asked.

"The women at the lodges are all certain that he hasn't. Besides, there are people waiting for him. And he gave a man, whom I know he's frightfully keen on meeting, an appointment for a couple of hours ago, and hasn't kept it. An appointment at the inn. No one has seen him for the last four hours. And his hat is still on the shelf where he always keeps it. Oh, please come up to the house!"

Pippa's racing-car, her Spaggetti, as it was called in the neighborhood, was a tight fit for Pippa even, but the three men hung on somehow, and she whirled them up to the house at a speed which made the chief constable, remembering sundry fires, feel like a whitened sepulcher.

"There's Mr. Jackson-Gupp," she said as they disembarked at the steps. "He—"

"—is doing his little best," he finished, coming towards them, his cool, clear, agate eyes dancing from one to the other. "After all, one can only do one's best. Though, as I said before, you Regulars scorn volunteer efforts."

"Not all," Pointer said promptly, "this disappearance of Mr. Rivers, for instance, I think you might be able to help us solve that."

Jackson-Gupp looked at him with those bright eyes of his.

"Disappearances are such tricky things," he murmured, "they don't give one a fair chance. They're almost always so different from what they seem. Possibly it's a publicity stunt. They generally are. In his case for his new gyroscope."

"It's nothing of the kind!" Pippa actually stamped her foot like a Victorian girl in a bad temper, "It's something very much more serious. Beaufoy and a publicity stunt!" She looked disgusted. "Nor is he working on a gyroscope, as you know perfectly."

Harold Danford came into the lounge. He looked very worried.

"I cannot understand this absence of Rivers. And this afternoon of all afternoons! He seems to have asked half the population of the British Isles to meet him in the office."

The usual questions of when the missing man was last seen had to be hurriedly put. A telephone inquiry to the station and to the garages of Norbury assured the police that he had not left by train or hired car, besides, the lodge keepers were certain, that he had not passed out of the grounds.

Farthing once more was hunted from attic to lowest cellar. No trace of the land agent was found.

Pointer asked Mr. Harold Danford for another look at the plans of the house. The safe in the estate office, now empty, was locked, but Harold Danford had the duplicate key which Edgar Danford had owned. He used it after a little fumbling, and hunted rather helplessly through the shelves.

Pointer's eyes were on the inside of the door where the print of four fingers showed. Someone seemed to have steadied the door open, it had a tendency to shut, due to the slope of the old floor, while he did something to, or more probably, got something out of the safe.

Pointer promptly asked Harold Danford to get him, without it being noticed, a piece of kitchen soap. He was insistent on the fact that it must be of the yellow, bar variety, aware that that commission would keep Mr. Danford out of the room for some time, and give himself plenty of time to examine those fingerprints.

Very much intrigued, Harold obligingly hurried off. Pointer then got a good close-up of the prints after dusting them with yellow powder. They must have been made by a slender hand with rather spatulate finger tips, and there was the mark of a cott on the middle finger. It was the left hand too. And Jackson-Gupp wore a cott around that finger of that hand.

He had, moreover, spatulate tips. But the marks showed more than mere pressure. Someone had either snatched the hand away in some movement of surprise or violence, or it had been snatched off the door by another person.

The chief inspector had barely finished replacing his tiny camera in his pocket, when the door was flung open and Pippa stood there, white faced and quivering.

"Surely you haven't given up already!" she asked, pleadingly. Then, before he could answer, she came in and shut the door. "Can't you do anything? Can't you even suggest anything? Oh, those miles and miles of awful underground passages!"

It was the first time that Pippa had ever found anything belonging to Farthing awful. "Mr. Jackson-Gupp says he's going to town. He seems to think that Beaufoy has slipped up without being seen or saying anything to anybody. Which is utterly absurd. He can't have left Farthing. Nor would he have!"

Pointer said nothing. At Farthing, or in town, Jackson-Gupp was always carefully shadowed.

"Chief inspector"—Pippa came nearer. "I can't get it out of my head that Mr. Rivers has been—been hidden or worse. I have an idea that I heard a call, or a cry, this afternoon, only I was too occupied at the time to think about it. But now . . ."

"When was this?"

"Around three o'clock."

That was the time that the letter from the clerk, of which Harold Danford spoke, had arrived.

"You aren't sure?"

She shook her head miserably.

"No. It's only a dim impression. If nothing had happened to anyone, I should never have thought of it again. It seemed to come from far away in the house, or deep down." A sort of spasm passed over her face. "I can't help wondering if I heard Beaufoy calling out . . you see, I've had an idea for days that Mr. Rivers has some sort of a suspicion. . ." She hesitated, then she broke out: "He's the second man to be missed since my stepfather's death. But Mr. Cox we think is the criminal, whereas, if anything has happened to Beaufoy"

"You say you think Mr. Rivers was suspicious?" prompted Pointer.

"I am sure of it," she replied, "though he didn't think I noticed it. There's one person whom he's always watching—watching. I don't mean eavesdropping or following around, but I don't think he ever took his mind off him, absent or present, for long."

"Well, jealousy, might explain that, mightn't it, Miss Hood. If I may speak quite frankly."

Which was a luxury that the chief inspector could never afford himself, while a case was on, when talking to anyone connected, even distantly, with the case.

She stared at him.

"I don't mean Mr. Ormsby!" she said impatiently and bluntly, "but—" She pulled herself up. That was Pippa all over. Veering now one way, now another. Then a look of resolution passed over her face.

"I mean Mr. Jackson-Gupp," she said under her breath. "I've never known Mr. Rivers act towards anyone quite as he does to him. Considering his position of course it sounds silly, but—" she gulped,—"but the fact remains that he did arrive at Farthing the evening just before—it—happened. And have you noticed the funny way he's searching for Mr. Rivers? As though he thought it all very funny. I hate Mr. Jackson-Gupp to-day! And I can't forget that . . ." again came that hesitation.

"That?" asked Pointer.

The door was opened. Jackson-Gupp looked in.

"Ah, there you are, Miss Hood! I wonder if there's any further place you can recommend us to look. Or do I interrupt?"

"I was just telling the chief inspector," Pippa said quietly, "that the search seems to amuse you." There was an unusual edge to her voice. Jackson-Gupp's eyes danced a trifle more than usual perhaps.

"Not amuse, no, but of course, in a way it's funny, this wild excitement over a chap for whom an hour before no one seemed to give a damn," and with the slightly contemptuous gallantry he always showed her, he held the door open for her to pass out.

She swished to the window instead, with a look that was positively sizzling. "The last I saw of Beaufoy, he and you were discussing a letter which he had just received," she spoke hotly.

"Discussing a letter?" Jackson-Gupp's face showed puzzlement. "A letter?" Then his face lightened as though by comprehension, "Oh, I see! Rivers jotted down on the back of an envelope some figures to do with his experiments. We discussed them. Not the letter."

She looked unconvinced. Pointer had closed the safe doors on her entrance. He saw Jackson-Gupp shoot a quick glance at them, and then look out of the window.

"I thought you were arguing over what was inside the envelope, not outside it—I heard the name of Cox mentioned—Mr. Rivers mentioned it," she said a little breathlessly, "and then you you both went down together into the basement . . . I heard you go."

"To look at the voltage," he nodded. "Rivers will prefer an alternating supply with valve rectifiers, whereas I am convinced, by my own experiments, that the running costs of a straightforward high voltage direct-current generator, say a 10,000 volt D.C. motor-generator as used by the 5 GB transmitter, is far cheaper. But isn't that Ormsby's step?" He opened the door. It was Ormsby passing.

"Found Rivers?" Jackson-Gupp wanted to know, with apparent anxiety Ormsby said they had not. That they were all gathering for something to drink in the inner lounge. He did not look at Pippa, Pointer noticed, nor she at him.

In the girl's case, however, she seemed barely conscious of the fact that anyone else had joined them. She faced Jackson-Gupp again, with a more determined look in her eyes than one usually saw there.

"But looking at the voltage doesn't undo the fact that you were the last person seen with Beaufoy Rivers, Mr. Jackson-Gupp," she challenged openly.

"No, no! Surely not," that man said carelessly, "it was after he and I had parted that I heard him and Ormsby here—talking together." The pause before the last two words was suggestive.

Ormsby flushed a little.

"You didn't tell us that!" Pippa now spun around on Ormsby.

"Because it was when he and I parted that Rivers said he had promised you"—this to Jackson-Gupp—"to show you something about the high tension supply in the cellars. After our talk!" He stared at Jackson-Gupp, who shook his head with amiable firmness.

"It looks to me as though Rivers must have been put to it for some civil excuse to end your chat," Jackson-Gupp remarked, "we had quite finished before you and he met outside this office. I strolled after him to add one more argument I'd thought of to back my, point of view, but decided to wait for another, and better, opportunity, and heard you—well, heard you both."

"Heard what?" Pippa asked, "you evidently want us to ask you what you heard. Well, what was it?"

Pippa had the gloves off with a vengeance, and Pointer was curious to hear the answer.

"A first rate quarrel," Jackson-Gupp said cheerfully, "Mr. Ormsby was suggesting that Rivers could work better on his experiments somewhere else, up in a cottage of his in Yorkshire I think it was. In any case, he pointed out that as soon as you and he were married, Mr. Rivers's position of land agent here would cease."

Pippa turned on Ormsby but she said nothing. She only drew a deep, quivering, almost a menacing breath.

"And you also heard Rivers suggesting that I leave Farthing instead," Ormsby said in his turn, "it was six of one and half a dozen of the other. Each of us lost our tempers."

"At any rate, I heard him threaten to spike your guns," Jackson-Gupp said, still in the same casual, conversational tone. "Threats always seem to come home to roost—like curses. Well, I must go to bed. After all, the world must sleep, even if some people are making a night of it away from Farthing." And Jackson-Gupp walked out, having done as much mischief as he could.

Pippa stood still a moment longer, then she broke out: "Oh how I hate that man. Why does he stay on here? He's only come to find out about Beaufoy's work, in my opinion. But don't try to explain things away, Mark. You didn't deny them to him—"

"*I'm* not in the habit of denying what's true," he said coldly, with a nasty accent on the personal pronoun, "but we all need rest and sleep."

"Rest? In Farthing? With Beaufoy perhaps entombed in those loathesome dungeons underground. I never knew there were so many, nor such quantities of beetles and horrid things with legs all over them. Ugh! I had no idea Farthing could be like that. Dank and slimy!" she was out of the room now with something like a suppressed sob.

Ormsby looked after her with a very black look on his face. Then he too went off.

Harold Danford hurried in with a piece of soap, yellow soap. He had finally obtained it at the garage.

Pointer thanked him, and did some quite unnecessary fiddling with it and a sliding drawer.

"There seems to be some bad feeling between Mr. Ormsby and Mr. Rivers," he said as he did so.

Harold Danford looked a troubled acquiescence.

"Ormsby wanted to leave us. But at this hour! Besides, morning brings counsel so often. Even to the very young." But Harold Danford's voice suggested that he was not thinking of what he was saying. After a pause he began again in a different voice.

"I cannot think that any trouble between the two can be connected with the extraordinary disappearance of Mr. Rivers." His tone suggested a question.

Pointer said nothing. He only looked very impenetrable as he stood aside and let Mr. Danford re-lock the safe.

That done, Harold Danford turned to him again.

"You don't agree?"

"It would depend," was the cautious reply. "Was there a violent quarrel?"

"Pretty bad," acknowledged the other. "My windows look out onto the sunk garden, and I had to shut them. Their voices disturbed me greatly."

"Did you hear what they were saying?"

"Not the words. But the tones of both were very far from soothing to listen to. I confess I wondered first of all whether Rivers had perhaps rushed off because of something Ormsby said. But that idea is quite fantastic. It's utterly unlike him to do anything hasty. He has the rather placid Rivers temper. If I may say so, the Danford temper too."

Pointer said good-night on that. Half way across the big lounge he met an utterly wearied, begrimed, Marjoribanks.

"The serpent's gait is very tiring," that young man re marked, "and frightfully bad on one's clothes. By Jove, Pointer, it begins to look bad for Ormsby!"

"Sure it doesn't cast a lurid light on Harold Danford?" Pointer asked.

Marjoribanks gave a generous chuckle.

"How you do harp on a joke! British bulldog won't let go. But Rivers—do you think he's in danger?"

A voice hailed them from the outer lounge. It was Jackson-Gupp.

"Any suggestions to make as to where we might find Mr. Rivers, sir?" Pointer asked lightly.

The wireless expert shot him one of his baffling looks. "You flatter me," he said, smiling a little.

"I don't think so," Pointer, replied without a smile. "No, I don't think so, Mr. Jackson-Gupp."

"Well, perhaps you don't," that young man conceded affably, "for, as a matter of fact, I was going to suggest just that—where Rivers may possibly be at this moment."

"And that is?" put in Marjoribanks.

"In Ormsby's car, which, with Ormsby driving, and his man besides him, is now speeding towards London town."

"Just what do you mean?" Marjoribanks frowned a little.

"It isn't outside the pale of things possible that Ormsby may have stunned Rivers this afternoon," Jackson-Gupp mentioned easily, "flung him into his car, left his man to keep guard over him, and when the hue and cry has died down a bit, has now driven off with him safely inside the tonneau. Driven off with his man and car he has. That much is fact. Thought the rest may be fancy."

"What were they quarreling about, you heard more than you told Miss Hood, I feel sure," Marjoribanks asked as they all passed down the drive, keeping close together and talking in low, hushed tones.

"Rivers threatened Ormsby with the telling of some facts to Miss Hood which would break the engagement. Something about another girl, I gathered, though, like all people in a temper, he was rather incoherent, and difficult to follow if you hadn't the key therefore. But that much was quite clear. And Ormsby got the wind up."

Marjoribanks plied him with questions and the two talked it over. Pointer said nothing. At the lodges they learned that Mr. Ormsby had driven through just now, his man beside him. The car was a closed one, and no inside lights were on.

"Well, here we part," Jackson-Gupp said, shaking hands. I'm afraid I haven't been of much use. But that's your own fault. I would have dearly liked to help you."

"By handing us the key?" Pointer was smiling now. His tone was light and casual.

"That might be beyond my powers," Jackson-Gupp protested modestly. "You will insist on rating me too highly, chief inspector."

"Nonsense," put in Marjoribanks, "we don't often get a chance at a chap of your caliber."

But Jackson-Gupp was not looking at Marjoribanks. He stared hard at Pointer's face which, in this light, showed up as tanned and hard and clean chiseled as bronze. The chief inspector's fine grey, eyes usually had a calm serenity, now they swept the other with a singularly cold and penetrating glance. The two parted in silence.

Marjoribanks walked on in silence too for some time.

"Do you think Rivers's sudden disappearance has anything to do with that letter he received? The letter that made such a difference to your reading of the case?"

"Mr. Harold Danford hasn't disappeared, and he had read the note, and told us of its contents. No, I don't see that letter as the cause of this."

"Personally, I still see Farthing as the great cause. The power for evil," Marjoribanks said dreamily. "Is Rivers in danger, do you think? Was he taken to town by Ormsby?"

"Well, if so, five tins of condensed milk, four glasses of various galantines, quite a high pile of tinned meats, a big jar of jam, and a large tin of plain biscuits, together with, probably, other unidentifiable groceries such as tea and sugar, seem to have accompanied him."

"What do you mean?"

"They're missing from Mrs. York's store-room, as she will find when she next checks over her list which is fastened inside the door, and very carefully kept up to date. The tin of biscuits only arrived this morning. I don't think the things were taken in the usual way, because their places are left vacant, the only vacant spots on the well stocked shelves and they're not marked off the list. Also, they were taken, the smaller tins, in whole files, just as they stood, one on top of each other. I asked Mrs. York if she could let me have an unopened tin of unsweetened biscuits if I needed one, and she told me that she could. One had just come in. She offered to have it fetched from her store-room for me. You heard me declining. It was just now."

Marjoribanks made some muttered exclamation.

"Now, as no one was seen roaming Farthing laden with tinned food, I rather think the edibles were taken into some underground room. In other words, I think Rivers is not in Ormsby's car, nor in danger of starvation."

"Was the lock of the store-room forced?"

"It's one of those locks that a button hook and a slight knowledge of mechanics and a little practice in the. use ofmlevers will open. At least I found it so."

"Ormsby has no talents in that line," Marjoribanks said thoughtfully.

"But Mr. Jackson-Gupp has." And Pointer refused to add another word to that, as he made for the police station, and Marjoribanks for the inn and bed.

CHAPTER TEN

POINTER at the police station heard the results of the inquiries which had been started as soon as he had learned the contents of the letter which had reached Rivers so oddly close on the time of that young man's disappearance, the letter which the chief inspector had never seen, but whose summary by Harold Danford had changed the whole aspect of the case for him. Ripon, the writer of the letter, had only been able to amplify his account of the day which he had spent some years ago in company with the deceased Mr. Cox, Mr. Plumptre, now retired, the then new partner Edgar Danford, and the senior partner's nephew, Digby Cox. His account of the last had not altered the one furnished by Mr. Plumptre. Nor had his story added anything new to what the police had already learned. Sure of that, Pointer once more retraced his steps and spent the night at Farthing, searching its foundations. He made a corner by the store room his hiding place, after he had patrolled passage after passage with no result. There he settled himself down to listen. Once he heard something brush against a wall not far away, and crept forth only to flash his torch on a very surprised black cat. Pointer apologized to the fellow-hunter and withdrew.

Again he heard a stir, too faint to be called a sound, and sallied forth. The sounds came clearer. A light step, but not a secretive one, was walking along a parallel passage. But after it came another, as light, but far more carefully subdued. Pointer branched into a cross cut and waited. Pippa passed him a moment later in some sort of dark gown, pale face lit by the electric torch she carried. She was sounding and knocking and now and then she called "Beaufoy! Beaufoy!" After she passed, there was a little interval, then a man's figure could be made out following her torch. He carried no light of his own.

Pointer purposely made a faint sound. The girl wheeled instantly and her torch caught the man following her full in the face. It was Mark Ormsby.

"You!" she said in surprise.

"Yes. I can't sleep, so I thought I would come and help you look," he said, a little over glibly. He had not been following her like a man who wants to help, but who wants to watch.

Pippa's voice sounded touched as she said:

"That's good of you, Mark. And you mustn't remember against me the horrid things I said a little while ago. This second disappearance is quite unnerving. What does it all mean? My stepfather killed. Mr. Cox disappeared, and now Beaufoy Rivers missing."

"I don't believe he's down here," Ormsby said, instead of trying to solve the apparently insoluble.

"Where else can he be?"

"With Cox. Wherever he is."

There followed a little silence.

"Mark," Pippa's voice sounded resolute but quiet, "you mustn't mind my asking you, but you really have no idea where Beaufoy is, have you?"

"None whatever," he said firmly, "upon my honor, none whatever. Frankly, I'm surprised at your asking me. Do you mean to say you credit Jackson-Gupp's rhodomontade about our having quarreled?"

"It's because you got Beaufoy to show you all the hidden places and secret rooms and where the old staircases used to run that I asked you. And I know you both went over the plans together and traced out as many as you could."

"That was curiosity," he said quickly, "and the merest coincidence that it should have come shortly before Rivers vanished, if you can call an afternoon's absence vanishing. Naturally, I'm interested in Farthing's hidden rooms. They always do appeal to the silly kid in one, don't they? Like smugglers' caves, or secret drawers. But now, Pippa, do be reasonable and go to bed. There's nothing to be done by prowling around here longer. It's nearly dawn already. We'll have another hunt in the morning, and you'll not be fit to help in it, if you don't rest now."

"I can't—I can't sleep!" she murmured brokenly.

"Of course. Of course," Ormsby said quickly and something in his tone suggested that he wanted to agree with her—at least outwardly—that he was eager to acquiesce. "Of course!" he repeated again, "and quite natural too in an old playmate. I quite understand."

"No, you don't!" came unexpectedly from the girl. "I don't, myself. Mark, I—I must speak to you—"

"No, no," he soothed, "you must go to bed. I absolutely refuse to hear anything from you to-night. To-morrow we'll talk over anything you please. But not now."

"No, no! Now!" she began, but as so often with Pippa, she let the will of another prevail. "I wish you'd let me say what I want to say now," she said weakly, instead of saying it.

He hushed her, and soothed her, and resolutely refused to listen to her, and so they passed out of hearing up the stairs leading to the corridor above.

No one came after they had passed to break the stillness below ground. Pointer patrolled the passages from end to end. many times, tapping and feeling. But there were whole corners and centers that had been blocked up he knew. Who would be aware of how the blocked parts ran, of—possibly—some secret way into or out of them? Harold Danford might be supposed to know of them. Though he had seemed genuinely baffled yesterday, and apparently had never set foot down here before. Rivers himself, a lad in an old house, would be almost certain to know if such entrances existed. And who else? What of the hand on the safe door, what, in other words of Jackson-Gupp? And Mark Ormsby, too, might have a wider acquaintance with this part of the house than one would expect, since he and Rivers had

gone over the house together. Just before Rivers
disappeared too.

When daylight came, Pointer snatched a few hours
sleep himself. Harold Danford sent in word that he would
like to see him when he was up. Pointer promptly
presented himself. Danford was walking up and down the
floor of the business-room looking very worried. His face
had thinned these last days of strain, but his smile was
as kind as ever.

"It's my niece," he began apologetically, "she will have
it that Rivers is shut up downstairs. If so, he must be
found. Her nerves won't stand much more. Besides—
who's done it?. What does it mean? What do you think,
chief inspector, has someone spirited him away, or is he
still on the premises?"

"I think he's hidden downstairs, but I may be quite
wrong," Pointer said at once.

"Then we'll find him, no matter if it takes all the
village and all the day," was the resolute answer. "Miss
Hood's eating nothing. All her color's leaving her.
Something must be done to find him."

You think that he matters so much to her?" Pointer
asked in that plain, matter of fact way that somehow
never gave offence.

"I do. And between ourselves, I think she's beginning
to realize as much. Personally I think she'll do well to
think things over a bit before marrying Ormsby. There's
something about him . . . well, he's not one of us down
here, and Rivers is. Perhaps it's that. Personally, I'd
rather she chose Rivers," and with that he led the way in
a most resolute and thorough-going effort to search every
nook and every corner below stairs.

He very certainly had had no hand in hiding the man,
for he worked like a navvy in the close and narrow
passages. He got a builder's foreman down, who had
superintended these very alterations, but it was all to no
end: Finally the search party had to own itself beaten.
But that was not until well on towards evening again.

They had taken it in turn to help, only Jackson-Gupp had excused himself on the plea of some experiment started by Rivers which must be finished or it would be spoiled.

"Why not take Farthing down stone by stone and brick by brick?" he suggested to Pippa once when he met her. She gave him a long, steady look.

"Why do you hate him so?" she asked. "Are you afraid of him?"

He in his turn looked at her.

"Not bad!" he murmured, "really not at all bad! But why delve into my conscience like that? I don't ask you if remorse is egging you on to take up this attitude, this quite unexpected attitude. Even Ormsby seems inclined to let sleeping dogs lie," and with that he drifted off again to the Tower where he really did do some hard work, judged, at least, by the close attention he gave it, and the time he spent there.

Pointer went to bed early that night, he intended to be up early—or late—according to one's computation of hours. But before one o'clock, the time he had told himself to wake, something sent him springing out of his bed. There was no sound outside his room, but something acrid and yet very faint reached his nostrils. It was smoke. In a second he slid down the banisters to the ground floor. There he found the butler just catching the switch of the big alarm bell into the notch that would keep it clanging, and rouse every inmate of the big house with its din.

Fire drill at Farthing was a weekly affair. The butler was the captain, and a very efficient man at his job. The servants tumbled into the line, hoses were straightened and connected, buckets passed, nozzles fitted. The fire itself, a bad one judging by the heat of the floor, was in the cellars. Exactly where, was not yet known, but all below the ground floor was alight.

Pointer tied a dripping towel around his mouth, and carried another in his hand, then he made for what looked like a tunnel of smoke.

The electric light refused to function, but candles had been stuck on to nails by the maids and fitfully lit the lower part and the staircase.

Pippa came running down. The head footman was busy at his task of seeing after the pictures. He had made a good beginning with the one over the east fireplace. He passed Pippa with his precious burden tenderly held in his arms. It was the portrait of Sir Amyas Rivers.

"Not a scratch on it, miss," he said reassuringly, and proudly too, misunderstanding her look.

Pippa took one leap forward, snatched the painting from him, and flung it with all her might down the stone steps into the flames that now were leaping up the lower stairs.

The panel seemed to shrink and cringe and curl away from the heat as might a living creature. It burned with a strange, hissing sound, as though a snake had been tossed into the fire.

The man gave a gasp of horror. She turned on him like a fury.

"Mr. Rivers is still cooped up somewhere downstairs. And you waste time on pictures! He's what matters—the only thing!" she was beside herself with anguish.

"Just as soon as we can get down those stairs, Miss Pippa," soothed the shocked but sympathetic butler. "He's not on the premises though. I'm sure of that after the search we've made. And, begging your pardon, miss, but the house is in danger. The safety of Farthing—"

"Hang Farthing!" sobbed Pippa in agony. "Oh, where is Beaufoy Rivers? Uncle Harold!" she sprang towards him as he appeared and clung to him for a moment.

"He can't be on the premises, dear child. Not a corner was left unsearched yesterday, and the day before," he tried to assure her.

She broke from him and vanished into the smoke that now began to fill the outer lounge.

Pointer had run down the passage that led to the storeroom. He knew these twisting passages now by heart. He heard steps ahead of him. They were reeling ones. He rushed on and caught at someone. It was Jackson-Gupp. A Jackson-Gupp whom it was hard to recognize. Black from head to foot, red-rimmed eyes and singed hair that stood in sooty stiffness in tufts all over his head. One sleeve was burning.

Pointer dragged him back by force, and twisted his spare towel over his scorched and blistered face.

"I've got the door into his passage open," the famous authority on air whorls and earth currents gasped, "the door of his room at the end is bolted on the outside only, but its blocked by a fallen beam. He's in the necromancer's hidden suite."

A shout came from behind the chief inspector. It was Harold Danford. Jackson-Gupp rushed back to where he had been working and was swallowed up instantly, in a wall of smoke and plaster fumes.

Pointer called out to Harold what Jackson-Gupp had said of the place where he seemed certain that Rivers was. The chief inspector would have followed the savant but his companion stopped him.

"You can't pass. We can cut down into that suite from the floor of the Pages' room. This way." The passage before them was now blocked with fallen timbers. Something red shone at the other end. Jackson-Gupp had got through just in time.

Together the two raced back and up the stairs. Harold Danford leading. The room into which he rushed was off in one wing. It too was full of smoke. They tore down a couple of two-headed axes from the walls as they ran, axes that had fought in the great battle of Hastings, the battle that had lasted from daylight until the setting of the sun, where not a *hus-carl* had been missing from his post of honor in the pile of dead men around their dead king. Farthing's owner had been one of them.

But even his axe had never worked harder than it did to day in the blistered hands of his descendant. Marjoribanks, the police superintendent, and a couple of men from Norbury joined the two, and the group sweated and hacked at the floor like demented navvies. It was hot to their feet already, as they chopped, and ripped, and up-ended, and tore.

They finally got the boards away and there in the hole, they quickly made, they saw below them two groping hands rising from the swirl of smoke.

In a second, Rivers was hauled out and laid on the floor. "Pippa?" he asked in a whisper.

"Safe!" someone assured him. Someone who had no idea where Pippa was.

"Thank God! But it was a near thing!" Harold Danford, bending over him, said, "the fumes from the mortar and stones, I suppose?"

The doctor who was working at top speed nodded breathlessly.

"Another five minutes and it would have been a case of off side not near," and with that the medical man gave directions for carrying the unconscious man out into the open air.

Meanwhile Pippa knew nothing of this happy ending. A question before the floor was opened up, a gasped answer from the sweating men, repeating what Jackson-Gupp had said, and she had run for one of the stone stairs that led below. It would have even a fireman pause. Pippa, the hesitating, the "will-I, won't-I," dashed down it, her gas mask, the butler had distributed them a moment before, was on. She looked like a young devil returning home, so unfaltering were her flying steps, so eager her shining eyes.

She was in a world of fire. It is a terrifying world beyond all imagining to flesh and blood. The body knows its peril and trembles.

Pippa the irresolute, drove her's forward, and refused to let it flinch. She only thought of the door bolted on the outside behind which Beaufoy might be dying. She reached the passage leading to it by some miracle. The beam was a pillar of fire now. In front of it the flags had opened and showed a depth below them of leaping flames. She trod on the edge. The stone on which she stepped was so hot that with a cry of agony she slipped off it—there was nothing below her feet—it was all over . . . Beaufoy would never know . . . But if only he were saved that would not matter . . . If . . . . .

A hand clutched her, all but missed her, caught at the girdle around her dressing-gown and pulled her up and back. An arm went around her, would have turned her, but Pippa pushed it away. It was too dark for her to see who was holding her down here where there was no light save the red, wild, dancing light of fire.

"Not that way! He's in there! In front," she shouted through her mask.

"Don't I know it!" came in a voice that seemed to break as it made its way out of laboring, pain-filled lungs. "Don't I know it! I've got the beam more or less in two, but the floor's given way now in front. We must try by the Pages' room from above. It's his one chance."

"No, no! That floor's much too thick. They'll never get to him in time."

Pippa launched herself with a spring across the flames. She landed on what felt like a shelf, a burning hot shelf, and crumpled up, overcome by the fumes, for her mask had torn as she fell. Luckily for her her dressing-gown was made of an artificial silk which had once been asbestos fibre in a far off Rhodesian mine. It saved her life. For anything else as light would have caught fire and flamed with the flames around her.

When she came to herself, she was lying out on the grass.

Someone was feeding her with a little iced milk. It was her maid. Pippa struggled, or tried to struggle, onto an elbow.

"Is Mr. Rivers saved?" she tried to say, but only the last word reached the ears bending down.

"Everything's pretty well saved, miss. Even to last year's jams."

"Beaufoy? Mr. Rivers?" came in an agonized whisper from Pippa.. ..

"They got him out, miss. Oh, how the gentlemen all worked! Mr. Ormsby too. Gallant, I call it, considering—well —considering. The floor all but gave way at the end. We screamed to them to come out, but they wouldn't. As for Mr. Harold, he looked like one of those pictures of an angel with a flaming sword. And how he stuck it in that heat. Mr. Harold who can't stand heat. Oh, he was splendid, miss. How the firemen cheered him!"

"Take me to him," Pippa whispered hoarsely, "no not to Uncle Harry, dear Uncle Harry, but to Mr. Rivers."

They laid her beside him on the grass, after bandages soaked in milk and methylated spirit had been laid over the ointment on her burned arms and hands, and her poor scorched feet.

As for Rivers, he was not quite sure what had happened, or was happening. He had a dreamy idea that there had been a fire . . . someone told him that everyone was safely out he had a blurred memory of Harold Danford carrying him like a baby out of a window, after he had been hauled up by scores of arms out of a hot bottle.

Something touched his hand. Something clung to it, furry like cotton wool. It was Pippa. Amazing how his head cleared then. She was close beside him now. No one was paying any attention to them. She lifted his hand to her cheek, a very red and blistered cheek in which there was a deal more of the tomato than the rose, but Rivers thought that he had never felt anything quite so soft and so smooth.

"Oh, Beaufoy"—her voice was as healing to him as the night breezes—"I feel as though I had waked out of a nightmare. I—I never expected to see you again in this world."

"But Farthing?" he croaked.

"Never mind Farthing! I hate the very name"—she burst out—"I thought it was going to be your tomb. How I shall always hate its endless dark cellars and passages! But they'll soon be all gone."

"Eh?" came in a startled gasp from the land agent. They could not see the building from where he had been carried.

"It's completely gutted. The collections are saved, I believe, or is it the jams? I forget! What does Farthing matter, or collections matter. But you look excited. Oughtn't I to have told you?"

"Oh well, it's a bit of a surprise." Things were now coming back to Beaufoy Rivers.

"Let's have some more iced milk," Pippa suggested. A jug had been set down between them on a block of ice in the earth.

"Farthing is done for," she repeated after a drink, "but don't let's talk of anything but ourselves." She did not even want to ask him, in this hour, who had shut him up in that underground old suite opening into a passage which all thought was blind, though it had turned out to have a secret door in the stones.

"Where's Ormsby?" he asked on that.

"Helping save the jam, I suppose," she said coldly. "I told him yesterday, when he would insist on trying to make us give up the hunt for you, that—well, that I cared for you, not for him."

"I knew that all along. But do you care for me more than for Farthing?" he asked, very quietly. "That's what I haven't felt sure of."

"Hang Farthing!" she repeated with a little choking laugh, and felt the tears, hot and salt, on her blistered cheeks. "You'll never have to ask me that again," she went on after a minute. "Even if it hadn't been burned, I should not keep Farthing, not now—not if I get you!" she added with a little gurgle. "Besides"—she hesitated, the reaction was beginning to come—"besides, somehow, since I've owned it, I've begun to feel about it a little as Ivory does. As though—well, as though it choked love —of people. As though one could only care for it—"

She broke off.

"Where are they?" Voices could be heard asking. Soon there was a cry of "Oh, here they are!" and friends clustered around them.

Had she known it, they had not been alone for a moment. To and fro among the trees behind them, round and round, the chief inspector had hovered, out of earshot, but always with an eye on Beaufoy Rivers.

Pippa was carried off in a friend's car to a neighboring house. Rivers was laid on his own sofa in his study, and doors and windows stood wide open. What he needed was air. Meanwhile, upstairs, Jackson-Gupp, swathed in bandages, for he had been badly burned, stirred at a sound close beside him. Chief Inspector Pointer took a seat by the bed. The man in it began to babble in a hoarse cracked voice. He seemed to have gone back in time, for his tones were those of despair.

"That's his girl. And I thought she had no grit in her. Must die with her if I can't get her out. He's done for. Not an earthly chance of getting that door open. God forgive me!" and a sob tore up as though from a breaking heart.

Some ice was slipped between hot lips A cool, kind hand, very pleasant to the touch, the hand of the chief inspector, adjusted the sheet.

"We got Mr. Rivers safely out of that underground room, Mr. Jackson-Gupp, and Miss Hood too. She's quite safe"

Jackson-Gupp opened blood shot eyes and stared fixedly at him. Then memory came back to him.

He saw again that underground hell in which he still hoped to free the door. In fancy he leaped back as the stones beneath him gave way. He saw Pippa Hood come running down the smoke filled passage, and stumble on the brink of the fiery gap. He saw her twist herself free from his detaining, saving arm, and jump the open space before them. He had jumped after her. Though he had not expected to land on any thing he had jumped after her. To find her behind the flames huddled on the flags. His outflung hand had touched a metal hinge. Red hot. He had groped for the bolt. Had found it by its very heat, and pulled it back regardless of singeing flesh. He had pushed the door open, dragged Pippa in, and flung it shut behind them. He was all but overcome himself. Lights showed overhead. They had broken through from the room above, and got Rivers out He had tried to call, but his throat would only let a croak pass his lips He took hold of a plate on a table in the center and with 'a last effort sent it whirling up through the opening overhead, to fall with a clatter and crash in the room itself.

He heard shouts, saw the opening thick with glittering helmets, the helmets of the Norbury firemen, heard cries of encouragement, a rope came down, a man followed, Pippa, still unconscious and he himself nearly so, were carried up it, and helped through the gutted lower rooms on to the lawns outside.

He had been attended to, and carried at once to the land agent's cottage, and his own bedroom there.

Once more he opened his eyes, this time they had some thing in them of the cool, dancing light peculiar to them when he was himself.

"Am I under arrest?" he croaked with interest.

Pointer smiled a trifle dourly. "You ought to be! At any rate I'm here to try and wring a confession out of you. I'm sorry to bother you before you've had time to recover, but time presses. Suppose I run over things as I see them. When I'm right, if you'll just nod, we can pass on, whenever I'm wrong, if you will shake your head, I'll make a note of the point, and we can discuss it later."

"This promises to be amusing," murmured the man in the bed, "but I foresee that my head will be shaken off my shoulders before long."

"You played the part of Cox on the night Mr. Edgar Danford was murdered," Pointer said as a beginning.

Jackson-Gupp did not nod. Neither did he shake his head. He merely fixed his eyes on the chief inspector and closed his swollen lips more firmly.

"You were an observer on a hush-hush plane of some kind, Mr. Jackson-Gupp, which crashed in the Danford woods that same evening," the chief inspector went on in his quiet, unhurried way. "Both you and the pilot, the man who called himself Mr. Hatter, escaped. He was very badly bruised, and had possibly fainted. You got him and yourself clear after some hard work—"

Jackson-Gupp shook his head. "He got himself and me clear and then fainted. Go on—I confess I hadn't expected this."

"As soon as you could move, you decided to separate. The greatest secrecy was to be observed about the plane. That evidently was of paramount importance throughout. You argued that two men together, in your condition, would arouse more comment than two separate, battered individuals. You left your airmen's overalls and soon in the wreck. Then you went south, he north. He reached a road, walked along it till he came to a house with a doctor's brass plate on the gate, crawled to the door, rang the bell, and collapsed. He was worse hurt than he thought.

"You were battered and torn and dirty, with getting the plane to pieces, and stacking it where it could be carted off next morning. Mr. Hatter, by the way, got the doctor to telephone a code word for him to someone, which decoded meant that they were to pickup the remnants of the plane before daylight, giving the place where it lay dismantled—"

"A moment! I must ask a question or burst. How do you know he did this?"

"Because you didn't," was the only answer. Pointer wanted to get to essentials. "You met a man who either took you for a tramp, or to whom you purposely posed as a tramp to account for your appearance."

"I stopped the first car that passed me on the road. It happened to be Danford's, and asked for a lift towards Farthing. He seemed surprised. I said that I had once done some electrical work, and that a Mr. Rivers lived there who would help me I felt sure." Croaked the man in the bed.

"Frankly, Mr. Jackson-Gupp, did you think he would help you? Or was it something to do with his work that brought you to Farthing?"

"A bit of both. I knew that if asked for help, he'd give it without questioning me. We're partners, all of us, a little band of searchers. But it's true, that there was something in the way we flattened out made me wonder if there might not be some wireless crash work going on. Oh, it is a possible prospect, you know. If so, it was Dame Nature's doing this time. I know that now. But I didn't know it then. For when I saw those powerful antennae radiating from the Roman Tower, well—I wondered!" Jackson-Gupp ended in another choke.

The chief inspector bent over with a bowl of jelly.

"I'm sorry to have to keep on," he said remorsefully, "but—"

"Like many a worse man, you've gone too far to stop now," whispered the patient.

"Your appearance on the road, all tattered and torn, was very welcome to Edgar Danford. You fitted into a scheme of his which had gone awry, saved it, he thought. He took you in his car, put his own top coat and cap on you to hide your soaked rags, and drove you to the Chantry. You hurried up to his visitor's room where you had a bath, and then changed into some clothes with which he supplied you. On the way he had offered you a fiver, let's say—"

"A tenner!" croaked the man in bed.

"—to play a little game. To represent a friend of his called Cox who couldn't come down himself. Of course, what reason he gave you, I don't know—"

"Said his wife didn't believe in Cox's existence; that he had really been coming down for the week-end, and now had wired to say that he couldn't come. Said he and this Cox were always off together golfing or fishing, and that his wife refused to believe he wasn't with someone more amusing than an old friend," Jackson-Gupp ended in a splutter and a cough.

Pointer fed him some ice.

"Just so. After he had talked to you he doubtless took you for a broken-down gentleman and decided to risk dinner. So he countermanded an order which he had given for a dinner over in the Chantry and lent you some dinner things. But the make-up?"

"Said he was a keen amateur actor, and by Jove he was! and could touch me up to resemble his friend," Jackson-Gupp explained. "Lent me a red wig which was a bit overpowering, gummed on a red heard, and so on."

"Then, after dinner, you and Mr. Danford went into the Chantry, and after, doubtless, bringing the talk around to it, he asked you to read over a part that he was taking in some theatricals shortly. I confess I wonder that didn't rouse your suspicions. Or, perhaps it did?"

"No. I was entirely concerned with speculating in what sort of wireless work was going on. Also, I had told him I was a broken-down actor. Mentioned drink as the cause of my downfall. I always spoke of my 'downfall.' It was so true a word," chuckled the wireless expert hoarsely.

"I see. That played into his hands, of course. I mean, about getting you to read over a part which would sound like quarreling. A part that had been written by him, I suppose."

"No. It was from *A Sprig of Wistaria*. I saw the name on the outside. Only he had scratched through lines and written in others which fitted better, when the servant heard us. Of course, his explanation was meant to sound untrue to the man, but true to me. But I forget—this is your confession. I'm only to see how it works. Go on. You certainly have surprised me. But I shall want to know how it was done!"

"Then, at some time, later, you went up on the roof to watch the Roman Tower?"

Jackson-Gupp nodded.

"I represented myself to Danford as dead from fatigue, for my pocket wireless detector had told me that some wonderfully powerful currents were about. I was keen to get a chance to make some notes. Danford said he was off for bed too. He took off my wig and beard and make up. He was very thorough over it, and extraordinarily deft and quick. Then he poured me out a stiff drink and, I thought, put something into it from a paper in his hand. I told him I'd drink it when I was in bed. I promptly poured it out of the window, by the way.

"I'm a teetotaler owing to my palate as much as to my principles, but he had seemed more than annoyed when I refused a bottle of some Italian wine he praised to the skies that came in while we were reading over that play. Well, on my taking up the tumbler, he told me to tie up all the clothes that he had lent me into a bundle and set it outside my bedroom door, other clothes would be left in their place in the morning. He even handed me a ball of string.

"I did as directed, putting on the pyjamas that I found laid out for me on my bed. But I didn't go to bed. I made for the roof instead. My detector, it's a little gadget of my own, works best in the open. I had noticed the trap-door. I slipped along to it, found it could be opened noiselessly, and stayed up on the roof, making notes and testing currents. By the way, the bundle which I had put out in the passage had gone when I got back. But I forget, after I had decided that I could learn no more on the roof, what did I do then?"

Pointer accepted the challenge.

"You came down again, had a look at Mr. Danford. Why?"

"I came down because my detector had done all it could do. I went to Danford's room because—well, things were a bit odd. Someone had been in my room. I had left the door on the latch. It was shut. I hadn't forgotten that drink which I thought had been doctored, you know. So I went to Danford's room to ask a few questions. I intended to play the drunken fool a bit. But everything was dark and quiet in his room. I switched on the light"—he gulped—"He was dead. Ghastly sight!" he said briefly, "and extra unpleasant for me for many reasons. I couldn't account for my presence there, in disguise, without telling a very cock-and-bull story. If I said who I was and how I came to be there, I should, of course, expect to be believed. But I couldn't do that. That plane didn't exist— to outsiders or civilians. So I—but go on, what did I do then?"

"You telephoned to the police station, and told them to hurry to the Chantry—"

Jackson-Gupp nodded.

"Then you tied up your own clothes which you had locked in the wardrobe, took them with you, went to Mr. Rivers and told him who you were. Or he knew you already by sight, of course, by reputation—"

"Modesty forbids my nodding, but you're right. Persevere!"

"He believed your tale, though he had recurring spasms of doubt."

"He believed me conditionally to nothing turning up to throw doubts on my story, so he told me frankly. Should that happen, he would tell the police the whole truth, he said. Up till then he agreed to pretend that I had arrived around nine. Now go on—only I want to make it clear that he felt the responsibility of shielding a possible murderer, frightfully."

"I thought, on the whole, that you and he were not in league together, in any way, though Marjoribanks had heard you speak of yourself to him as a 'sort of partner' the night of the murder."

"Did I? Oh, yes, I remember! When I pressed him to stand by a fellow-worker, a partner in the field of scientific research." Jackson-Gupp nodded.

"Neither of you were sure of the other," Pointer went on. "You, for one, weren't satisfied about the nature of his work. You watched him more or less night and day. As he did you—because of the murder and the amazing tale you told him of your connection with it. You found his safe open yesterday morning, and looked at some plans of Farthing which also showed the way the cables ran at the Roman tower. Am I right?"

"You are. Seems to be a habit of yours."

"He came in and found you at the safe, and made up his mind to bear the responsibility of being responsible for you no longer?"

Again Jackson-Gupp nodded and looked intensely indignant.

"Did he speak of laying your story before us?" Pointer asked.

"He did. I decided, as you say, to prevent his doing anything foolish by locking him up for a while. But apart from that, I wasn't quite sure about his work, and some of its possible effects. You see, he was pledged to secrecy too. In his case, by Cox and Plumptre. I decided both that I had no time to lose, and that I needed more time—to work out the principal experiment of his my own way.

"I was quite sure that I had located the Necromancer's suite, as I believe it was called, while studying the run of the electric wires, and if so, I had an idea where a hidden door could be found. There was a part of the wall down there which seemed to have stones too old for the rest' of it."

"Too old?"

Jackson-Gupp nodded "Doubtless taken from some old rubbish heap when the suite was constructed. It was a well made secret door, closing flush with the rest of the stones, only, as I say, the stones were Saxon or Norman-hewn, in a wall of not earlier than the early days of Victoria. I had got the door open. Rivers was so surprised when I showed it to him that he stepped on into one of the rooms—inside at once, like a canary into a cage. I shut the door and bolted it. Then I closed the secret door at the end of the little passage and connected up the electrical heating of the suite with the main switch. He was quite comfortable, I assure you."

"You had already put in your supply of provisions? I thought so. And next came the fire, which upset your plan? How long were you going to keep him down there?"

For a moment Jackson-Gupp did not reply. He went very white under his burns. The fire held memories of awful emotion, when he had believed that Rivers could not be saved, when he had feared that Pippa Hood was doomed.

"For another week at any rate." He tried to speak lightly. "I had an idea that you had an idea on which you were working. And I rate you as a man who thinks swiftly and uncommonly clearly. And since once you got the murderer I could come forward and explain myself as 'Cox,' I decided to be patient—and see to it that Rivers should be patient—for awhile longer. I meant to slip down as soon as I had worked out a certain test and found his experiments weren't dangerous, unbolt his door while he was asleep, slip a card under it with some merry greeting on it such as 'Why not walk out? People think it's funny of you to be so shy,' and be off before he woke."

Jackson-Gupp ended in a prolonged racking cough, but he insisted on the talk continuing.

"You haven't any idea yourself as to who the criminal is?" Pointer asked.

"My first idea was that it was Harold Danford. Because he could have got out and back unnoticed, from his room Sunday night. Then probabilities seemed to me to point to Ormsby. Now I suspect no one and only wait on my betters, for no murderer would have worked as both those men did to get Rivers out of that death-trap."

"And you think they exhaust the possibilities—" Pointer murmured. "But time is passing, and I want to get your part in the tangle clear. Had you looked out of the window before your disguise was taken off you? Was it to you that Mr. Danford spoke those words that the gamekeeper overheard?"

"Certainly not."

"I'm not keeping anything back from you mean now?" Pointer asked dryly. Jackson-Gupp grinned and nodded.

"Heaven helps those that help themselves. And unto him that hath, and so on. I'm only telling you all this because you know it. I heard nothing whatever while I was on the roof. But I was deeply engrossed, I confess, in my work. But I want to know how you found this all out, and whether you found out any more. But you must have."

"Going back to the night of the murder," 'Pointer continued, "you telephoned at once when Rivers put you up to the same address in town to which the man who called himself Hatter afterwards phoned—"

"Have you any idea what his real name is?" asked the man in bed.

"Herriot Crawfurd."

Jackson-Gupp laughed outright. His burns made the laugh half a shriek but he was obviously amused.

"You make me feel as though I were made of glass. But go on—" he urged.

"Your mutual friend in town—I fancy it was someone connected with the plane you were both trying—"

"Possibly," assented Jackson-Gupp with a very discreet look.

"Let you know at once where Crawfurd was, and under what name he was going. You took him the clothes the night: after the murder, the clothes which you were wearing when Danford had first met you and taken you for a tramp, the clothes you had had on under your airman's overalls—and under your dressing-gown when I first saw you. He let down a string from his window, and hoisted them up, sending them into safety next morning as soon as a friend should call in his car. A good part of that night, like many later ones, you spent watching Rivers at work in the Roman tower through a periscope that you rigged up in a rain-water pipe."

Jackson-Gupp jumped, also he flushed.

"Look here, how the dickens did you track all this up? I'm sure you didn't—couldn't—see me when I was looking through that periscope. How did you find this all out? No one followed me to the Hatter's, that I'll swear. Then how was it done?"

"Just a bit of routine," murmured Pointer modestly.

The sick man stiffened. "If you don't explain fully and freely I shall develop a temperature and double pneumonia at once. Was it my arrival you found fishy? Did Rivers boggle at telling a full-throated lie like a gentleman?"

Pointer looked at his watch. He still had plenty of time. "It was very simple, really—"

"Routine work, in fact!" snapped Jackson-Gupp.

"I can't explain everything—yet awhile—" Pointer's eyes were on his boots. "Even if I had the time, I couldn't."

"Kindly tell me why, since you guessed that I was the much wanted, much suspected, 'Cox' of Sunday night, you didn't arrest me on the spot? It was what I was half prepared for more than once."

Pointer fed him some ice, arranged him more comfortably, and then began:

"The trouble with arresting you was the lack of motive, sir. Nothing, turn and twist it as I might, fitted you as a murderer, and yet I had come to the conclusion that you had, must have, played the part of Cox that fatal night, however incredible that seemed for a man in your position. My puzzle was to find some reason why you should have consented to play it. Were you and Edgar Danford working together on something? Connected in some interest? I could find nothing to prove this. But I felt certain that you played the part you had. And there was another point. Rivers was helping you. Why? Could it be that his help was given to you, not because you were implicated in a murder case, but in spite of it? Because of your scientific attainments? If so, then what had brought you down to Norbury as Cox was something unconnected with the murder too. But what could bring you down in such a way that you couldn't come openly? And was that sodden tramp, whose marks in the Chantry puzzled us so, connected with you? With the real reason why you were here? In other words, was 'Cox' a chance? Had Danford come on you by chance? Was that possible? I believed, for reasons, that he wanted someone to play the part of Cox that night—"

"Other reasons than those he gave me?"

"More or less," was the highly insufficient answer with which Jackson-Gupp had to be content.

"But what would make you accept such a proposition?" Pointer went on. "What would make him dare to offer such a proposition to you? And the tramp . . . where did he belong? Then I saw that if I dovetailed all three men whose arrivals and departures were such odd conundrums together, they explained themselves. If you were playing the part of a tramp, then he was explained, and Danford's proposition would be explainable. Had you disguised yourself to come and find out on what Rivers was working? Had Danford met you as a tramp, offered you a sum to play the part of Cox for a night.? My reason for doing all this was highly, improbable, but the facts fitted, so I decided to keep to the theory that you were the tramp, until it became untenable. It fitted too the peremptory tone in which Edgar Danford was heard to speak to you, as one speaks to an inferior. And those grimy hand marks on the tub—"

Jackson-Gubb gave a throaty chuckle. "I did make your brain work a bit, didn't I? But do go on!"

"I wasn't happy over the reason for your disguising yourself," Pointer went on. "Suppose I was wrong about your having come as a tramp? Could you have been mistaken for one, looked like one, and yet not have intended to act any such part? Could some mischance have overtaken you which would make you look the outcast? What about the mud? Then I learned that it was leaf mold. Chiefly beech mold, from at least five feet under the surface, and the truth burst on me. No motor goes five feet down, but a crashed aeroplane might. And you are connected with planes. And above all, Mr. Crawfurd! I am quite vexed with myself that I hadn't guessed his job at sight of him. He's a typical flyer."

"You needn't be too hard on yourself?" murmured Jackson-Gupp.

"Ah, but I had recognized the look really, but hadn't worked it out. That idea, the idea of a plane-crash accounted for his injuries and shock, and your possibly bedraggled appearance, and your need of fresh outfitting—"

"Bedraggled! Need!" Jackson-Gupp again chuckled. "From the muddy crown of my head to the soles of my burst shoes, there wasn't a hand's patch of whose material or clean skin on me!"

"So I sent Mr. Hatter's snapshot off to all the flying places to be identified, and had it sent back to me as Mr. Crawfurd, known as the Mad Hatter at Spittlegate where he took his ticket. Meanwhile other things fitted. The storm on that Saturday afternoon and evening would account for the crash having passed unnoticed, and its marks would be taken for those of some upheaval. But if you watched Rivers as you did, that meant that you were suspicious of his work. But since you did not explain your presence except as having come to visit Rivers—which I did not believe—that must mean that you were on some work about which you must be silent. Which would explain Crawfurd's alias. And since nothing was said by those who took the plane away, it must concern a hush-hush plan. And now, I must go. I wanted to check up my facts as soon possible, those that concerned you, so as to get on with case. The real case."

Pointer put things handy for the injured man, and slipped from the room.

CHAPTER ELEVEN

MEANWHILE on the scene of the fire, work was still going on apace. The greater part of the collections had been saved. The only irreparable loss was the portrait of Sir Amayas. Much of the furniture had been carried off by friends and given house-room under their several roofs. Covers were being stretched over what remained. Tents were put up, and things hastily, but carefully stacked inside them under Harold Danford's guidance. Ormsby helped him well but with a certain indefinable air of it being no concern of his that Harold noted. It did not grieve the elder man. He was not at all keen, as he had told the chief inspector on Ormsby marrying Pippa Hood.

As for Farthing itself, it was completely gutted. Gone were its beautiful carvings, its noble ceilings, its leaded casements. Nothing remained but its stout old walls.

Suddenly a rumor began to run among the busy workers, in that headless, tailless way that rumors do run. At first vaguely, then with more detail came the whisper that something had happened to Mr. Rivers. Then that there had been an accident. Then that he was dead, had just been found dead in the garage at the back of his cottage. And close on its heels came a dreadful whisper, the whisper of suicide. It was said, guardedly, that he had started the engine of his car. That he must have closed the doors, and that the fumes had overcome him, weakened as he was by his stay in his extraordinary—as yet unexplained—hiding place among the cellars of the house. Why he had committed suicide was a matter for speculation in still lower murmurs. He could not have had anything to do with the fire, for that was due, so said the fire brigade's captain, to the disturbing of the earthing of the wireless aerial, due to the determined efforts of the last day to find the missing land agent.

So since Rivers could not have gassed himself because of the outbreak of fire . . . here the gossip stopped with a significantly raised eyebrow and portentous nod. The inference on both sides—being that it was because of something more important still. And here and there sharp eyes had noticed, and sharp tongues now mentioned what sharp eyes had noticed, that the chief inspector from Scotland Yard had kept very close to the land agent ever since the latter's rescue.

Harold Danford finally caught the rumor. It was Ormsby who mentioned it.

"They're saying a most extraordinary thing." The latter's face was impassive, but his voice told of his suppressed excitement. "They're saying that an accident—or, well, some thing—has happened to Rivers in his garage."

"What?" This was evidently the first time that the report had reached Harold. "Impossible! I must go to the cottage at once."

Danford hurried off with him. On their way they saw a police inspector in the distance.

"Let's ask him," Ormsby suggested.

"The idea is ridiculous! Impossible!"

But Harold Danford spoiled the assured effect of the words by adding "surely!"

The inspector was very formal and non-committal. Hints only rebounded from his polished coldness. Asked point-blank by Ormsby, he said stiffly that the police could not understand how the rumor had got about, then he softened, sufficiently to beg them to do their best to keep the report from spreading.

"But we must know whether it's true or not!" expostulated Harold Danford.

"Sorry, sir, but the utmost secrecy about the affair has been ordered. Just for the time being, sir," he added soothingly.

"But you can't keep this sort of thing quiet!" Ormsby pointed out with some heat.

"We must all try to, sir," was all he got in reply. The inspector hurried off with a very important air.

"It's true!" Ormsby said laconically, as he watched the figure in blue disappear into the gray morning light.

"It can't be!" Harold Danford said in the tone of one assuring himself rather than another.

At the land agent's cottage they found a housemaid breathless with having run back from a long talk with the servants at the "house." She was nearly in hysterics.

Mr. Rivers had been found gassed in his garage about half an hour or less ago, and had been taken to the mortuary on a stretcher by the police. She had seen them carry his body off.

Who had found him?

"A constable had noticed that the doors were shut, though he heard an engine running, and had opened them—they were not locked—to find the master's dead body, sir. Oh, what a night of horror!" And she burst into tears.

Ormsby murmured something shocked.

"But what on earth was Rivers doing in the garage?" he asked Harold Danford, as they turned away. "Or was it—?" Harold Danford looked very shaken.

"Must have been an accident!" he said hurriedly. "Oh, must have been! To think we saved him only for such an end!" he murmured brokenly. "I must see the chief inspector at once."

But that was easier said than done. Constables abounded; but their superintendent, and the officer from Scotland Yard were nowhere to be seen. Nor was Marjoribanks.

"Busy with the body, probably," Ormsby suggested. "I'm very sorry for Rivers's end. I didn't care for the chap, but I'm very sorry indeed. It looks very bad . . . or rather very strange."

"I don't see that!" Harold Danford said stoutly.

"Well, I do," Ormsby said tersely. "Coming on top of the unsolved mystery which Mr. Edgar Danford's death is still, I do. Well, I was leaving anyway this morning—you know that Pippa broke off our engagement last evening? I'll go on up to town now. It's hardly worth while turning in for a couple of hours' sleep."

Harold Danford came closer.

"There's no use pretending that this news—about Rivers—won't be a terrible blow to Pippa. If I can't credit it, if I can't realize it in the least, what of her? Don't you think you might arrange to run down later on again? She may need you, badly!"

Ormsby's eye and set of mouth suggested that Pippa might indeed, and miss him too. A very unkind person might have connected his cold glance, his silence, with a letter in his pocket. A letter from a Miss Naomi Tigerstein, the only child of the only Tigerstein in existence—financially speaking. Naomi wrote to ask Mr. Ormsby to come to Blair Cowan for a cricket match, the house against the crofters. She said some pretty things about his game, and he really was quite a good batsman, and could at times play genuinely offensive cricket.

She went on to say that her father was looking forward to meeting him again, she had been talking to him about the new wireless aeroplane director he— Ormsby—had described the other day. She meant the one which was being worked out down where he was staying, the one that he was financing. Her father etc., etc.

It was a very nice letter, Ormsby thought, and Blair Cowan was a very nice place, ten thousand acres, and some of the finest stag shooting to be had in the Highlands. And with the Tigerstein millions to keep it running. . . . Naomi too quite charming girl, Naomi . . . docile, gentle, bidable. In fact, charming . . . Tigerstein was to get a peerage in the New Year's honors.

After all, Mark Ormsby thought quite kindly of Pippa Hood and poor, burned Farthing, as he waited for his car.

Suddenly he caught sight of the superintendent and hailed him eagerly, hoping to learn more of what the police thought of the strange fatality in the land agent's garage. But Lang too gave out no information whatever. He only wanted to know, he said, whether Mr. Ormsby had by chance seen Rivers enter his garage, or whether he had heard of anyone who had seen him go in. He was asking everyone at Farthing the same question. Ormsby said that he had not.

"There's one more thing we want to find out," the superintendent went on, producing a half sheet of paper on which some words were scrawled in a wild and shaking hand. "Can you explain, sir, what this may mean? It was lying on the floor of the garage beside Mr. Rivers's body. Looks as though he had torn out a sheet from a note-book in his car, and meant it as a last message to the world."

Ormsby took the paper. It ran: "Paper explaining every thing is in—" There the hand seemed to have failed, and the pencil had only made a sort of illegible squiggle.

"I've shown it to everyone already," the superintendent. went on. "No one can seem to suggest what the paper can be, or where it can be. Do you know anything about it, sir?"

"Of course I don't! He's referring—obviously—to a confession!" Ormsby looked staggered at his own words, but the superintendent took them calmly.

"Well—a message left like that—under such circumstances—certainly needs looking into," he agreed.

"I should say that when looked into it would solve the mystery of Mr. Danford's death," was the reply. "Rivers! Well —though I'm terribly shocked, yet in a way I'm not surprised. Not entirely."

"You're quite wrong!" Harold Danford had joined the two. He, too, had been shown the paper and had nothing but ejaculations to offer. "You're forgetting Cox, Ormsby!"

"Cox? Cox, in my opinion, came back after Danford was murdered, and helped himself to some money or bonds, something valuable and fairly safe, which he found on Danford or near his body. Then he telephoned to the police and made off. Either some accident has happened to him, or he's lying low somewhere, and will come forward later on with a good, and well backed-up excuse. I never have believed Cox the murderer. Too risky," Ormsby said in his dogmatic way. "But this! Why, it's clear enough. Find the paper and we shall understand everything."

He was getting into his car. Then he turned to Danford. "You say that you want to see the solicitors about the insurance claims. Can I give you a lift? It's on my, way."

Harold Danford thanked him and accepted. His own cars were busy transporting valuables to safe custody.

Finally Ormsby asked his companion where he should put him down. Harold Danford had decided to go to Rivers's chambers in Kensington. He happened to know the address, and the chambers were on the way to the solicitors.

There might be a chance of finding some papers in the flat which might be the one that Rivers had meant.

Ormsby said he thought that the chance was worth trying, and stopped the car at the address. There Harold's card and a few words of explanation admitted him to the flat. The porter knew that Rivers was land agent at Farthing.

Harold Danford did not expect to say long. He was turning to let himself out, when a noise in an adjoining room made him turn.

"Mr. Harold Danford, I arrest you on the charge of murdering your brother, Edgar Danford, on the night of Saturday to Sunday, July fourth, and the attempted murder of Mr. Rivers just now. I caution you—" The usual words followed.

It was Chief Inspector Pointer speaking. Behind him was Marjoribanks. Behind both were a couple of men in plain clothes.

A face that was utterly unlike the Harold Danford that anyone was allowed to see, twisted round at them.

"Are you mad? How dare you attempt this kind of a joke with me? Murder my brother! What possible motive could I have to harm him? What would I gain by such an act?"

"Farthing, Mr. Danford, was what you thought you were to gain. Farthing which your brother had left you in a later will than the one giving the property to Miss Hood."

"I know nothing of such a will." But the man's face was gray.

"It was in the book of maps which you locked inside a valuable desk and carried out yourself into safety before joining in the search for Mr. Rivers," Pointer said quietly. He thought it only fair to an arrested man to know how the case stood against him. "Superintendent Lang was watching you."

"I knew nothing about it," Harold Danford said firmly. "Besides, why should not my brother have left me the place? Though, mind you, I knew nothing of his having done so."

"I will tell you why you thought that he should—why he had promised you that he would. And that was in return for playing the part of Digby Cox from time to time so as to give that young man 'body.' Oh, not all the time. We know about the man helped back from Mexico, and so on. I won't go into that now. But when the original plan had to be given up, because of its resemblance to Mr. Fairbairn's idea, and when an accident, a mortal accident, had happened to the other sham 'Cox,' your brother improvised still a third 'Cox,' a tramp as you both thought, whom he had providentially found, who was to act the part for one evening."

Harold Danford's face twitched. His burning eyes asked a question—which was not answered.

"You were told that he had left after dinner. Going later over into the Chantry you found no trace of him. He was on the roof. You then entered your brother's room, his exclamation at the sight of you was probably because he mistook you for the tramp, until some word or sign of your's told him that it was you. Coming close up to him you strangled him where he stood, burned your own wig and beard in the downstairs which had often been used for burning inconvenient papers, and returned to your bedroom, passing in, as you had let yourself out, by one of the many side-doors to which you had a key. There are two which open without a sound supposing you know how to reach them.

"The tramp on the roof came down shortly afterwards, found Mr. Edgar Danford dead, and telephoned for the police."

"A tissue of lies!" Harold Danford managed to articulate, but he was shaking violently.

Pointer went on calmly: "In the course of routine work, suspicions fastened on you, and to test those suspicions, a letter was sent to Mr. Rivers, reaching him the morning after he had disappeared, when you were asked to deal with his mail. You handed over the correct envelopes, but instead of the letter we had concocted, you enclosed an invitation to a private view. That letter which you kept purported to come from a friend of Mr. Rivers, in answer to a mythical letter which Mr. Rivers was supposed to have written. In this letter, the one which you suppressed, the writer spoke of the safe-keeping of 'the deed of sale to you of Farthing,' mentioning the document as being in a safe of Mr. Rivers's up in town. The latter went on to speak of the promise of secrecy on the affair which he had given Mr. Rivers. That, Mr. Harold Danford, I am afraid is why you worked as you did to get Mr. Rivers out of the fire; and where you could speak to him alone. When he was freed from his cellar-room, you waited until everyone—as you thought—was busy with the work of salvage, and then went over to the land agent's cottage with what purported to be a message from me, a message asking him to hand you—for me, of course—Farthing's deeds of purchase. You told Mr. Rivers that you had been aware of the sale to him all along. Oh, this isn't guessing—!" in reply-to the opening of Mr. Harold Danford's white lips. "Captain Boodle and. I were in the next room. A hole had been knocked between the two, behind one of the pictures. Mr. Rivers handed you the keys of his bag inside which you would find a deed box, and asked you to get it from his rooms in Chelsea Chambers and bring it to me.

"You demurred at doing that, and suggested that he had better come too. That the drive in the open car would do good. The idea appealed to him. You went on ahead to the garage. He tottered down after you. You had started his carethyl spirit too! You had screwed the window shutters together outside before going to speak to him, now you slipped out and turned the key on him. At the same time starting up the motor bicycle of some helper near by to drown the noise from the garage, and possibly of Mr. Rivers's pounding on the door. But having used him as bait—by means of that letter you opened, which I had written—we naturally guarded him. Until he handed you key or papers he was safe, more than safe that we knew. Now we watched him every second of the time. Mr. Marjoribanks was on top of the garage. He had climbed up there when you were busy with the shutters, and lifted that trap-door inside, covering the opening with a car cover. He watched all you did.

"There was a man of ours hiding in the bushes outside. As soon as you were out of sight, the man opened the door, and together with Mr. Marjoribanks got Mr. Rivers out, on a stretcher and covered up, it is true, but quite unharmed.

"The rumor of an accident to him, of his death was spread. You, Mr. Harold Danford, denied before witnesses all knowledge of his having gone to the garage, of any paper of importance belonging to him.

"Mr. Marjoribanks and I took a car and got here to the Chambers ahead of you. Here we watched you open the bag and take out the papers from the despatch box inside, the papers that are now in your pocket.

"I don't think I should say anything, if I were you. The case is complete."

"A tissue of nonsense. A series of police traps which will rouse England from end to end when they are recounted. I am innocent. Of course, I am innocent. And I shall be able to prove it."

Harold Danford carried his head high. His voice did not falter.

As soon as Pointer had begun to speak, two plain clothes men had each laid a hand, and kept it there, on Harold Danford's arms. He did not attempt to struggle, and he was not prepared with the means for suicide. He turned and glared at the chief inspector as he stepped out of the room.

"The portrait!" Marjoribanks ejaculated. "As I told you!" And in truth the face had been the face of old Amayas Rivers.

"He'll be taken to Norbury jail. Now I must report at the Yard." Pointer turned to leave the rooms.

"I must hear your report," begged Marjoribanks. "There are lots of things I want to know."

"By all means come, if you don't mind my being too busy with my notes to talk on the way."

The two drove off in the car that had brought them, quite an ordinary car to look at, but one that had had the mysterious "hotting-up" process applied to her vitals, and would not have disgraced herself at Brooklands.

A quarter of an hour later they entered the room of the Assistant Commissioner, at New Scotland Yard.

"Got him, sir!" the detective officer said quietly. Pointer was looking very grave, and rather pale. To arrest a man for murder was no light task. It always left its mark on him.

Marjoribanks and the assistant commissioner were old friends. Major Pelham waved them both to seats. Marjoribanks perched himself on the window ledge instead. He was aquiver with the excitement of the last hour.

"Harold Danford!" he now murmured. "A man who seemed only to care for his music. I still can't grasp it!"

"He only took up music when money-making failed, Pointer reminded him. "Though I understand that he is a very remarkable musician. But he's a businessman first, in my belief. It was Edgar Danford of the two who really wanted to be free to enjoy art—in luxury."

"And to think I felt his wrongness at the beginning, and let myself be deflected because it didn't seem to fit when he took it so quietly about the property passing to Miss Hood. Of all the asses!" Marjoribanks smote his brow. "He that has eyes and *won't* see!

"And to think, too, that it was he himself who told you about Edgar Danford having met the original Digby Cox. A fact that let you steam full speed ahead on your idea about Edgar Danford's schemes! How it will gall him when he finds that out! He made no other slip."

"That was only because Mr. Rivers's accounts made him absent-minded," Pointer thought.

"I gather that your oracular words the other day about bait to catch a tiger referred to this?" Major Pelham asked the chief inspector. "I carefully refrained from inquiring too closely into them, for fear lest it be some of your—er—routine work."

"He set an awfully good trap," Marjoribanks said, lighting up. "But what beats me is how you came to suspect Harold Danford in the beginning. I did. But I went by instinct. I stuck to Farthing. And I was right. But you?"

Pointer said nothing.

"Come now, work it out on the blackboard for us!" laughed Major Pelham, "It's the workings that interest us."

"Well, there was always Farthing," Pointer agreed with Marjoribanks. "As much present to my mind as yours, though —to me—merely an object of great value.

In other words there were two reasons why Edgar
Danford might have been killed. One connected with
Farthing, one unconnected. If the former, if possession of
the magnificent place was at the root of the crime then—
obviously—the criminal would have to be someone who
could, or would, only gain possession of Farthing by
Danford's death—and without rousing suspicion. That
suggested the brother at once and with this fitted the fact
that no effort had been made to disguise Mr. Danford's
body, or take it away. Quite the contrary. Though the
possession of a red wig and beard looked like
premeditation, the bottle of sulphuric acid in the place
wasn't used, nor the building itself set on fire, though the
means for that too were on hand. In short, Mr. Danford's
identity was clearly to be known at once.. Only there was
the complication of the two young men and the supposed
heiress of Farthing. I believed the murderer was one of
the incarnations of 'Cox,' because of the man in the red
beard seen by the gamekeeper, and because also,
obviously, that man must be deep in the plot with
Danford. He might be Ormsby, and the motive for the
murder be loot, the loot piled up for the nonexistent Cox
by Danford for some five years. But I did not see how
Ormsby could have got away from Farthing the night of
the murder.

"Also the elaborate story of the forgery of the annuity
paper—if true, and Mr. Ormsby's account of it rang true,
was supported by Miss Hood—let him out of being the
accomplice. Nor did Ormsby account for Mrs. Danford's
suspicions. She never went to her husband's offices, but
she had ample means of overhearing some chance
incautious word between the two brothers. Then too—it
was only a trifle—there was the fact that the chief
constable, speaking for outsiders in general, had an idea
that the brothers lately were not on the best of terms. If
they were hatching a plot together that would be the
effect they would be sure to try and create. But Mrs.
Danford in the house with them, and a very clever

woman, thought they were the best of friends. Also we have no record of Mr. Ormsby having known Mr. Edgar Danford until this year, until the time when they are supposed to have first met. Yet Mr. Danford would sometimes have had to talk things over with the sham Cox, in his real person, in order to arrange the next 'official' interview. This would be quite easy if they were brothers. Mr. Harold Danford, too, is about the height of the Savoy 'Cox,' is a gourmet, and has no idea of the turf. Though that latter meant little, the ignorance might have been assumed, like the affection for Montepulciano."

"Neat touch, that!" murmured Major Pelham appreciatively.

"But the problem to me was what inducement would make Harold Danford help his brother in his thieving. He had plenty of money. Mrs. Danford? I did not think either of them cared for the other—in that way. The only thing I could think of that Harold could not have while his brother was alive, and could have without any suspicions being roused, if his brother were dead, was Farthing. So I assumed it to be Farthing—supposing Harold to be the criminal. And learned that, though he always spoke as though he disliked the place, yet he had given it some very rich treasures, more and more frequently of late, when the arrangement with his brother about the promised—never to be carried out of—handing of it over and final legacy of it to Miss Hood, let him ostensibly present her with his offerings—as his caretaker had she but known it. And if his indifference to the will leaving Farthing to Miss Hood was genuine, and I thought it was, that could only mean—supposing Harold Danford were guilty, and guilty because of the property—that he had a later will carefully put away, to be produced when the trouble about his brother's murder had blown over. His words to Miss Hood about carrying out implicitly a dead man's wishes, seemed to me to fit in with that possibility."

"Yes, that will of Edgar Danford's that you told Lang to look out for," Major Pelham picked it out of some papers in front of him, "is dated a week after the Miss Hood will, and leaves everything, real and personal of which he dies possessed to his brother, saying that he had made up his mind that it is not fair to Miss Hood to leave her a place which exposes her to the danger of being married for its possession."

"Smug hypocrite!" murmured Marjoribanks. "So you thought Harold Danford guilty all along? You tight-clamped oyster!"

Pointer disclaimed that at once. "There was Rivers," he pointed out. "Rivers fitted the Cox impersonation fairly well. In his case money might be the motive, for Farthing seemed rather a dangerous legacy—supposing he were Edgar Dan-ford's murderer. He could have slipped over to the Chantry from his cottage. I had very grave doubts of him—until his attitude about the will. That seemed to me inexplicable on the part of the murderer. For whatever else a murderer does one expects him to do nothing peculiar—to always melt into crowd."

"I still can't understand Rivers's attitude about that will!" muttered Marjoribanks. "But don't let me interrupt you."

"Had the trap for Harold Danford not worked, I should have set one, a different one naturally, for, first Rivers, and then, if he had proved himself guiltless, for Ormsby, and even for Mr. Jackson-Gupp and each of the men servants in turn," Pointer went on.

"But supposing it had been Harold Danford who had hidden Rivers away, for some reason of his own?" the assistant commissioner asked.

"I thought that absolutely unlikely, sir. You see, I had one end of the Jackson-Gupp, Hatter, Rivers connection by then. Mr. Harold rather favored Mr. Rivers as a suitor for Miss Hood, in preference to Mr. Ormsby. The latter would be sure to cut up very rough when the will taking Farthing away from his fiancée—and from himself—was eventually produced. Mr. Rivers is a different character altogether. Still, I was on tenterhooks after I had written that letter, I confess. But Harold Danford was watched day and night by myself and one of my men, inside and outside. That's how the fire was discovered quickly. It was Williams, as you know, sir, who woke the butler. But I'm thankful it's over. It was an awful risk to run, using a man as bait. But I *knew* that nothing else would catch the murderer—if he was Harold Danford. You see, it was no use in this case pretending that a clue had been found, or that someone had seen the crime committed. Whoever killed Edgar Danford *knew* that there were no clues left, no witnesses."

"I only hope you're prepared for the roasting you'll get when it's known that you set a trap," Major Pelham said grimly.

Pointer was.

There was a short silence. Marjoribanks broke it.

"What *did* make Rivers act so strangely about Miss Hood's inheriting Farthing. You don't really think that Rivers owns the place do you? That was just to bait the trap?"

"I shouldn't be surprised if it were true," Pointer said.

"But—" Marjoribanks evidently was. "But! I thought he was badly off. Only hope lay in the future, in his wireless work and patents."

"We learned, you remember, that Mr. Rivers had an uncle who died in a nursing home in town last spring, within a month of his return to England, after half a lifetime abroad."

"And left something like two hundred pounds." Marjoribanks finished. "I remember."

"He may not have been a poor man all the same. The Yard has learned that he bought, and eventually sold just before his return, some very fine mines and workings in Afghanistan. Originally he and his brother, Colonel Rivers, Mr. Beaufoy Rivers's father, started life well off. The uncle had no relatives left but Mr. Beaufoy. It's not outside the pale of possibilities that he handed our Mr. Rivers' some securities before he died. And since Mr. Rivers seems as poor now as before, it is possible that he had spent any money so given him, in buying Farthing. It would explain some odd trifles."

"Such as his lifting his hat to that painted devil," Marjoribanks ruminated. "But the secrecy!"

"Ah!" Pointer lit his pipe. "That would have to be part of the bargain, wouldn't it. If Edgar Danford had already promised it to his faithful 'Cox' brother? I can imagine him letting Rivers have it below its market value under some pledge of absolute secrecy—for a certain time. Long enough for Danford, who would be supposed to be dead, to get away. He didn't dare make a condition mentioning death, for fear of arousing suspicions, of course, but I shouldn't be altogether surprised if Rivers owned Farthing. It would be just like Edgar Danford to have done his brother out of the promised reward. Personally, I think this idea alone explains Rivers's attitude since the will was read, his efforts to get Miss Hood to become engaged to him, regardless of any suspicion of being a fortune hunter, his efforts, crude though they were to prevent Ormsby getting into deep waters on the security of his coming marriage with an heiress."

"Yes," Marjoribanks agreed. "It sounds mad, but it really does rather fit things, even to why no death-duties were entered on those accounts that so upset Harold Danford."

"I shouldn't wonder," Pointer went on, "if it was the copy of the will that Mr. Rivers had taken from the safe, I when nearly caught him doing it, just after the murder was discovered. If he believed that he had just bought what would doubtless figure as the great prize in the will, he might have taken it, hoping to delay the reading."

Rivers had done just that, and for that reason.

They found afterwards, in due time, that Beaufoy's uncle, Guy Rivers, had handed him on his deathbed quite a fair fortune, with the request to buy back, if it should ever be possible, the old place which was threatened with passing into outside hands, since there were no Danford heirs, not likely to be any, for Harold Danford was professedly not a marrying man.

Rivers had tentatively approached Edgar Danford on the point, and had found to his delighted amazement that Danford was quite willing to sell, and at the same reasonable figure which he himself had originally paid to Beaufoy's father for it, on the pledge, however, of three months' absolute secrecy. The secrecy to be part of the purchase as it were, and, if broken, to invalidate the sale. Two months were just over when he was murdered.

Rivers's horror when he thought that Pippa Hood did not care for the place was because it was chiefly for her sake that he had bought Farthing. It had only been a request, not a commission, on Guy Rivers's part.

Farthing, by the way, was fully insured, but in Rivers's own name, and with another firm. The insurance money would not have compensated any worshiper of the original building, but it would furnish the means of acquiring a home without any tragic memories.

A ring came on the telephone. The chief inspector was wanted. He sprang to his feet.

"There's been an accident. . . . The car taking Mr. Harold Danford down to Norbury jail has been run into by a lorry. One of the constables with him was killed outright, and he's not expecte. to live. The chief constable says he's asked for me. Perhaps I can make it!"

A word from the assistant commissioner and Pointer was running down the stairs, Marjoribanks beside him. In the courtyard the Yard's fastest car was ready in a second. This time it was a British Mercedes Benz, 36-220 h.p., a Grand Prix sports supercharger, model, as yet invincible on the road.

Pointer leaped into the seat, and a moment later was threading his way through London traffic, and then, once in country roads, went roaring along at ninety miles an hour in safe stretches.

There was no landing place near the spot where Harold Danford lay dying, if not already dead, or he would have flown. The car could have done a hundred and twenty-five easily once it got into its stride, but Pointer was careful. The noise the great Mercedes makes saved him using the horn. Every car on road was passed, some to their obvious amazement. At length its six noisy brakes, acting with the precision which alone makes such a car allowable, he drew up beside a little village outside Norbury at a place where an overturned lorry and smashed closed car told their own tale. Red flags marked off a little spot, inside which knelt some figures around something on the ground covered with a coat.

It was Harold Danford. He was still breathing. To move him would mean instant death.

The dying man looked up at him.

"You don't often have people slip through your fingers, I fancy. I shall," he said in little jerky gasps.

"Would you like to give me any messages?"

"You mean a confession?" Again the face suggested the portrait.

"No, Mr. Danford, I didn't mean that. Though that harms no one who has come to the place where you are," Pointer said gently.

"Beginning or end?" Harold Danford said slowly. "Overture or finale.?"

There was a pause, as someone moistened his lips.

"You shall have your confession," the man on the ground said suddenly. His voice was fainter, but with his glance beckoned Marjoribanks and the chief constable to bend lower. Captain Boodle had hurried out from Norbury as soon as he heard of the accident to the car.

"I killed my brother. For the sake of that infernal house. That picture got me. Somehow. In the beginning I didn't care for it, house, I mean, or picture, both perhaps—but more and more, it got me. I knew Edgar wouldn't keep faith, if he had the chance he would cheat me out of it. And for its sake I helped him in all his schemes—embezzlement, fraud—Digby Cox died a week before his uncle. I was 'Cox' for a while you guessed. Then I thought it dangerous. With Edgar." A shudder passed over him. Then his words came faster. More jumbled. "I didn't trust him. Less and less. He got hold of a chap in Mexico. Man wanted go to Sidney—consumption, doctor said. Didn't look it but was. Edgar brought him to town three months or so. Then he fell into the docks just when I was wanted. Just at the end. You know about the Fairbairn. There followed some words no one could catch, then the voice went on. "Know Edgar meant mischief. Knew it all along. Play me false somehow. Farthing—" His eyes widened, a smile flitted across his twisted face. Then it faded. "It was that portrait. A curse on it? It changed Edgar. It changed me. I use to feel at times as though I wasn't myself, but it. Or that it was some dreadful partner of mine. But the partnership is broke — now."

Again there came a silence. Then he said clearly and loudly:

"Edgar's gone. The picture's gone. Farthing's gone. And—" Another shudder caught him, and shook his spirit free from his torn and mangled body.

"He's gone!" ejaculated Captain Boodle, in a tone of relief. "Better so . . . 'straordinary story, and 'straordinary painful for everyone concerned. You took the confession down didn't you, Marjoribanks? I thought so. He couldn't sign, but we were all present and heard him."

It was Mrs. Danford who broke the news to Pippa. Pointer had called on her with the news at once. He learned nothing fresh from her. He had not expected to. Whatever she knew or suspected of the truth was her own secret—as far as he was concerned.

She hurried down by car as soon as the chief inspector had told her of Harold Danford's arrest and death. She had found it hard to believe in his guilt. Pippa too at first scouted the idea. But his confession, even more than the arrest, was something that no doubter could get around.

Pippa stared at Ivory.

"Horrible! Harold Danford killed his brother! I thought him devoted to him."

"No Danford was ever devoted to anything but himself," the widow of a Danford said a little wearily. "Like you, I never thought Harold Danford was other than straight when he seemed to dislike the place so much. Yet that last night before—before it all happened, when he played for us, I should have guessed. It was a warning to all of us. A warning unconsciously welling up from Harold Danford's innermost self, a warning misunderstood by us all, victim and listeners."

"Oh, horrible!" muttered Pippa, with a shiver. "And all the time he was plotting and practically stealing. . . . Did you suspect what was going on?"

Mrs. Danford stretched a length of ribbon between her hands. She was not in mourning.

"I suspected that Edgar was staging something. But I never dreamed of linking Harold with it. I thought it was aimed at our money, yours and mine. I found a sheet of paper with some notes on it in his writing which I thought meant something of that sort. I burned it, and began to pay attention to things. I was quite sure that Edgar was crooked. I had been sure of that for a long time.

"And I heard odd messages over the telephone at times when he thought himself quite alone and safe. But they weren't linked in my mind with Harold, because Harold was often in the house, though not always. Now we know that they were directions sometimes to the 'Cox' who fell into the river, but sometimes to Harold himself.

"But I thought Edgar was planning to go off with some other woman. I rather hoped he was. I should have divorced him like a shot. Then came the laugh, and I was sure that he intended to stage some sort of a disappearance—death—and then get away.

"I saw him slip a plug out of the wall just after the second laugh, and I found a bit of flex poked into the gilt openwork of a little table. I was certain that there was a gramophone hidden inside, though I couldn't test it, as I didn't want him to guess that I had found him out. I wanted to see what the reason was. If he intended to disappear I was sure that he must have help. I had an idea that Ormsby was in it, when Edgar pressed his engagement to you so keenly. Edgar Danford never did anything without a reason for himself."

"He made me think it was care for me. Oh, surely it was—just a little bit? Just mixed in with other things?" Pippa had tears in her pretty eyes. She had been very fond of Edgar Danford.

"I shouldn't wonder if it had been," Ivory agreed. "But don't forget the mixed-in. He wanted Ormsby on his side, I suppose. To fend off inquiries. The chief inspector thinks he meant to stage a death scene and then Harold Danford turned it into the real thing."

Both women were silent a moment.

"Love of money, love of it, is the root of evil, the old teachers were quite right," murmured Mrs. Danford, half to herself. "And it grew in both the Danford's hearts."

"Was that why you wanted me to marry Beaufoy?"

"To spoil Edgar Danford's plan?" Ivory Danford shook her head. "Oh, no! I felt sure that you and he loved each other."

"We do," breathed Pippa blissfully. "We shall be fearfully poor at first, until his royalties begin to accumulate but we don't mind. Farthing, of course, and its collections, go to the Crown."

She did not know, neither woman knew, that Farthing's insurance was going to start the young couple in comfort, and that the sale of the collections would make them quite comfortably off.

"I'm glad I burst that picture!" Pippa said suddenly. "I suppose it's only superstition, but I had a feeling that Beaufoy wouldn't be saved if I didn't get rid of it. That's why I flung it down the steps into the flames!"

"And I'm glad too that it's gone." Ivory spoke with a little shudder. "It used to suggest dreadful things to me. I left Farthing because of it. Ran away from its horrible promptings."

She rose and put an arm through Pippa's.

"You see, I married Edgar because of Farthing. That was why I grew to hate the place so afterwards. And hate gave that picture power, my father would have said, just as greed did. I never tried to fight it with love. You did. And you won!"

The two young women went out into the sunlight together to where Rivers was waiting for them.

THE END

Other Resurrected Press Books in *The Chief Inspector Pointer Mystery* Series

Murder at Bridge

When an afternoon bridge party attended by some of Hamilton's leading citizens ends with the hostess being murdered in her boudoir, Special Investigator Dundee of the District Attorney's office is called in. But one of the attendees is guilty? There are plenty of suspects: the victim's former lover, her current suitor, the retired judge who is being blackmailed, the victim's maid who had been horribly disfigured accidentally by the murdered woman, or any of the women who's husbands had flirted with the victim. Or was she murdered by an outsider whose motive had nothing to do with the town of Hamilton. Find the answer in... **Murder at Bridge**

One Drop of Blood

When Dr. Koenig, head of Mayfield Sanitarium is murdered, the District Attorney's Special Investigator, "Bonnie" Dundee must go undercover to find the killer. Were any of the inmates of the asylum insane enough to have committed the crime? Or, was it one of the staff, motivated by jealousy? And what was is the secret in the murdered man's past. Find the answer in... **One Drop of Blood**

AVAILABLE FROM RESURRECTED PRESS!

THE EDWARDIAN DETECTIVES
LITERARY SLEUTHS OF THE EDWARDIAN ERA

The exploits of the great Victorian Detectives, Poe's C. Auguste Dupin, Gaboriau's Lecoq, and most famously, Arthur Conan Doyle's Sherlock Holmes, are well known. But what of those fictional detectives that came after, those of the Edwardian Age? The period between the death of Queen Victoria and the First World War had been called the Golden Age of the detective short story, but how familiar is the modern reader with the sleuths of this era? And such an extraordinary group they were, including in their numbers an unassuming English priest, a blind man, a master of disguises, a lecturer in medical jurisprudence, a noble woman working for Scotland Yard, and a savant so brilliant he was known as "The Thinking Machine."

To introduce readers to these detectives, Resurrected Press has assembled a collection of stories featuring these and other remarkable sleuths in The Edwardian Detectives.

- The Case of Laker, Absconded by Arthur Morrison
- The Fenchurch Street Mystery by Baroness Orczy
- The Crime of the French Café by Nick Carter
- The Man with Nailed Shoes by R Austin Freeman
- The Blue Cross by G. K. Chesterton
- The Case of the Pocket Diary Found in the Snow by Augusta Groner
- The Ninescore Mystery by Baroness Orczy
- The Riddle of the Ninth Finger by Thomas W. Hanshew
- The Knight's Cross Signal Problem by Ernest Bramah

- The Problem of Cell 13 by Jacques Futrelle
- The Conundrum of the Golf Links by Percy James Brebner
- The Silkworms of Florence by Clifford Ashdown
- The Gateway of the Monster by William Hope Hodgson
- The Affair at the Semiramis Hotel by A. E. W. Mason
- The Affair of the Avalanche Bicycle & Tyre Co., LTD by Arthur Morrison

RESURRECTED PRESS CLASSIC MYSTERY CATALOGUE

Journeys into Mystery
Travel and Mystery in a More Elegant Time

The Edwardian Detectives
Literary Sleuths of the Edwardian Era

Gems of Mystery
Lost Jewels from a More Elegant Age

E. C. Bentley
Trent's Last Case: The Woman in Black

Ernest Bramah
Max Carrados Resurrected:
The Detective Stories of Max Carrados

Agatha Christie
The Secret Adversary
The Mysterious Affair at Styles

Octavus Roy Cohen
Midnight

Freeman Wills Croft
The Ponson Case
The Pit Prop Syndicate

J. S. Fletcher
The Herapath Property
The Rayner-Slade Amalgamation
The Chestermarke Instinct
The Paradise Mystery
Dead Men's Money

The Middle of Things
Ravensdene Court
Scarhaven Keep
The Orange-Yellow Diamond
The Middle Temple Murder
The Tallyrand Maxim
The Borough Treasurer
In the Mayor's Parlour
The Saftey Pin

R. Austin Freeman
The Mystery of 31 New Inn from the Dr. Thorndyke
Series
John Thorndyke's Cases from the Dr. Thorndyke
Series
The Red Thumb Mark from The Dr. Thorndyke Series
The Eye of Osiris from The Dr. Thorndyke Series
A Silent Witness from the Dr. John Thorndyke Series
The Cat's Eye from the Dr. John Thorndyke Series
Helen Vardon's Confession: A Dr. John Thorndyke
Story
As a Thief in the Night: A Dr. John Thorndyke Story
Mr. Pottermack's Oversight: A Dr. John Thorndyke
Story
Dr. Thorndyke Intervenes: A Dr. John Thorndyke
Story
The Singing Bone: The Adventures of Dr. Thorndyke
The Stoneware Monkey: A Dr. John Thorndyke Story
The Great Portrait Mystery, and Other Stories: A
Collection of Dr. John Thorndyke and Other Stories
The Penrose Mystery: A Dr. John Thorndyke Story
The Uttermost Farthing: A Savant's Vendetta

Arthur Griffiths
The Passenger From Calais
The Rome Express

Fergus Hume
The Mystery of a Hansom Cab
The Green Mummy
The Silent House
The Secret Passage

Edgar Jepson
The Loudwater Mystery

A. E. W. Mason
At the Villa Rose

A. A. Milne
The Red House Mystery
Baroness Emma Orczy
The Old Man in the Corner

Edgar Allan Poe
The Detective Stories of Edgar Allan Poe

Arthur J. Rees
The Hampstead Mystery
The Shrieking Pit
The Hand In The Dark
The Moon Rock
The Mystery of the Downs

Mary Roberts Rinehart
Sight Unseen and The Confession

Dorothy L. Sayers
Whose Body?

Sir William Magnay
The Hunt Ball Mystery

Mabel and Paul Thorne
The Sheridan Road Mystery

Louis Tracy
The Strange Case of Mortimer Fenley
The Albert Gate Mystery
The Bartlett Mystery
The Postmaster's Daughter
The House of Peril
The Sandling Case: What Would You Have Done?
Charles Edmonds Walk
The Paternoster Ruby

John R. Watson
The Mystery of the Downs
The Hampstead Mystery

Edgar Wallace
The Daffodil Mystery
The Crimson Circle

Carolyn Wells
Vicky Van
The Man Who Fell Through the Earth
In the Onyx Lobby
Raspberry Jam
The Clue
The Room with the Tassels
The Vanishing of Betty Varian
The Mystery Girl
The White Alley
The Curved Blades
Anybody but Anne
The Bride of a Moment
Faulkner's Folly
The Diamond Pin
The Gold Bag
The Mystery of the Sycamore
The Come Backy

Raoul Whitfield
Death in a Bowl

And much more!
Visit ResurrectedPress.com
for our complete catalogue

About Resurrected Press

A division of Intrepid Ink, LLC, Resurrected Press is dedicated to bringing high quality, vintage books back into publication. See our entire catalogue and find out more at www.ResurrectedPress.com.

About Intrepid Ink, LLC

Intrepid Ink, LLC provides full publishing services to authors of fiction and non-fiction books, eBooks and websites. From editing to formatting, from publishing to marketing, Intrepid Ink gets your creative works into the hands of the people who want to read them. Find out more at www.IntrepidInk.com.

Made in the USA
Middletown, DE
28 March 2023

27847046R00166